MURDER AT THE HIGHLAND GAMES

BOOKS BY DEE MACDONALD

KATE PALMER MYSTERY SERIES

A Body in the Village Hall

A Body in Seaview Grange

A Body at the Tea Rooms

A Body at the Altar

A Body on the Beach

A Body at Lavender Cottage

A Body in a Cornish Village

ALLY McKINLEY MYSTERY SERIES

Murder in the Scottish Highlands

Murder at the Loch

A Very Bookish Murder

The Runaway Wife

The Getaway Girls

The Silver Ladies of Penny Lane

The Golden Oldies Guesthouse

The Sunshine Club

DEE MACDONALD

MURDER AT THE HIGHLAND GAMES

bookouture

Published by Bookouture in 2026

An imprint of Storyfire Ltd.
Carmelite House
50 Victoria Embankment
London EC4Y 0DZ

www.bookouture.com

The authorised representative in the EEA is Hachette Ireland
8 Castlecourt Centre
Dublin 15 D15 XTP3
Ireland
(email: info@hbgi.ie)

ISBN: 978-1-83618-254-2
eBook ISBN: 978-1-83618-253-5

ONE

Turning up the collar of her jacket at the cool breeze that hinted at the end of summer, Ally McKinley looked around at the idyllic setting. The heather had now covered the foothills of the Western Highlands of Scotland in a purple haze, against the backdrop of her old converted malthouse, the castle and the blue-grey mountains above, not yet iced by layers of snow. The leaves of the trees were rapidly morphing into various shades of gold and copper, and the nearby river could be heard as it tumbled its way over rocks and stones towards the sea.

Nestling amidst the mountains, she was standing in what was one of the region's rarities: a completely flat four-acre field where Jimmy McCrae normally grazed his sheep, or so she had been informed. Not today though. Today this was the setting for the Locharran Highland Games, and the field was packed with hundreds of onlookers, laughing and shouting in anticipation. Everyone appeared to be supporting someone who was competing in something. The mood was jovial and good-natured, particularly among those who'd spent considerable time in the hospitality tent where the whisky and beer flowed. There was an assortment of stalls around the perimeter, some selling hot or cold drinks, some selling Scottish souvenirs and another selling shortbread in half a dozen flavours. No one could possibly have forecast what was to come.

The summer had been busy and now, mid-September, Ally was beginning to feel a tad weary. Was it her age? She was now seventy-one after all, and she'd been living here in Locharran for over two years, much against the advice of her son and daughter, who both initially thought she'd lost her senses when she decided to move to this isolated spot and convert the old, neglected malthouse into The Auld Malthouse B&B.

She had been very glad to welcome a family who'd come all the way from Canada for the games a couple of days ago because summer was coming to an end, and the bookings had begun to drop off.

The village still buzzed with visitors, of course, many of whom had actually come just for the Locharran Highland Games, which, for no apparent reason, always took place on a Wednesday. And to gape at the spectacular castle up there, the historical home of the Earls of Locharran.

When Ally, along with her friend and lover, Ross, had arrived at the field, they found themselves standing next to Morag McConnachie, her cleaner, along with Morag's husband, Murdo, the village postman. Between them, these two knew everyone and everything that took place in the village.

'Well, look who's here!' Morag exclaimed, nudging her husband.

'Aye,' said Murdo, squinting against the sun. 'Just a pity ye had to bring that bloody Canadian with ye!' He referred to Archie Armstrong who, Morag had told her earlier when she'd seen the booking, was some sort of champion sportsman. He was known as the 'Atlantic Warrior'.

'I didn't bring him with me,' Ally protested. 'He just happens to be staying under my roof!'

'Aye, well,' Murdo muttered to no one in particular.

'Murdo's only worried, ye see, because *that man's* goin' to be winnin' everythin'!' Morag said.

Now Morag nudged Ally's arm. 'Look, there are my boys! Our lads have been trainin' for this all year, and it's not fair. Our Micky's awful mad about that Canadian being allowed to take part.'

Morag had told her several times that their eldest son was a builder, known at these events as Muscles McConnachie, who'd won several contests of strength throughout Scotland, including caber tossing. He'd fully believed he'd be winning this event too, until Archie Armstrong had unexpectedly arrived on the scene. Micky's younger brother, Bobby, known in these same circles as Braveheart Bobby, still lived at home and was another hopeful.

'Our Bobby's up and runnin' all mornin', *every mornin*',' Morag informed Ally, 'and then he's off to the gym for his weight trainin'!' As she spoke, Morag's eyes glowed with pride, and Ally could only wonder if Braveheart Bobby ever found time to do any work.

'There was no word of a Highland Games *last* summer,' Ally had remarked, giving a wave to her friend, Linda, who was helping in the hospitality tent at the far end of the field.

'Ach,' replied Morag, 'we didn't have them last year cos Jimmy McCrae's field was flooded and so they had the games at Clachar instead – and a bloody poor job they made of it!' She shook her head sadly at the memory of it all.

Now there was further cheering from the crowd, including Morag and Murdo, as the elderly Earl of Locharran, in his green tartan kilt and tweed jacket, stepped jauntily up onto the podium. The earl, Hamish Sinclair, was a tall, handsome man in his seventies, with more than a passing resemblance to Sean Connery. He had white hair, a neatly trimmed white beard and a roguish twinkle in his eye. He'd finally settled down after years of womanising, due to meeting a young lady who'd provided him with not just one heir, but two at once! Kenneth and William the twins were called and they were the legal inheritors of everything the eye could see – and a lot it couldn't – including the land for miles around *and* the entire village. The lady in question, Magda, was now watching him proudly alongside her twin baby boys, fast asleep in an enormous Silver Cross pram – an item rarely seen amongst all the strollers and buggies these days. Had it once transported the earl himself? Ally could only wonder and admire how Magda – once a nanny herself – coped so efficiently and calmly with these babies.

The earl wrestled with the microphone for a moment and did some throat clearing before finally addressing the crowd. 'I am delighted to see you all here today, to continue the tradition of our beloved Highland Games, and welcome everyone!' Much cheering. 'I am proud to announce the games are now *open*!'

Immediately this was followed by the skirl of the pipes as the pipe band marched around the field a couple of times in their black jackets, red tartan kilts and plaids, playing 'O Flower of Scotland' – the unofficial Scottish anthem – and, as the pipers droned their way out of the field, Callum Dalrymple, manager of the Craigmonie Hotel and one of the organisers of the games, ascended the podium. He was a stocky, good-looking man in his mid-fifties, with hypnotic blue eyes which, when Ally had first met him, reminded her of Paul Newman's. She'd rather fancied him then, in spite of him being much younger than her. But that, of course, was before she met Ross.

Callum announced that the first event today would be the tug of war against the Fort William team, which elicited more whoops and cheers from the crowd. The Locharran team had an enormous asset on their side: the so-called Atlantic Warrior, as well as Muscles McConnachie and Braveheart Bobby.

Ally could not recall ever having seen so many muscular bodies in the flesh, so to speak, and couldn't help but wonder how many hours of training went into the maintenance of these gleaming torsos.

Ross put his arm round Ally. 'Stick your eyes back into your head!' he instructed with a laugh. 'You would never be able to cope with that much testosterone!'

'Just as well I don't have to then!' Ally replied, leaning against his firm body. 'You've got as much testosterone as I need!'

What would she do without Ross?

Ally recalled their first meeting, when she'd taken her new black Labrador puppy, Flora, into the vet's surgery for her inoculations and, instead of finding Will Patterson, the usual vet, she'd found his supposedly retired father. It had been a lucky day for Ally, and their relationship had gone from strength to strength.

Ally turned her attention to the tug of war, which was accompanied by much grunting, groaning, some swearing and a great deal of muscle flexing. The Locharran team, thanks to the Atlantic Warrior, won easily. After hammer throwing was announced as the next event, Hamish made his way across to where Ally and Ross were standing.

'Foregone conclusion, I suppose,' he said, pulling a face. 'That Canadian is as strong as an ox!' He turned to Ally. 'I believe they're staying with you at the malthouse?'

'They are,' Ally said, 'and I understand that his wife has a relative around here?'

'Oh indeed,' Hamish confirmed. 'She's Angus's niece.'

Angus was the earl's senior ghillie, in charge of all the equipment for stag hunting, fishing and shooting, as well as being in charge of the dog kennels. An elderly, gruff old fellow, he'd been with the earl for countless years.

'As it happens, Angus is in a terrible state as we had a break-in at the castle yesterday!'

'A break-in?' Ally and Ross asked in unison.

'Was anything taken?' Ally continued.

'Just a rifle. They broke into the gun cabinet, and Angus is most cut up about it. That's the reason he's not here today – he has the police to deal with.'

'Poor Angus!'

'Yes, and no doubt he's disappointed because he was always very fond of his niece. I remember the girl well – Patti, she calls herself now,' the earl continued. He looked around. 'I'd best be going – got things to see to! See you both later!' With a wave, he made his way back to the hospitality tent.

Many of the same contestants who had taken part in the tug of war were also about to take part in the hammer throwing and the caber tossing. Another popular contestant was Ivan, known as Ivan the Terrible, since no one could pronounce his surname. He was the Lithuanian barman at the Craigmonie Hotel who, when he wasn't imbibing vast amounts of whisky, spent his time bodybuilding. And there was Forby McKinnon, son of Finlay, the local fisherman, who didn't believe in giving himself a silly name.

The 'hammer' was actually a metal ball attached with a steel wire to the 'grip', which weighed around sixteen pounds and was basically a test of who could throw the thing furthest. There was a red flag stuck in the ground to show the current record.

The earl's foregone conclusion was correct – Archie Armstrong's hammer was the only one which sailed past the red flag.

'What a farce!' Ross muttered. 'The local lads didn't stand a chance.'

The earl reappeared to present Archie Armstrong with a medal, the tourists providing most of the applause. Archie had accepted the medal and returned to the sidelines with a swagger, looking at his rivals with undisguised disdain.

The other contestants had by now also retreated to the sidelines, preparing for the caber tossing, which was the event that really got the crowds interest.

But first it was time for the Highland dancing competition.

When the so-called Atlantic Warrior had arrived at Ally's guest house, he came accompanied not only by his glamorous wife Patti but also his two pretty daughters, Julie and Janey. They were tall, slim girls with green eyes; attractive enough except that, every time Ally had set eyes on them, they were always chewing gum, and with their mouths open, which wasn't a good look. With them was Archie's sister Wendy and her husband Greg Watson, on their first visit to Scotland.

The pipe band marched on again and played 'Oh, Campbeltown Loch, I Wish You Were Whisky', followed by the music for the Highland dance competition. First there was the sword dance, then the Highland fling, all performed with arms aloft, kilts and plaids swirling, toes tapping.

'Aw, that was grand!' said Morag, gazing at their granddaughter with pride. 'Our Katy's done right well!'

After a moment while the judges conferred, Hamish stepped up to the microphone again. 'Ladies and gentlemen,' he boomed. 'We can now announce the three winners for the Highland dancing.' He paused to let this sink in. Then: 'In third place, we have Miss Katy McConnachie!'

Much applause followed, particularly from the proud grandparents, Murdo cheering loudly, although Morag was muttering under her breath, 'She should've been *first*!'

Janey Armstrong was the winner, Julie Armstrong the runner-up.

Ally heard both Morag and Murdo groan. The Armstrongs provided most of the applause, as the two girls went up to collect medals from the earl. Then, after shaking their hands, and probably aware of some disgruntlement amongst the spectators, the earl headed swiftly back to the hospitality tent.

'That's not fair,' moaned Morag. 'Not fair at all.'

'Well, I suppose a little competition is no bad thing?' Ally suggested.

'A little competition! Are you serious? They'll take all the bloody prizes!'

At last it was time for the caber tossing. A long, tapered pole, usually cut from a larch tree and between sixteen and twenty feet long, the caber usually weighed somewhere around a hundred and fifty pounds. To execute it perfectly, the competitor had to balance the caber upright, tapered end pointing downwards, supported by stewards while it was placed in position. They were then meant to crouch, slide their interlocked hands down the caber and under the base, then lift it in their cupped hands – not an easy feat with the heavier end at the top. They then had to walk or run a few paces forward to gain momentum, and flip the tapered end upwards so that the large end hit the ground first, falling directly away from them.

The first contestant was Ivan the Terrible. He got into position, cupping his hands to receive the narrower end of the caber. It was a very wobbly business, and Ivan tottered a few paces to gain momentum, before tossing the caber with all of his might, plainly hoping it would fall with the large end hitting the ground first, end over, the ultimate aim.

Unfortunately, it fell sideways, as so many did. He had two further attempts. One fell sideways again, and the other successfully did land, end over, to much applause from everyone. Ivan was popular.

He was followed by Muscles McConnachie, who didn't do so well, only managing three sideways falls. Nevertheless, this had Morag and Murdo jumping up and down, still cheering wildly, along with the rest of Locharran.

Braveheart Bobby, Muscles's brother, was next. He had great style, but, according to Murdo's reaction, he hadn't done too well either. 'I dinna understand it,' he said gloomily. 'He's been practisin' and practisin'...'

'He'll be awful disappointed with that,' Morag said sadly.

Now it was the turn of Forby McKinnon. Forby, like Ivan, had one successful toss and two which landed sideways.

The fifth, and final, contestant was none other than Archie Armstrong, the Atlantic Warrior, winner of the hammer throwing and father of the Highland dancing champions. He appeared from somewhere out of sight, full of confidence and wearing a blue-and-green tartan kilt. The caber was hoisted up and lowered into his hands. He flexed his muscles, smiled benignly, and took a couple of steps forward to gain momentum but, as he ran with the caber, there was an ear-splitting shot and the Atlantic Warrior tumbled to the ground, the caber crashing on top of him.

People came running from every direction. Ally and Ross had pushed their way to the front, and Ross kneeled by Archie Armstrong's prone figure, gently turning him over and checking his pulse. The sound of the shot had plainly unnerved him and caused him to fall, the falling caber striking the fatal blow.

'Oh my God!' Ally exclaimed as she realised what had happened.

'There's nothing we can do for him,' Ross said flatly, turning to the crowd now gathering. 'He's dead.'

As Ross laid him gently back on the ground, Ally noticed a fresh graze alongside the dead man's right ear. She had limited experience in this area, but unless she was very much mistaken, this was a bullet graze. It had missed him by a fraction of an inch, but there was little doubt that it had been intended for him.

This was murder.

TWO

Ross stood up and looked around. 'Where is this man's wife?'

As he did so, Archie's two daughters and their aunt, all crying, had elbowed their way through the rapidly gathering crowd.

'Mom! Where's Mom?' the older girl shrieked, while the younger one sobbed in her aunt's arms.

Patti had obviously been told because she appeared from somewhere beyond where the others had been standing.

'Oh my God!' she screamed, kneeling down beside her husband. 'Oh *no*! Oh God!' She was kissing him now and moaning loudly. 'Who would *do* this?' she shouted, pointing at the graze on Archie's ear. 'Oh, somebody *do* something! Girls, come here!' She stood up, and both girls rushed into her outstretched arms. 'You shouldn't have to see this!'

'I'm so sorry,' Ross said, walking towards her. 'It's too late to do anything for your husband, but I'm calling the police now, and they'll be here shortly.' He looked around at the gawping crowd. 'Please stand well back, or go away!' he shouted. 'There'll be no more events today!'

Patti, the girls and Archie's sister were huddled together alongside Archie's body, weeping inconsolably. Suddenly, Archie's sister, Wendy, yelled out, 'Greg! Where the hell *are* you?'

Her husband emerged from the hospitality tent looking slightly bewildered, accompanied by the earl. Greg rushed towards the weeping family. 'Oh, Wendy!' He embraced his hysterical wife, while staring down at his brother-in-law's body. 'How the hell did this happen?'

The police arrived promptly, but the two young constables appeared to be out of their depth, phoning frantically for senior intervention. One of them had taken Patti, Wendy, Greg and the girls away to the hospitality tent, which was now empty, to await the arrival of Detective Inspector Kandahar. The other one stood alongside the body shooing everyone away. The crowd had evaporated rapidly, most of them heading towards the Craigmonie Hotel to recover with a stiff drink. A few remained, standing well back, gawping with ghoulish fascination.

When Amir Kandahar appeared with the forensic team, he took Ally and Ross to one side.

'What on earth has happened here?' he asked, shaking his head and staring at the body. 'Isn't this supposed to be a light-hearted, enjoyable, sporty event?'

'Good question,' agreed Ally. 'A shot came out of nowhere and caused him to lose his balance completely. It was obviously meant to kill him!'

'Well, indirectly the caber *did* kill him, and that shot came out of *somewhere*!' Amir said with a faint smile. 'Forensics need to study this – we have to get more idea of the exact direction the shot came from, and the constables are combing the area back there right now looking for the gun.' He turned to Ally. 'Where were you two standing when this happened?'

Ross pointed back. 'Around there somewhere.'

'And you saw nothing unusual going on? People coming or going? The family, for instance, where were they?'

Ally tried to think, wishing now that she'd paid more attention to the spectators than to the brawny bodies. She shook her head. 'If I'd known...'

'We're always wiser after the event,' said Ross.

'Well, have a think,' said Amir. 'I'll have to question the family now, which I'm not looking forward to. I'll bring them back to you later.'

Amir Kandahar was a tall, good-looking South Asian man in his mid-forties who hailed from Glasgow. Earlier that year, he had replaced Detective Inspector Bob Rigby, who had retired due to heart problems. Ally had had a good relationship with Rigby and had helped him with his investigations on several occasions. He'd been impressed with her sleuthing skills and had sung her praises to Amir. As a result, she and Amir had struck up a friendship, and he was inclined to use her as a sounding board. Ally knew, from their conversations, that Amir had been widowed two years before, and struggled at times to bring up his two teenage daughters on his own, albeit with the help of his extended family.

Back at the malthouse Ally lit the log burner in the kitchen, and she and Ross sat on either side of it, sipping large gin and tonics.

She was dreading the Armstrongs coming back to the malthouse later. What on earth could you say to the widow, daughters and sister of a man who'd just been killed in front of their very eyes in a foreign country?

There must be a certain stigma, Ally reckoned as she sipped her drink, attached to having your most famous guest murdered on day three of his stay in your guest house. It could be off-putting, to say the least, as far as future bookings were concerned. Not that it had happened *under* Ally's roof, of course, but nevertheless...

She recalled the previous Sunday morning's conversation with Morag, when she'd mentioned that a family called Armstrong were about to arrive.

'So long as it's not that Archie Armstrong!' Morag had exclaimed, raising her eyes to heaven and her mug of tea to her lips.

'Well, I think it just might be because that is the name they booked with – Mr and Mrs Archibald Armstrong, their two daughters and another couple who I believe are related.'

At this, Morag had to sit down, hand on heart. 'Did you not know that he's the champion Canadian hammer thrower and caber tosser? Oh my God, just wait until I tell our Micky and our Bobby! We knew *that man* was over here earlier in the year competing at other Highland Games, but we thought he'd gone home by now. He calls himself the Atlantic Warrior!'

Ally had no idea about Atlantic Warriors. She'd taken their booking, delighted to have her three guest rooms booked for a week so late in the year. Atlantic Warrior or not, he, along with his wife, two daughters, sister and brother-in-law were all staying in The Auld Malthouse.

Standing at the kitchen window as Morag bustled off to finish cleaning the rooms, Ally had looked out over her garden and the purple hills stretching out behind in the morning sunshine. It was a good end to the season, and she braced herself to cope with the months ahead. Sometimes she wondered if her children had been right when they'd tried to dissuade her – then in her late sixties – from purchasing the old, empty malthouse. Her son, Jamie, had been particularly sceptical about the whole thing, not least because he'd lived close to her in Edinburgh and liked to keep an eye on her. Her daughter,

Carol, down in Wiltshire, was a little more encouraging, knowing about her mother's love of adventure, but also possibly thinking of free holidays with her family.

For hundreds of years, the building had been used for storing malt for the whisky which had now been moved to more hygienic premises. She'd come up on holiday and fallen in love with the old place in its glorious setting halfway up the hill beneath the huge, turreted castle towering above and the village straddling the river below. Should she have stayed in her comfortable Edinburgh flat instead of moving up here and converting this old building?

Good Lord, no, *no*! Particularly not on this golden September day!

'What are they like as a family?' Ross asked now as he refilled their glasses, comfortable in their seats by the fire.

'Pleasant enough,' Ally said, sipping her gin. 'They were very complimentary about the place, and said that, while they were touring Scotland anyway, they'd decided to visit Locharran to compete in the games. Archie had Scottish parents and liked to visit often.'

'When did they get here?' Ross asked. He lived a few miles away in a converted barn, closer to the coast, where he had a thriving holiday business. When they'd become lovers, it was normally more practical for him to sleep at the malthouse where, most of the time, Ally had guests. On Sunday evening, however, when the Armstrongs had arrived, he'd been at home dealing with some of his own guests who'd arrived very late.

'They arrived on Sunday evening, as scheduled, in a people carrier. Archie and Patti have Room One, the two girls are in Room Two, and Archie's sister, Wendy, and her husband Greg Watson, have Room Three.'

'There was no sign of them being at daggers drawn with each other or anything then?' Ross asked.

'No, not at all. They all seemed very happy and friendly,

and enjoying staying here. They've had the full Scottish breakfast every morning. Except for Patti, who only has tea and toast, or cereal.'

'So, no problems?'

'Well, no, but when I asked them if they'd slept well, one of the girls said she'd wakened in the night and heard some funny noises coming from the bathroom and thought it was the wind. Except there was no wind on Sunday night, so need I say more?'

Ross rolled his eyes. 'God, not *Willie* again!'

Wailing Willie was the ghost Ally had inherited when she bought the malthouse. A couple of hundred years back, Willie, a local piper, had broken into the malthouse one night because he'd been told, correctly, that there was a stash of bottles of the end product locked away in an upstairs storeroom. He'd taken his bagpipes with him and, as he'd drunk his way through the golden liquid, he'd played a few tunes to celebrate. That was fine until he'd hit the second bottle when, drunk as a skunk, the 'music' had evolved into a series of drawn-out wails. Willie had died a very happy man in what had now become the en-suite bathroom to Room 2. And his wails always signalled an imminent death.

Ally had been sceptical at first. Ridiculous! Typical village gossip! Until, that is, Willie's wails had actually forecast several deaths since Ally had moved in.

Ally was becoming more and more concerned about the return of the remaining guests and, draining her glass, stood up. 'I think I'll suggest they go into the sitting room when they get back,' she said, glancing at her watch. 'Although I've no idea when that's likely to be. I think I should leave some bottles of spirits and mixers in there for them to help themselves because they must still be in a state of shock.'

'They walked down to the games, didn't they?'

'Yes, so I expect it'll be the police who bring them back,' Ally said, watching as Ross set up a tray with bottles and glasses.

'I think I can hear a car out there now,' Ross said, lifting up the laden tray and making his way towards the sitting room.

As Ally followed him, she opened the front door to see Detective Inspector Amir Kandahar standing there. Behind him, the Armstrong family were slowly getting themselves out from the police car.

He looked somewhat weary this evening, and who could blame him? The family had now formed a line behind him: Patti, tearful, make-up smudged, hair hanging limply round her shoulders, was supported by her equally tearful two daughters, with the other couple walking slowly behind.

'Please come into the sitting room and relax, if you can,' Ally said, stepping aside to let them enter. 'Help yourselves to anything you want, and do let me know if I can get you any hot drinks or anything.'

Patti nodded, let out a wail and collapsed on the sofa. The tear-stained girls plonked themselves down on either side of her, holding her hands. The only person who seemed to be in control was Greg Watson, husband of Wendy, who was still weeping openly.

'This is real kind of you,' he said to Ally. 'I guess we just need to sit here quietly for a while in this beautiful room of yours and get our strength back.' He took a deep breath. 'These four gals have been through hell this afternoon.'

One of the girls – was it Janey or Julie? – stood up suddenly. 'Someone's just killed our *daddy*!' she shouted before falling back onto the sofa again and cuddling up to her mother.

'I am so sorry,' Ally said. 'I really don't know what to say other than if I can help with anything in any way...' Her voice tailed off.

'I guess we'll all have a nightcap before bed,' Greg said. 'How about it, everyone?'

Nobody paid much attention to him, and so Ally thought this was a good time to take her leave. She retreated to the kitchen where, to her surprise, Amir and Ross were drinking tea together.

'Just thought I'd wait and have a quick word with you,' Amir said. 'Obviously these people are in a state of shock at the moment, but tomorrow might be telling.'

Ally frowned. 'What do you mean?'

'Just watch them. They might revert to type,' Amir replied.

Ally was aghast. 'You don't think...?'

'I don't think anything. But someone shot Archie Armstrong, even if it was indirectly, and we can't rule anyone out, not even his own family, not all of whom were close by watching, I'm told. Can you remember seeing them *all* watching Archie?'

'I remember seeing the girls at the front, and Archie's sister was somewhere behind but, now you come to mention it, I don't remember seeing Patti, but I think I saw the brother-in-law somewhere around the hospitality tent. But they're all *devastated*!'

'That's as may be,' Amir said enigmatically. 'Thanks for the tea. I'll probably call in again tomorrow.' He stood up and walked towards the door. 'Sleep well!'

Unlikely, Ally thought as she closed the door behind Amir and stood for moment in the hallway. When she'd had the old malthouse converted, she'd had this spacious hallway made, with an oak staircase leading up to the three en-suite bedrooms. The rooms on either side on the ground floor had become a dining room and sitting room respectively. To her right, she could hear the murmur of subdued voices from the sitting room as her guests drank their nightcaps, still shocked at the day's events.

Ally, lingering for a moment longer in the quiet hallway, had never dreamt that she'd be plunged into another murder investigation and realised, as she headed to the kitchen to tidy away the tea things, that she was feeling extremely apprehensive about what tomorrow might bring.

No, it was *very* unlikely she'd sleep well.

THREE

Ally predicted that breakfast was likely to be a shambles, and it was. She'd given the Armstrong family the usual spiel about breakfast times when they'd first arrived and, for the last couple of days, they'd all trooped down at nine o'clock, had full Scottish breakfasts and then gone out by ten, leaving Morag sufficient time to do their rooms without interruption. This morning, however, the only person who appeared at nine o'clock was Morag.

'Where *are* they all?' she asked as she removed her purple anorak and tied on her apron.

'Still upstairs, I'm afraid,' Ally replied. 'I should think we can write off any normal routine this morning.'

Hands on hips, Morag surveyed the kitchen. 'How am I supposed to do their rooms then?'

Ally shrugged. 'We'll have to play it by ear. See who comes down first, and then perhaps you could nip up and do a quick tidy while they're eating. *If* they're eating.'

'Tsk, tsk,' said Morag grumpily, heading for the kettle to make herself a cup of tea. 'I suppose it's to be expected.'

'Of course it is. They've just lost a husband, a father, a brother – killed in front of their very eyes.'

'Aye, well it wouldn't be anyone from round here that would have tried to shoot him. It was probably one of them that pulled the trigger!'

'I doubt that very much,' Ally said, 'because they were in such a state when they got back last night. They were really absolutely shattered and weeping. They all needed a drink, even the girls, and, in fact, there are probably still some glasses lying around in the sitting room.'

Morag wasn't finished yet. 'They was all standin' well back when *that man* started off with the caber! Come to think of it, I only saw the daughters and the sister cheerin', and nobody was lookin' at them, was they? Everyone was gawpin' at that big brute, Armstrong!' She pursed her lips into a tight line. 'That's *all* I'm sayin'!'

At this point, Ross came in with two damp and exuberant dogs. He'd taken them for an early morning walk across the moors as he usually did when he stayed overnight. He grabbed an old towel and dried them off in the lobby at the back, where they'd stay while breakfast was being served.

Morag had gone to check the sitting room for any stray glasses and returned, wide-eyed. 'My God, there's a bloody woman asleep in there!'

'There *is*?' Ally rushed out across the hallway and peered around the sitting-room door. There was indeed a woman, fully dressed and fast asleep, draped across the sofa, and it took Ally several minutes to identify her as Wendy Watson. She had plainly fallen asleep in there the previous evening, and the rest of the family had decided to leave her to it.

Ally sighed. What to do now?

'It's Archie's sister,' she said as she re-entered the kitchen.

'So how am *I* supposed to get my work done?' Morag asked,

gulping her tea and running her hand through her mop of dyed-blonde hair.

At that moment, there was the sound of footsteps in the hall, and Ally looked out to see Greg, Wendy's husband, heading towards the sitting room.

'I'm sorry,' he said when he saw Ally. 'My wife fell asleep in here last night. She was exhausted from crying, and I thought it best to leave her.'

'That's not a problem, Greg. Do you fancy breakfast?'

'Don't think I could eat much,' he said, 'but I'll have some cereal, and coffee would be great.'

'Same for me,' said a female voice, and Ally turned to see Patti Armstrong had padded silently downstairs in her socks. She was wearing tight jeans and an oversized sweater, and she was perfectly made-up, her blonde hair immaculate. Ally tried not to gawp at this newly bereaved widow who, only last night, had looked a total wreck.

'Have you managed to get some sleep?' Ally asked solicitously.

'Oh yeah,' said Patti. 'A little. The girls are still pretty upset though.'

How on earth had Patti recovered so rapidly, Ally wondered, from the death of her husband of twenty years, or whatever it was? Ally remembered then two points: Detective Inspector Kandahar saying something about 'reverting to type', and Morag's suggestion that one of the family had fired the gun. Was that possible?

If nothing else, at least now Morag could do two of the rooms upstairs.

Amir Kandahar arrived at ten o'clock, just as Wendy had woken up and staggered into the dining room to join her husband and sister-in-law.

'I'll talk to them later,' Amir said as he sat down at the kitchen table and opened up his briefcase, accepting a mug of tea. He sighed. 'Let me know when they're *all* in the dining room,' he said, 'but, in the meantime, could you take me through yesterday again in more detail – where you were standing in relation to the caber tossing area, and what, if anything, you saw going on among the other spectators?'

Ally looked at Ross, and they both shrugged.

'The thing is,' Ross said, 'everyone's eyes were riveted on Archie Armstrong. He'd already won the hammer throwing, his daughters had won the dancing and I guess that people were either grudgingly admiring the man, or hoping he'd trip up.'

'Well, he certainly did that,' Amir said drily. 'According to the post-mortem, judging from the grazing on his ear, the bullet was fired from somewhere due east to where he was staggering around with the caber. Thank God a couple of people were videoing the event so we have a little film footage.' He frowned and passed a piece of paper across the table. 'This is a rough map of the field, with the tossing area marked off. Where exactly would you say you were standing?'

Ally studied it for a moment. 'We were sort of south-east, I suppose,' she said, pointing her finger at the likely spot and handing him back the sheet of paper.

'We think the killer must have been hiding in the trees at the top of the hill, above where the mobile toilets were, but can you remember some of the people standing on this east side near you?'

'Most of the competitors and their supporters were near where we were standing because it was the best viewpoint, and the Armstrong family, of course.'

'Hmm,' said the inspector, 'that's interesting. I think it's time I spoke to them again.'

Ally could hear some movement in the dining room. 'Let me have a look in there,' she said.

There was still no sign of the two girls, but Wendy, looking dishevelled and blotchy, was pouring herself some fruit juice, her husband at her side. She was tall, like her brother, but gangly and not very strong-looking, with dark hair tied back in a ponytail. Patti was seated, ramrod straight, at the table toying with a bowl of cereal. They could probably manage coffee and toast, they said in unison, but nothing else. The girls did not want to come down and so they'd take some fruit upstairs to them, if Ally didn't mind. Ally didn't mind at all.

She went back into the kitchen and related the conversation to Amir.

'Did you tell them I was here?' he asked as he prepared to head towards the dining room.

Ally shook her head. 'No, I didn't.'

'I'll have a word with them then.' Amir picked up his files and, as he got to the door, asked, 'What about your cleaner? When can I speak to her?'

'She'll be down as soon as she finishes the bedrooms,' Ally said.

'Good,' said Amir. 'Don't let her leave until I've spoken with her. And watch out for reporters because they're likely to be here in force and probably knocking at your door. Tell them absolutely nothing.'

'The girls are still in their bedroom,' complained Morag as she arrived in the kitchen shortly afterwards, 'but at least I've had a chance to tidy up the other two rooms—' She stopped short as she saw Amir come in from the dining room.

'Can I have a word, please, Mrs Mc...'

'McConnachie,' said Morag. 'Just a moment while I have my much-needed cuppa.'

He looked slightly taken aback as Morag made her way to

the kettle and made herself a large mug of tea. 'I *always* have a cuppa when I've done the rooms,' she told him.

'Just a few questions, Mrs McConnachie, if you don't mind. I believe you were at this event yesterday?'

'Aye, *of course* I was. With Murdo, my husband, the postie.' She looked at him as if he should have known this. 'I'll have ye know I had two boys competin' in them events, and a wee granddaughter in the dancin', and—'

'And where were you standing in relation to this map?' Amir interjected, handing her the field plan.

Morag scowled. 'I was standin' right next to Ally here. Wasn't I, Ally?' She looked across to where Ally was loading the dishwasher.

'Yes, you were.'

'And you stayed there all the time?' asked Amir.

Morag gave him another of her looks. 'Of course not! As soon as the caber tossin' started, Murdo and me moved over to where our lads had been standin'.'

'You saw or heard nothing suspicious?'

'Nobody was runnin' around with a gun, if that's what ye mean? Whoever it was, it wouldn't be anyone from Locharran, let me tell ye *that*! This is a peaceful place with law-abidin' folk, but, of course, I canna speak for all them *foreigners*.' She shook her head and took a large gulp of tea.

'Foreigners?' asked the inspector. 'What foreigners?'

'*That man's* family, of course. All Canadians, them. And some folk from Fort William who could have been foreigners too. How would *I* know?'

'Oh, indeed,' said Amir, exchanging glances with Ally. 'And your husband stayed at your side throughout this time?'

'Well, he went for a pee at some stage, I canna remember when.' Morag frowned. 'Me and Murdo don't go around shootin' people, you know? We have better things to do.' She paused. 'Even though he bloody well deserved that bullet!

Cavortin' around at village gatherin's and winnin' all the prizes, when our lads have been practisin' all year! And they're *locals*! It's not bloody fair! Just as well I *don't* have a gun! Have you done with me?' Morag scowled as she drained her tea.

'Oh, indeed, Mrs McConnachie. Thank you for your help.'

Morag disappeared into the porch to remove her apron, hang it up and put on her purple anorak again. 'See you tomorrow!' she yelled at Ally. 'If the good Lord spares me.'

'Well, that's *me* told,' said Amir with a grin as he left.

Ally didn't really think that Morag could be involved, but she couldn't say the same for Morag's two sons. Or any of the other competitors, for that matter. There seemed to be quite a few people who might have wanted Archie dead.

FOUR

Ross was helping his son at the veterinary surgery for part of the morning. 'I must go too, love, so see you later,' he said to Ally, kissing her, as he and his black Labrador, Ebony, made their way towards the back door, where Morag was still pulling on her boots.

Just at that moment, Murdo arrived with the post, and Morag trundled back into the kitchen.

'Have ye heard the *latest*?' Murdo asked hopefully as he laid a couple of envelopes onto the kitchen table.

'I expect you're needing some tea?' Ally said, knowing that Murdo liked to stop off on his rounds for constant refreshment.

'Aye,' he said. 'I'll just have a wee mouthful, if ye please.' He nodded towards the front of the building. 'I see the police car's outside there?'

'Yes, Detective Inspector Kandahar's just leaving. He's been talking to the Armstrongs,' Ally replied, handing him a large mug of tea, which was Murdo's idea of a wee mouthful.

Morag stood, hands on hips, and glared at her husband. 'Have we heard *what*?'

'The earl's goin' potty cos of that break-in they had at the castle when someone stole a rifle, and the police think it'll likely be the one that was supposed to kill that Armstrong bloke.' Murdo took a couple of long gulps. 'And poor old Angus is awful worried cos he's supposed to be lookin' after all the guns.'

'And are they certain that was the rifle that fired the shot?' Ally asked.

'Well,' said Murdo, '*you're* the one that's pally with that inspector! Did he not tell you?'

'No, he didn't!'

Murdo nodded. 'They found that bullet stuck in the caber. I heard they're runnin' tests, but it looks like being the right kind of bullet to have come from one of the earl's rifles.'

Ally was horrified. So *was* that the weapon? It was too much of a coincidence not to be surely? She had no idea in which part of the castle the gun cabinets were, but she guessed that they were probably somewhere in the utility area at the back or in one of the outbuildings.

When they'd finished breakfast, Patti asked Ally if it would be all right to use the sitting room for most of the day. They'd do their best to take their minds off the horrendous tragedy by watching TV or trying to read. The girls had their phones, of course, and would be glued to those.

As predicted by Amir, the media had arrived in force – reporters, film crews and photographers all hanging around in the lane between the malthouse and the village. Two of them ventured to the door to ask the whereabouts of the Armstrong family, and Ally politely told them that she was not at liberty to give out that sort of information, hoping that none of them would leave the sitting room while she was dealing with the press. One reporter was particularly persistent. 'Surely,' he said, 'it's not going to harm the case if we just have a chat with Mrs Armstrong?'

'Mrs Armstrong does not want to be disturbed at this sad time,' Ally said, repeating one of Amir's suggestions.

In spite of their grief, everyone got hungry around lunchtime, and Greg was dispatched to find some pizzas, which he did, after directions to Concetti's from Ally. The reporters presumably didn't know who Greg was, so he was able to walk down to the village, returning with a mountain of boxes, in every imaginable flavour, plus two bottles of wine, and they all moved to the dining room after Ally produced some plates, glasses and cutlery.

Back in the kitchen, she was making herself a sandwich when there was a knock on the back door and in walked the earl.

'Oh, Hamish. Good to see you! Can I make you a sandwich?'

'That's kind, Ally, but no thanks. I just wondered how the Armstrongs were bearing up?'

'They've recovered enough to be eating pizza in the dining room,' Ally replied, 'if you want to go in there.'

Hamish shook his head. 'I don't particularly want to see them. Just wondered how you were coping with a bereaved family, and to tell you that the rifle we had stolen has been found and believed to have been the weapon that fired the shot. Would you believe the bullet was found in the *caber*?'

'Murdo told us this morning,' Ally said. 'I think he saw Angus on his travels.'

'Poor Angus! He's beside himself!' Hamish sighed. 'He just can't understand how anyone could have broken into that cabinet without him being aware of it.'

'And is that definitely the gun that fired the bullet that indirectly killed Archie Armstrong?' Ally said.

'Yes, the police are now certain it was actually *that* rifle, and they found it in the woods that adjoin the field. Whoever fired that gun was a very good shot indeed, even if they didn't *quite* hit their target, but no one appears to have seen anything. No fingerprints yet, of course.' He stroked his beard. 'Ghastly business.'

'I understand that Angus is related to the Armstrongs,' Ally remarked.

'Yes, he's Pat's uncle – although I'm told we must call her "Patti" now apparently.'

'Did you ever meet her?'

Hamish nodded. 'I remember her well because she used to come up and stay with her uncle Angus for a week every summer. She was always a bit of a girl, man-crazy in her youth. She was just plain "Pat" back then, when Archie met her at the Glenfinnan Gathering eighteen years ago, according to Angus. Archie was competing, and Pat was serving drinks at the bar. They haven't been over much since, but Angus was pleased that she and the family had visited him at the castle a couple of times earlier this week after they arrived.'

'You don't think...?'

'No idea. Just saying.' Hamish gave a hint of a smile.

'Fancy some tea or coffee?'

'I'd rather have a wee whisky,' he said.

As Ally poured the whisky, she asked, 'How's Magda?'

'She's very well, thank you.'

Ally was glad that Hamish had abandoned his old, somewhat lecherous ways. When she'd first arrived in Locharran, Ally had been warned about the earl and his penchant for the ladies. As predicted, he had made advances in her direction, and she'd had to tell him firmly that there was to be no hanky-panky but that she'd like him as a friend. Much to her surprise, he'd agreed, and they had indeed become firm friends.

When Magda arrived on the scene, it had been during a really difficult time for her, during which she'd not bothered much with her appearance, and it was Ally who had driven her to Inverness for a great haircut and some smart clothes and make-up. This had proved so successful in bringing Magda out of her shell that it hadn't been long before she and Hamish had struck up a relationship and the twins were on the way. Since only legitimate heirs were allowed to inherit, a delighted Hamish had wasted no time in putting a ring on Magda's finger and seemed to be embracing first-time fatherhood in his mid-seventies, despite having little idea of what it might entail.

'I'm longing to see the babies again,' Ally said.

'Well, you know you can come up to see them any time you fancy,' Hamish said, knocking back his drink. 'We're always delighted to see you – and Ross. Now I must go!'

Concetti's pizzas appeared to have revived the Armstrongs a little, even the girls. One of them knocked on the kitchen door that afternoon. 'Could my sister and I take your dog for a walk, please? Or play with her in the garden?'

Ally was taken aback for a moment. 'Yes, yes, of course,' she said. 'I know Flora would be delighted.'

Flora was. She came bounding out into the hallway at the mention of the magic word 'walk'.

'We just need some fresh air,' her sister said.

'Can you tell me which one of you is Julie and which one is Janey?' Ally asked, pleased to see some return to normality.

'I'm Julie,' said the slightly taller one. 'I'm seventeen.'

'And I'm Janey,' said her sister, 'and I'm fifteen, and we're trying not to think about yesterday.'

'We're missing our daddy so much,' said Julie, her eyes brimming with tears.

'But he wouldn't let us have a dog,' said Janey, dabbing her eyes with a tissue, 'and we love dogs.'

'Well, you can love Flora as much as you like,' Ally told them, smiling. 'She's a good dog, and she'll come back when you call her. You won't need a lead so long as you keep away from the main road.'

'We thought we'd walk across the moor,' Janey said. 'Mom said it's beautiful up there, but we don't know which way we should go.'

Ally accompanied them to the door and pointed out the well-trodden path through the heather and across the moor to Loch Soular. 'That will take you to a wee loch, one of my favourite walks,' she said, hoping they'd find it as therapeutic as she herself did.

As she closed the outside door behind them, Greg emerged from the dining room.

'May I have a word?' he asked.

'Of course. Come into the kitchen.'

Ally led him in, and, like most first-time visitors, Greg looked around and whistled. 'Wow, this is real nice,' he said.

This was always music to Ally's ears because she loved her kitchen and, against all odds, had been successful in making a large room feel cosy and welcoming.

The kitchen was very much Ally's domain. Off it was a little 'snug', also featuring a wood-burning stove, a large TV and a large sofa, where she and Ross spent many a cosy winter evening. The door at the back led to the rear porch, a toilet, and the stairs to Ally's own bedroom and bathroom.

'Coffee?' Ally asked.

'Thank you. Just a small cup,' he replied.

'Is your wife feeling a little better?'

He sighed. 'It's difficult. He was her only brother.'

'It must be awful for you all.'

'It's going to take time, particularly as that bullet must have been fired real close to where I was. It's unbelievable.'

'Where were you exactly?' Ally asked.

'In the hospitality tent,' he replied.

Ally poured some coffee. 'Milk and sugar?'

'Just a dash of milk, please,' he said, accepting the cup. 'Do you have *any* idea who might have done such an awful thing?'

Ally shook her head. 'I've no idea whatsoever. I know that some of the villagers were upset because Archie was the Canadian champion and they didn't think it fair that he was allowed to compete. But I very much doubt that any of them would go so far as to try to kill him.'

Greg took a sip of his drink and nodded. 'Great coffee. I'm a little concerned about Patti's uncle,' he continued. 'That's the old guy in charge of the guns, you know. We met him a couple of days ago; strange fellow.'

'Oh, Angus is all right,' Ally said defensively. 'He's been with the earl for fifty years and he's a little eccentric, but there's no harm in him.'

Greg didn't look particularly convinced. 'Angus didn't like Archie, you know.'

'Didn't he?'

'No, apparently he never approved of Patti marrying him. He thought she should have stayed home and married a Scotsman. But Archie *was* a Scotsman! Both of his parents were born and bred in Scotland. So I guess he just didn't like Archie for some reason.' Greg shook his head. 'What about the earl? Could he have had any reason to want Archie dead?'

Ally frowned. 'The earl's a good man. And what possible reason could there be for him to kill the star competitor? And apart from that, he would have been in the hospitality tent at the time. Didn't you see him?'

'No.' Greg shook his head.

'The earl's a great advocate for anything to do with tourism around here, you know, and this killing isn't exactly likely to pull in the crowds.' Ally poured herself a coffee and sat down. Did this man really think that she might know who'd fired that damned bullet? 'Were you close to your brother-in-law?'

'Not so much on a personal level,' he replied, 'but we were in business together. We make log cabins which sell all over North America, and it's very much a thriving business.' He hesitated for a moment. 'His personal life wasn't so great though. His marriage wasn't too happy.'

'What? Weren't they well suited?' Ally asked.

'He shouldn't have married her because he was known to play around.'

Ally didn't really think she should be hearing this because it was none of her business, but she couldn't help but be fascinated. She remembered that it was only a short time ago that the earl had been sitting in that very chair saying that Patti had been man-mad in her youth, but she'd heard nothing about Archie...

'Well, Greg, I'm sure the police will find the killer before too long. Detective Inspector Kandahar is very efficient.'

'Let's hope you're right. I'm not sure we're gonna be able to leave here until they do,' Greg said. He looked out of the window. 'It's beautiful here, but we need to get home; I got a business to run single-handed now. Anyway, I must go to see if Wendy's OK, but it's been good talking to you.'

Has it? Ally wondered. Why on earth had he thought that she might have known who killed Archie? He'd definitely been pointing a finger at poor old Angus and even the earl himself. But where had *he* himself been when the shot was fired? *Had* he been in the hospitality tent? Ally was beginning to wonder if he could just be deflecting suspicion away from himself. For that matter, where had Patti been as well? She'd told Amir that she'd just gone to get a coffee – he'd mentioned this to Ally just before he'd left. And Wendy. Had Wendy gone for a coffee too? Was the rifle definitely fired from the woods? Who knew?

Ally sat mulling this over for a good twenty minutes and got nowhere, so she remembered she needed a few groceries and her time would be better spent if she paid a visit to the shop. She was reluctant to face Queenie and Bessie because she had no idea how fast the rumour mill might have been spinning. But needs must.

FIVE

The Locharran Village Post Office and General Stores was run by two aged spinster sisters: Queenie and Bessie McDougall. Queenie was the elder and the boss, and spent most of her day stretched across the counter, so as not to miss any conversation which might be taking place between the aisles of canned goods and Locharran souvenirs – mainly tea towels sporting an unlikely tropically coloured depiction of the village and the castle. And Queenie was the font of all knowledge when it came to village gossip.

'Och, it's yersel',' Queenie stated as Ally walked in.

'I just need a few bits and pieces,' Ally said, picking up a basket and bracing herself for the barrage of questions to come.

'Ye was at the Games yesterday, I hear,' Queenie stated.

'Yes, I was,' Ally said, popping a jar of marmalade and one of raspberry jam into her basket. 'And, before you ask, yes, I did have the honour of accommodating the poor man who was killed, and his family, under my roof.'

'And they're still *here*?' Queenie asked.

'Well, *he* isn't, of course, but *they* are! Where would you expect them to be? This only happened yesterday!'

'I'll tell ye somethin',' Queenie said, leaning even further across the counter. 'That wife of his was a local lassie.'

'Yes, I know that,' Ally replied, placing her purchases on the counter. 'Angus's niece, I believe.'

'Pat McKay she was before she went off with that Canadian. She always liked the men.'

'Yes, well, she's very upset at the moment, naturally.' Ally wasn't sure that Patti was all that desperately upset, but she certainly wasn't going to tell Queenie this.

'Ach, she'll soon be findin' someone else,' Queenie retorted. 'Bessie,' she yelled into the depths of the storeroom. 'Did ye hear that?'

Bessie emerged from the room with some packs of toilet rolls. 'No, I didn't hear,' she said. She climbed a couple of steps up a ladder to best display the wares, at the same time tugging at her grey, droopy skirt in the hope that no one would see her voluminous pink knickers.

Queenie sniffed loudly. 'We was just talkin' about that shootin' yesterday.'

'Aye, well they'll no win any popularity prizes round here,' Bessie said as she lowered herself carefully down the steps.

'Our late brother's granddaughter was dancin',' Queenie said proudly. 'She's a grand wee dancer is Dolina. And she should have won! She's the best dancer for miles around! How come thae two girls of Pat's won? Eh, tell me that? Everyone's sayin' how well Dolina was dancin' better than the McConnachie lass, and a bloody sight better than them girls of Pat's! Just a shame our Charlie, God rest his soul, is no' here to see her. Did I ever tell ye about poor Charlie?'

'Yes, you did,' Ally got in quickly. She recalled hearing from Queenie, not so very long ago, all about their late brother who, in his normal inebriated state, had met his demise by stepping out in front of the bus from Clachar. That had been the end of him. But – Queenie had added with much satisfaction – it had been a 'grand funeral', although someone called Ecky, who'd been driving the bus, was never the same again.

Ally got her purse out, paid for her purchases and beat a hasty retreat.

When Ally got home, she found the girls sitting on a garden seat, concentrating on their phones. Occasionally, one or the other would toss the ball for Flora to retrieve.

'We had a real nice walk,' Janey said.

Ally was amused to see them wearing their dancing medals around their necks. 'Do you do much Scottish dancing in Canada?' she asked.

'Oh sure,' said Julie. 'We keep lots of Scottish traditions. And Daddy took us all over Scotland before...'

'But we're not going to be coming here again, *ever*,' said Janey. 'Not after this.' She blew her nose.

'I can hardly blame you,' Ally admitted, 'but it's such a shame because there's so much to see.'

'Will they ever find who did this?' asked Julie, her voice breaking.

'I'm sure they will,' Ally replied, 'and we have a very good detective on the case.'

'Is he the cute one with the lovely smile?' asked Janey.

Ally smiled. 'Yes, Detective Inspector Kandahar.'

'Mom says she quite fancies him,' added Julie.

Their mother has recovered mighty quickly, Ally thought.

'It's got to be one of the competitors,' Janey said, 'because, let's face it, they were all jealous of Dad. I overheard two of them talking, saying that Dad should have stayed in Canada, where he belonged. And the other one said, "I'd like to send him home in a box." Isn't that a mean thing to say?'

'Yes, it's a horrible thing to say,' Ally agreed.

'Mom's upset for Uncle Angus too,' Janey said. 'Did you know he was Mom's uncle?'

'Yes, I did know,' Ally said. 'He's a nice old boy.'

'Well,' Janey continued, 'nice or not, everyone's blaming him.'

'Because he's got the keys to everywhere,' added her sister.

'But the gun cabinet was broken into,' Ally said, 'so the keys weren't needed.'

'And who else would know where to find that gun store?' Janey asked. 'So it's got to be someone in this village! Because it sure as hell wasn't any of us.'

'Unless it was Uncle Greg,' Julie said with a snort.

'Don't say that!' Janey nudged her sister and looked somewhat guiltily in Ally's direction.

'Well, he and Daddy weren't getting on too well, were they?' Julie persisted. 'And he wasn't with us when Daddy was killed.'

'Oh, for God's sake!' Janey snapped. 'He was bored, wasn't he? He'd only gone over to the tent for a drink!'

'So far as we know,' said her sister ominously.

Ally hadn't liked Greg all that much, but she certainly wouldn't have considered him to be a suspect. Until now. Was it time to work on the board again?

The board was actually the back of a painted wooden picture – a still life of fruits brought back from Italy years ago by her grandmother – which hung on the wall behind the kitchen table.

Ally had once been a researcher on a TV programme in Edinburgh. When she'd done her research, she'd always put the problem in the middle and the possible solutions around the centre, like the numbers on a clock face – the most likely candidate at the top of the dial, at twelve o'clock, and the least likely at the foot, at six o'clock. When she'd used her board previously, she'd found it helped to clarify her own thoughts. She would glue a large piece of paper to the back of the picture, write the victim's name in the centre of a circle and place the suspects – on Post-it notes – all the way around, as on an imaginary clock. The Post-it notes could be moved, or removed, as necessary.

Ally found a large piece of white paper, drew a circle on it using a dinner plate and wrote 'Archie Armstrong' in the centre. Then she got out her Post-it notes for the suspects. But who *were* her suspects? Who might have killed the Atlantic Warrior? Ross would tease her for her efforts, of course. 'You and your board!' he'd say, laughing. 'You've become addicted to sleuthing!' And she couldn't deny that she had.

Let's face it, no one at the castle had any need to break into the cabinet when they could have helped themselves to the key which hung in Angus's office. Unless, of course, they wanted to make it appear to have been someone else. There were two under-ghillies: the older of the two, Gordon Soutar, was in his late forties or early fifties, and would one day be taking over from Angus. The younger was called Tom Hamilton, who Ally had never met but who set the hearts of the local female teenage population into frenzy mode apparently. She'd heard that he was friendly with Micky and Bobby McConnachie, so either of them could have visited the castle and sussed out the whereabouts of the gun cabinet. Unlikely, but they couldn't be ruled out. Then the Armstrongs had all visited Angus the day before Archie was killed. Was Patti perhaps having an affair and fancying her freedom? Then there was Greg, who appeared all too keen to point the finger at both Angus and the earl. Furthermore, according to the girls, Greg hadn't been getting on too well with Archie. All these thoughts were whirling round in her head. It could have been any of them.

Ally supposed she couldn't exclude Angus from the suspects, but she'd place him as low as possible at six o'clock, right down at the bottom of her 'clock'. Then she decided that, due to a lack of any other likely suspects yet, she'd place Patti up there at twelve o'clock because of her connection to Angus and the likelihood of her being able to get a gun from him, and Greg at three o'clock, mainly because of what the girls had told her about him not getting on with their father. After all, he'd gone up with the family to see Angus, so perhaps he'd sussed out the whereabouts of the gun cabinet while he was there. And then there was Wendy Watson, but how likely was it that she would want to kill her own brother? That left the competitors at the games, none of whom had been exactly delighted at the prospect of competing against this Canadian champion. But surely none of them felt strongly enough to attempt to *kill* the man! It was, after all, only a sport!

Ally wrote the names on her Post-its: Micky McConnachie, Bobby McConnachie, Forby McKinnon and Ivan the barman. She placed Micky at four o'clock, his brother at eight o'clock, and Ivan at five o'clock. Forby she placed at seven o'clock. After some thought she placed Tom Hamilton, the young ghillie who was friendly with the brothers, at seven o'clock too. She had no further suspects yet. She'd seen the girls watching the caber tossing, and she was pretty sure she'd seen Wendy nearby somewhere. Or had she? To be on the safe side, she'd place Wendy at five o'clock, alongside Ivan.

As she placed the picture back on the wall, the painting facing outwards again, she gave it a good dusting. If Morag espied a cobweb anywhere around, she'd have the thing down and would see her two sons as prospective suspects, in Ally's estimation at least.

She stared at the oranges, lemons and grapes in the picture for a moment and then decided that what she really wanted was to have a chat with Angus. But what excuse could she have for going up there to see him? Angus wasn't someone who you might call on for a cup of tea and a chat – far from it! He was a curmudgeonly old fellow who viewed most people with suspicion. And he must be feeling extremely guilty that anyone could have broken into the gun cabinet without him hearing or seeing something.

Ally decided to take her mind off it all by visiting her friend, Linda.

Linda was an Englishwoman who'd married a Scotsman, came to live in Locharran and, a few years back, had been widowed. She then had to decide whether to head back south of the border or make a life for herself here in the village. Fortunately, she'd chosen the latter option and, thanks to her considerable culinary talents, was now the proud owner of The Bistro. All summer, her five tables were continually booked, but in the quieter season, she concentrated on making desserts for the Craigmonie Hotel. Which was how, earlier this year, she and Callum, the manager, had begun dating. 'For years,' she'd told Ally, 'we only lived about three hundred yards away from each other but never really seemed to be in the same place at the same time!'

When Ally arrived at The Bistro, Linda had just made a coffee cake, a recipe which included Baileys and goodness knows what else, and was one of the most delicious cakes Ally had ever tasted. It was difficult to ration herself to just one slice, but she had her figure to consider and she was trying hard to be careful.

As she sipped her coffee and valiantly refused that second, delicious slice, Ally asked, 'Has Callum said anything to you about Ivan since Archie Armstrong died?'

Linda refilled their coffee cups. 'Are you sleuthing again?' she asked, grinning.

'I suppose I must be,' Ally replied. 'I guess I'm just nosy! Besides, the family are living under my roof, so I'm naturally interested.'

'Apparently, the bullet was fired from the rifle that came from the castle,' Linda said.

'I think I should be having a chat with old Angus, up at the castle,' Ally said, 'but he's not very sociable, and I'm trying to think of an excuse to visit him.'

'Isn't he the wife's uncle?'

'Yes, he is Patti's uncle,' Ally confirmed.

'Perhaps that's your cue. You could say you're a bit worried about her or something. Perhaps suggest he calls in to see her?' Linda said.

'That's not a bad idea,' Ally admitted. 'Why didn't I think of that?'

Linda shrugged. 'Perhaps you don't eat enough cake. *Sure* you won't have another slice?'

'Oh, go on then!' Ally said. 'Just a *tiny* piece.'

'It was Linda's idea,' Ally told Ross later as she prepared their evening meal.

'Which idea was this?' Ross asked as he shoved a log into the stove.

'About trying to approach Angus by saying that I'm rather concerned about Patti and that perhaps it might be a good idea for her dear uncle to visit her. What do you think?' Ally asked. 'It would give me a reason for going up there, and if we got into conversation, he might then open up about who he thinks might have been prowling around.'

Ross sighed. 'Ally, you must realise that anyone in the village could have access to any of his keys because he never locks his office door – the keys are hanging in there, and so why would they need to break in to get a rifle?'

'But he might have some idea who'd been lurking around, mightn't he?'

'Well,' Ross said, 'Hamish and the under-ghillies would be

the only people who would normally be up there, so it stands to reason that they, the earl and Angus himself are the main suspects.'

'But if Angus and the other two were out and about, feeding the dogs for instance, then anyone could have gone in and helped themselves surely?' Ally was beginning to realise that this was far from being as simple as she'd hoped.

'That's about it,' said Ross. 'And young Tom Hamilton spends his free time down in the village. He's a great friend of both of Murdo and Morag's boys. I've often seen them in the Craigmonie Bar playing darts together.'

'I told you about Greg's little chat, didn't I?'

Ross nodded. 'Yes, and he was supposedly in the hospitality tent when this happened, but he could have popped out for a moment – as could anyone.'

'But surely someone might notice if you arrived at the games carrying a rifle?'

'Of course they would,' Ross replied, struggling with the corkscrew to open a bottle of wine. 'But it would have been pre-planned. Whoever it was would have hidden the rifle in the bushes or the bracken in front of the trees above and behind the portable toilets. And bearing in mind that most of the guys in the village would have had a few pints of beer beforehand, most of them would have needed to have a pee!'

Ally had a thought. 'But if you were going to shoot someone, aiming for their head, you'd need a very steady hand, wouldn't you?'

'You certainly would,' Ross agreed.

'So you wouldn't be doing much drinking beforehand, would you?'

'Very true,' said Ross. 'Hamish is an excellent shot, of course, and so is Angus. But so far as we know, Angus wasn't there.'

'So far as we know,' Ally repeated.

Ross handed her a glass of wine. 'Cheers!'

'Cheers!' Ally took a sip. 'The girls said something quite interesting when they were in the garden with Flora. They hinted that Greg hadn't been getting along too well with their father.' She paused. 'Did I tell you that Archie and Greg were in business together, making log cabins?'

'Yes, you did,' Ross replied. 'Maybe it's not a very good thing to go into business with an in-law. Who knows?'

'Well,' said Ally, 'my mind is made up. I'm going to walk up to the castle tomorrow afternoon and have a chat with Angus.'

Ross rolled his eyes. 'Good luck with that then! Make sure you're wearing your bulletproof vest!'

'You don't mean that!'

Ross smiled. 'OK, I don't, but be careful anyway. Don't forget you are now known to have this talent for sleuthing, and there's a crack shot around!'

SIX

The following morning, Morag had a lot to say after breakfast.

'You wouldn't believe how many times that detective has been round to our house,' she said as she sat down with her mug of tea, having just completed cleaning the bedrooms.

'I suppose he has to question everyone who was there,' Ally said as she brought a tray of empty dishes in from the dining room and set it down on the kitchen table.

'He's even questioning Murdo,' Morag went on. 'Maybe Murdo did use those toilets, but not when *that man* was shot! And as for my boys...' Words seemed to fail her for a moment. 'He must have spent half an hour on our Bobby, and Micky says he spent ages on him too. For God's sake, they didn't have anythin' to do with shootin' *that man*, did they? They'd only just thrown their own cabers and was dryin' the sweat off therselves.'

'He has to be thorough,' Ally remarked in what she hoped was a comforting tone.

'Aye, well he's certainly that!' Morag sniffed and took a large gulp of her tea while Ally began to load the dishwasher.

'I was chattin' to Forby yesterday and he's been through the same. And poor Ivan was tellin' everyone in the bar last night that it certainly wasn't *him*! He was sayin' that he's never fired any kind of gun in his life and wouldn't know where to start.' Morag took another gulp.

'Well, he would say that anyway, wouldn't he?' Ally replied.

Morag ignored her. 'And ye don't need me to tell ye that Ivan's never proper sober, is he? So how would he go shootin' a target like that? Last time we had a funfair here, he couldn't even hit a bloody thing at the duck-shoot stall. And why would Ivan want to kill him anyway?'

Ally wanted to reply that none of the competitors thought that Archie should be there at all, so any one of them might have been sufficiently incensed to take a shot at him. But that would be unlikely as it would have to have been planned in advance, in such a way that would necessitate getting and positioning the rifle. Instead, she shrugged and shook her head.

Morag wasn't finished yet. 'And Angus wouldn't do it but, mind you, he was a champion caber tosser in his day – near fifty years ago.' She chuckled, then narrowed her eyes. 'And what about the earl, eh?'

'Knowing Hamish, he would have had a few drinks, so his aim wouldn't have been too good. And what possible motive could he have anyway?'

Morag ignored the question. 'And where was that wife of his when *that man* got shot, tell me that? Why wasn't she there cheering him on? Was she havin' a cup of tea maybe? Did you go for a hot drink?'

Ally shook her head. 'No, neither Ross or myself went in the hospitality tent.'

'Aye, well there was the hospitality tent and all those stalls selling shortbread and the like; it's hard to be sure where anyone was.' Morag drained her tea and stood up, making her way towards the porch outside the kitchen door where she removed her pinny and donned her purple anorak. 'See you tomorrow! If the good Lord spares me!'

Ally smiled. This was fast becoming Morag's catchphrase.

After Morag had gone, Ally finished stacking the dishwasher and tidied up the dining room.

Only the two girls seemed eager to go for a walk; none of the three adults appeared to be overkeen on exercise. They'd taken over the sitting room, where they spent most of the day reading or watching TV. Ally had also overheard them arguing about Archie's body – should they have him flown back to Canada or have him buried here in Scotland? Patti thought he should be buried here, whereas Wendy wanted him flown home. Greg didn't appear to have an opinion.

Ally was unaccustomed to her guests hanging around all day and was beginning to wish they'd booked in at the Craigmonie. Only Greg was sent out periodically for supplies, mainly takeaways, which they ate in the dining room, and so both of Ally's main downstairs rooms were constantly in use and had to be cleared and cleaned whenever possible.

She'd noticed today that Patti still seemed quite perky. However, Patti's devotion to her uncle Angus did not seem to extend to walking up the hill to see him.

As she came out of the dining room, Ally almost collided with Greg, who was heading towards the stairs. 'Another sunny day!' she exclaimed brightly. 'Just right for a walk!'

'Oh, it would be,' he said morosely, 'if it wasn't for the press.'

'Are they *still* outside?'

'Yeah, we've been mobbed by reporters and cameras every time we go out of here,' he said, rolling his eyes. 'I don't want the girls to have to deal with that. Maybe the detective could get them to move?'

'They won't follow you if you go out the back door and take

the moorland paths up to the castle or Loch Soular,' Ally suggested hopefully. 'They normally hang around on the road between here and the village.'

'We ain't taking any chances,' he said before he disappeared into the sitting room, shutting the door firmly behind him.

Ross had gone home to supervise a new central heating boiler being installed, and Ally had the afternoon free. She'd do what she said she was going to do and visit Angus. She'd even practised what she was going to say to him: she was concerned about Patti and how she was dealing with her grief, so perhaps Angus could see his way to calling in or inviting her up there? In fact, of course, Patti was just fine, made up to the nines and exhibiting a shapely thigh.

'Come on, Flora – we're going for a walk,' she said to her excited dog.

They set off on the moorland path about half past two. Ally had reservations about leaving the family on their own in the malthouse; not that they'd be likely to do anything stupid, but she just wasn't used to their constant presence all day long and needed to get away for a bit.

It was another lovely day, the sun shining with a gentle breeze, Flora romping ahead. It was the kind of day that would make anyone feel better, no matter how low they were. And there wasn't a single reporter or a photographer in sight.

Halfway up to the castle was the little hut where she liked to sit and admire the view all around. It was a ramshackle old building with a long bench seat inside, out of the wind, and had been used as a shelter for the earl's shepherds in the days when he had sheep grazing on the hillside. He still did have a few sheep, but they were in a fenced-off field down in the village. There were still a few other sheep around, mainly in the smallholdings and crofts where families

– like Morag and Murdo – kept chickens, a cow and sometimes a goat or two.

Ally sat down for a few minutes and wondered where she was likely to find Angus. He was usually around somewhere, frequently at the kennels or – unlikely at the moment – cleaning his guns. After a few minutes, she and Flora set off again, uphill.

They found Angus oiling the hinges of the tractor shed, dressed in his usual uniform of tweed plus-fours and hefty boots. He glared at them, his bushy white eyebrows and moustache bristling with curiosity.

'Ye come for another dog?' he asked, staring at Flora.

'No, no,' Ally replied hastily. 'I'm more than happy with the one I've got.'

'Aye, I daresay. Another one would cost you.'

She knew he was referring to the fact that when she'd first visited Angus to buy a puppy, the earl had refused to take payment. It was his welcoming gift to her, he'd said, a fact that circulated around the village like wildfire. Ally knew what everyone thought but didn't let it bother her, knowing no one would believe it was purely a friendly gesture.

'No, it's such a lovely day I thought we'd have a little walk,' she said.

He continued glowering at her. 'Is that so?'

Ally cleared her throat. 'Well, I was hoping I might run into you,' she admitted.

'Why's that?'

'I'm a little concerned about Patti,' she said.

'*Pat!*' he corrected her.

'OK, Pat then. Your niece.'

'What's wrong with her?'

Not much, Ally thought. 'I'm a bit worried about her because she seems to be acting a little strangely.'

Angus had a way of looking at you as if you were

completely deranged. 'Well, her husband's just been killed, as I expect ye've noticed.' He continued oiling the hinges.

'I know that, but I think it would be good for her to have some contact with you. I've tried to suggest they take a walk up here, but none of them seem keen on leaving the malthouse.'

'Lazy lot,' he said.

'I wondered if you might pop in sometime – just have a little chat with her perhaps?'

Angus grunted. 'She wants to talk to me, she can come here.'

'I think they're afraid of the press,' Ally said. 'There's been a few reporters and TV crews around.'

'We all have our jobs to do,' he said, laying down the oil can.

Ally realised she was getting nowhere. 'It was just a thought,' she said lamely.

'Let me tell ye somethin',' he said. 'My niece is as tough as one of my old boots. She comes from a strong family.'

'Well, she's pretty vulnerable at the moment,' Ally said.

'She'll soon recover and move on. That's what Pat does. Don't go wastin' any tears on *her*!' He continued looking at her. 'Between you and me, I never liked her husband; he was far too fond of himself. She should've married a local lad.' He thought for a moment. 'Och, maybe it's as well she didn't because she was never any good at keepin' her knickers on.' He spoke completely matter-of-factly. 'Let me tell you, Mrs Malthouse, that bullet was meant to look as if it came from the earl or myself because we are both crack shots. Or maybe the two lads workin' fer me, Gordon and Tom.'

Angus had never taken the time to find out Ally's real name.

'And you didn't get down to the games at all?' she asked.

'I had more important things to do. And so did the lads. Did ye not know we had a break-in and that rifle taken? I had the police here for most of the day, so I went nowhere. Nowhere at all. And certainly not taking potshots at some bloody Canadian!

I want that rifle back when they're finished with it! And let me tell you this – we save our skills for the deer and the rabbits,' he added before turning on his heel and disappearing into the tractor shed.

Ally sighed as she and Flora made their way back home. The meeting had not been a great success, and it was obvious that Angus hadn't the slightest intention of visiting the malt-house to console his wayward niece.

Flora gave an excited bark as she spied a rabbit, and Ally decided *she* was barking up the wrong tree.

When she got home, Ross phoned.

'There's been no end of trouble with getting this damned boiler fitted,' he said. 'What with bits missing, a pipe cracked and the plumber swearing. Just as well this cottage isn't booked until the end of the month because it's going to need some replastering and redecoration at the very least.' He sighed. 'I'm feeling worn out, so why don't we go down to have a drink and something to eat at the Craigmonie tonight?'

'Great idea,' Ally agreed.

'I need to get away from the chaos here, and you need to get away from your stricken guests. How did you get on with Angus by the way?'

'Waste of time – tell you later.'

'See you around six, my lovely,' he said.

After she finished the call, Ally made herself a cup of tea and sat down in the armchair. The house was warm, and Flora was already stretched out on the fireside rug, fast asleep. She felt weary too as she sipped her tea and relaxed.

The next thing she knew it was half past five. There was a hungry-looking dog waiting for her dinner on one side of the chair and a cold cup of tea on the other.

. . .

By the time Ross had parked up, at five past six, in his big, black Mercedes, Ally had had a quick shower and a change of clothing.

They decided to take a drink in the Craigmonie Bar first, as opposed to the hotel's cocktail bar, before going into the restaurant. This popular bar was manned by Ivan from Lithuania, his only help being a girl who went backward and forward to the main hotel kitchen to collect epicurean delights such as pies, sausage rolls and chips, greatly welcomed by the locals as they stopped off for a few pints of beer on their way home from work. They'd be back later after what they called their 'tea' and would put the world to rights with a further few pints. This group normally included Murdo and his two sons.

'Ah,' said Ivan, hastily placing his whisky glass under the bar. 'Good to see you both. What can I get you?'

'We'll have two gin and tonics, please, Ivan,' Ross said, 'and make them doubles! And put another shot of Scotch in your glass!'

'Thank you!' Ivan retrieved his glass and did just that before he poured their drinks. As he placed them on the counter, he said sadly, 'The past few days have been so quiet, ever since the games.' He pointed at a group huddled together in the far corner of the bar. 'See them? They are from the television, the newspapers, and they hope, I think, that the Armstrong family will come in here for drinks maybe. But not yet.' He turned to Ally. 'Perhaps they do not drink?'

'Yes, they do drink,' Ally replied. 'Certainly when they're stressed.' She recalled the evening after the games. 'But they don't seem to like going out.' She pointed at the group in the corner. 'Because of *them*. They're avoiding the press.' She and Ross clinked glasses as she took her first sip.

Ivan nodded. 'They ask me where the family is. Why don't they come out? Do they have something to hide?'

'No idea,' Ally said. 'I've suggested they go for a walk, but...' She shrugged.

'Have the police been here a lot?' Ross asked.

Ivan raised his eyes to heaven. 'Oh yes. And they ask me over and over again the same questions. Where was I standing? Who was I with? I tell them that yes, I am watching this champion, but no, I'm not at the very front because I am with friends and I am putting on my sweater. You know what else? That bullet went right by my ear too! I am in shock! Then the police ask if it might be meant for *me*! And then I get worried. Who would want to kill me?' He shook his head and uttered what might have been a Lithuanian swear word. 'Who wants to shoot *me*?' he repeated.

'You can't think of anyone, Ivan?' Ally asked jokingly. But, of course, you never quite knew.

'No, no,' Ivan said, 'because they like me here in the bar I think.' He shook his head at the very idea.

'It also had to be fired with great precision,' Ross added, 'and not hit the wrong person. Which makes sense, as the police think that the shooter was up on the hillside, hidden by the trees.'

'You weren't standing with the McConnachies then?' Ally asked.

Ivan shook his head. 'No, I am on my own with a couple of friends.' He leaned across the bar, having taken a large gulp of his Scotch. 'But I do not know one end of a rifle from another! That is the truth! I do not like guns!' He pulled a face. 'Unless they are in American westerns!'

Ally and Ross sat down with their drinks while Ivan dealt with a sudden influx of customers.

'Do you think it's at all possible you could shoot accurately if you were way over the alcohol limit?' Ally asked.

'I very much doubt it,' Ross replied. 'In any case, I don't think it was Ivan who did it.'

'Neither do I,' Ally agreed.

Callum espied them as they crossed the reception area on their way to the restaurant.

'I've got you a nice wee table by the window,' he said as he ushered them in.

'Thanks, Callum. How are you?' Ally asked.

'I'm OK,' he said, 'but feeling sorry for you being saddled with your unfortunate guests.'

'Yes, they were booked in for a week, but I've no idea how long they will need to stay now. Good job I don't have any further bookings this month and the rooms are free.'

As they sat down, Callum added, 'I'm amazed the police haven't made an arrest by now as it's very obvious who did it.'

Both looked at him in surprise.

'You know who did it?' Ally asked, feeling a little excited.

Callum looked around to make sure that none of the other diners were eavesdropping. 'Angus, of course,' he replied.

Ally's frisson of brief excitement took a plunge. 'Oh, really?' she said.

'Why do you think it's Angus?' Ross asked.

'No end of reasons,' Callum said. 'First of all, it's well known he's a fantastic crack shot, can shoot targets from miles away. Secondly, he's got the key to the guns and could access them any time he fancied without anyone turning a hair.'

'So why would he have to break in then?' Ross asked, looking puzzled.

'To make it seem like it was someone else,' Callum replied. 'And, thirdly, he was the wife's uncle and, according to rumour, he never wanted her to marry Armstrong in the first place.'

'But he said he wasn't even at the games,' Ally protested.

'*Of course* he'd say that!' Callum scoffed.

'I believe the police were there most of the day, because of the rifle being stolen,' Ross said.

Callum pulled a face. 'Not *all* day.'

'But why would he suddenly decide to kill Archie Armstrong after all this time?' Ross asked. 'They were married for the best part of twenty years, weren't they?'

'Because he finally had an ideal opportunity,' Callum said. 'He probably hoped his niece might decide to stay in Scotland with her daughters perhaps. He hasn't got many relatives, you know.' He grinned at them. 'I'd put my money on Angus! Anyway, I must go now, so enjoy your meal!'

As they examined their menus, Ally's brain was racing. Callum's remarks had provided food for thought. Perhaps she should check up on Angus? His alibi had been that he was being questioned by the police about the break-in, but could he have got to the games before or afterwards? Would Amir be able to confirm the time that Angus was actually being questioned?

SEVEN

As they walked up the hill arm in arm, Ally asked, 'What do you know about the two under-ghillies who work with Angus?'

'Not much,' Ross admitted. 'The senior gamekeeper, Gordon Soutar, is almost a younger version of Angus. Keeps himself to himself, a bit like Angus in that respect.'

'What about the younger one?'

'Oh, that's Tom Hamilton,' Ross replied, looking thoughtful. 'He came out of agricultural college a year or so ago and has been sending the local girls' hearts aflutter ever since. Good-looking lad, favours *very tight* jeans.'

'So they'd both easily be able to get their hands on the gun cabinet keys?'

'I expect so,' Ross said. 'I didn't see either of them at the games, but I believe that Tom, the heart-throb, is quite friendly with the McConnachie lads and often drinks with them in the Craigmonie Bar in the evenings. He would have access to the gun cabinet keys, so it's unlikely he'd fake a break-in. Have you ever been in Angus's office?'

'No, I haven't,' Ally replied.

'Well, I have, and it's total chaos in there!' Ross said. 'It's like someone set off a bomb! There's all sorts of paperwork strewn over the desk, the floor, every available surface. That's Angus's filing system! But I'll tell you something: any document you might want, Angus will find it – on the floor, under the desk, anywhere! In an instant. No problem.'

'I think I need to talk to these under-ghillies,' Ally said. 'Because I'm not likely to get much help from Angus.'

'Your best bet would be Hamish,' Ross said. 'He does all the hiring and firing, with Angus's help and approval, of course.'

'Good idea,' Ally said. 'It's time I paid him a visit. Apart from anything else, I'm longing to see the babies again. Now I must update the board.'

'*The board*?' Ross repeated. 'I'd forgotten about the board! Do you really think it's helpful?'

'Well, yes, I do,' Ally admitted. 'It's been helpful in the past, and it could be useful now!' As they entered the malthouse door, Ally added, 'Let me show it to you!'

She removed the painting from the wall, turned it over and laid it on the kitchen table.

Ross studied it for a moment or two. 'You've put Angus very low down.'

'Well, I didn't think...'

'You heard what Callum said. It could be Angus.'

Ally moved Angus up to four o'clock and resolved to double-check his alibi with Amir.

'And while you're at it,' Ross said, 'you need a Post-it for the earl too.'

Ally pulled a face. 'I don't somehow think Hamish would have had anything to do with it.'

'Ally, if you're going to do this properly, then you can't rule anyone out without good reason.'

Ally sighed but placed Hamish at five, alongside Ivan and Wendy. That didn't look right somehow.

'And both of Angus's trainees,' Ross said, frowning at the

board. 'You've only got Tom, though I'd have him much higher up, say at ten o'clock.'

'OK,' said Ally, pulling a face as she moved Tom up from seven. 'I'll add Gordon at six too just to keep you happy.'

Ross went home in the morning to supervise another day of boiler-fitting, and Ally decided to visit Hamish and Magda later.

The spell of good weather showed no signs of ending and, much to Ally's surprise, the Armstrongs finally decided to venture out. It was while they were breakfasting that Patti announced that they might go for a walk in the afternoon.

'I'm sure Angus would be pleased to see you,' Ally said.

'No, we thought we'd go to that loch place,' Patti said, 'where the girls went, you know?'

'Oh, Loch Soular you mean,' Ally said.

'You'll be glad to see the back of us for a while,' said Wendy with a faint smile.

'Not at all,' Ally lied, thinking of finally being able to give the sitting room a good clean.

Wendy was the quiet one of the family. The death of her brother had plainly hit her hard, and she'd rarely joined in the conversation at breakfast time. She was also the antithesis of her sister-in-law – a tall, somewhat gangly woman in casual, comfortable clothing, and if she was wearing any make-up at all, it was barely perceptible.

When Morag had finished her stint and was making herself a cup of tea, Ally said, 'Believe it or not, our guests have finally decided to go for a walk.'

'What, *now*?' Morag asked.

'No, I think they said this afternoon.'

Morag stirred her tea and thought for a moment. 'You'll be wantin' to give that room a good tidyin' up,' she said.

Ally nodded, a little disappointed because she'd planned a visit to the castle.

'Well, I could do with some overtime,' said Morag. 'If you wanted any help, that is.'

'Oh, Morag, would you be able to come back this afternoon?'

'Aye,' Morag replied, gulping some tea. 'If I could do a couple of hours, I could give all of downstairs a real good clean.'

'You're an angel! Of course you can do a couple of hours. I was planning to go out, so it suits me fine.'

Just don't turn over that picture, she thought, gazing at the oranges, lemons and grapes.

'Of course you can come up; we'd love to see you,' Magda said when Ally phoned a little later. 'Come for tea and see our beautiful babies!'

And squeeze some information out of your husband, Ally thought. She needed to know as much as possible about Angus's helpers. She was also very tempted by the daily afternoon tea ritual, with so many delicious confections that were hard to refuse.

As always, when Ally approached the castle in the afternoon, she was impressed by the sheer size of the building, with its turrets and its huge oak door, complete with a bell which, when the rope was pulled, she felt sure could be heard all over Locharran.

It was Mrs Fraser, the housekeeper, who appeared.

'Ah, Mrs McKinley,' she said. 'The earl and the countess are taking tea in the south garden as it's such a beautiful day. Do you know how to get round there?'

'Yes, I do. Thank you.'

Ally made her way round the castle walls to the south

garden where, on the patio, Magda and Hamish were sitting in the sun, with the pram in the shade behind them.

'Just in time for tea!' boomed Hamish.

Ally smiled and walked straight over to the babies, amazed at how quickly they'd grown since she last saw them. 'Wow!' she exclaimed. 'Aren't they getting big?'

'I think she's feeding them steak!' said Hamish.

'Just mother's milk,' said Magda proudly.

Mrs Fraser and her trolley, piled high with dainty sandwiches, scones, cream, jam and luscious-looking cakes, emerged from the door. She poured Assam tea for Hamish and Ally, and Earl Grey for Magda, before distributing plates and passing round the sandwiches.

Ally had started on one tiny cucumber sandwich when Hamish asked, 'So, how's life down at the malthouse at the moment? It's never-ending up here, with Kandahar arriving every five minutes to question us all. God knows when I'll get my rifle back. It's being kept for evidence and further tests, of course. And I'll never understand who could have broken in and taken it from the cabinet.'

'Not much happening with us at the moment,' Ally replied. 'But my guests have finally taken themselves out for a walk, up to Loch Soular.'

'Shouldn't they be visiting poor old Angus?' Magda asked.

Ally shrugged, wondering if she should have a scone. 'Angus doesn't appear to be a priority. And when I saw Angus yesterday, he didn't seem particularly interested in popping in to see Patti either.'

'I expect they've fallen out,' Hamish said, standing up and handing round the sandwiches again. 'He was very fond of her as a child, but I don't think he approved of her later in life.' He paused. 'I'll tell you one thing though – when Pat would come out with us for a day's shooting, she certainly knew how to handle a gun!'

Oh, *did* she indeed? Ally reckoned she'd probably been taught by Angus, the expert. Interesting...

She declined a sandwich, still unsure about the scone. 'I was just thinking the other day that I've never seen either of your under-ghillies close up. Is under-ghillies the right word? Or should it be trainee gamekeepers?'

'Call them what you will,' said Hamish, smiling.

'Yes, I wondered who'll take over from Angus eventually,' Ally prompted.

'Oh, you mean Gordon?' Hamish added extra cream to his scone and sipped his tea. 'Gordon's the one who'll take over. He's a bit dour, keeps himself to himself, doesn't do much socialising – very much like Angus really. But he's a good ghillie, and he works bloody hard.'

Magda leaned forward with a grin. 'But have you seen Tom, our newest recruit? He's causing a bit of a stir!'

Hamish snorted. 'He's clever, and he's got all the right qualifications, but he couldn't be more different from the other two. He shares a cottage with Gordon, but I don't think that's going to work out for long because Tom keeps bringing girls back. Apparently, they all fancy him!'

'So, presumably he *does* socialise?' Ally said.

'He certainly does,' Hamish replied. 'He goes down to the Craigmonie most evenings, I believe. But he's young and needs some lively company, I suppose.'

'Would either of them have keys to your gun cabinet?' Ally asked casually.

'They don't have keys themselves, but both of them are in and out of Angus's office where the keys are kept.' Hamish hesitated. 'But do I think that either of them would have faked a break-in and could have fired that rifle? No, I damn well don't! Just for a start, neither of them had the faintest idea who this Armstrong fellow was, and neither of them had a great deal of interest in the games, although young Tom did go down to have a look. I've told the police this a hundred times!'

'But neither Angus nor Gordon went down there?' Ally asked.

'Of course not! I'd have seen them if they did,' Hamish retorted. 'I made a point of seeing everyone.'

Except the sniper, Ally thought. *And when you were sampling the whisky...*

'That's how I know that Tom was there,' Hamish continued. 'He was with a couple of local girls, and they were in and out of the hospitality tent all afternoon.'

'Tom was with the two girls all the time then?' Ally asked, wondering if perhaps she was overdoing the questioning.

'Yes, yes,' Hamish replied impatiently. 'That's enough about him! Now, have you had a scone yet? They're delicious! Newly baked, still warm...'

At this point, one of the twins began to wail, and Magda, with the speed of light, was picking him up. 'He'll set his brother off if I don't act quickly,' she said, holding the infant to her shoulder.

After a minute, she carried the now pacified baby over to Ally. 'This is William. Would you like to cuddle him?'

'Oh, I would!' Ally said truthfully, accepting the little warm bundle and praying he wouldn't start howling again. William looked up at her with big blue eyes, and Ally was won over, all thoughts of sleuthing abandoned for the moment.

'He obviously likes you,' Hamish said, 'so he's plainly a man of taste. But you haven't had your scone yet!'

'I'll settle for William!' Ally said, laughing.

As she walked home a little later, Ally realised that she hadn't gleaned a great deal of information from this visit either. She knew, however, that both Gordon and Tom had access to

Angus's office and the keys so, in theory, wouldn't have needed to break in, and that Tom had actually been at the games. She also now knew that Patti was an excellent shot. Any of them, and even Angus himself for that matter, she supposed, could have been the killer.

Unlikely but possible.

Was there going to be sufficient space on the board to add a few more names if necessary? And when was she ever going to be able to eliminate some of these suspects?

EIGHT

Her guests had returned when Ally got home. She could hear them talking in the newly cleaned sitting room as she walked into her pristine kitchen. It didn't appear as if Morag had taken the painting down from the wall, but you never knew. She'd done it once before and been so incensed to see her sons there as suspects that she'd given in her notice. Fortunately, Morag needed the job as much as Ally needed a cleaner, and so it had been resolved amicably.

Ross phoned to say he wouldn't be able to come up to the malthouse tonight because he'd got guests coming to one of his cottages and, furthermore, the boiler still wasn't connected.

Ally decided she'd have an early night.

Ally had never seen Morag so angry as when she arrived after an uneventful weekend at the malthouse on Monday morning.

'They're questioning our Bobby again!' she ranted. 'Just cos he said somethin' a bit silly!'

'What did he say that was silly?' Ally asked, only too aware that a great deal of what Bobby said was silly.

'Well, after he'd thrown his caber, he went into that hospitality tent for a quick pint with a couple of his mates, but he came out before they did because he wanted to see *that Canadian* doin' his tossin'. So they're treatin' him like he's a suspect anyway, and then he goes and tells them that he won a rifle-shootin' contest a year or two back.'

'Why would he tell them that?' Ally asked.

Morag sighed. 'I know, I know, he shouldn't've done. He was only havin' a wee boast!'

'No wonder he's a suspect,' Ally said. 'I hope Micky didn't win any shooting contests?'

Morag looked uncomfortable. 'No, but he always went out on the stag-huntin', and he's known to be a good shot. I mean it was Angus who trained him, for goodness' sake!'

'I thought your two were together at the time of the shooting?' Ally asked, slightly puzzled.

'Och no. Micky was with his missus, and they was watchin' the dancin'. Then, after he'd done his caber tossin', Micky goes off for a wee beer, then he nipped to the toilet, but he came straight back to watch *that Canadian.*' Morag pursed her lips in disapproval.

Another one in the toilets! Ally thought. These loos were certainly well patronised. And as the killer had to have been in the elevated position above and beyond the toilets, how come nobody saw him or her? Surely someone would have seen somebody up there or even glimpsed the metallic glint of a rifle in the bright sunshine, even through the trees?

By later in the day, it had clouded over, and the Armstrongs opted to remain in the sitting room. They had commented at breakfast time about how much they'd all enjoyed their walk to Loch Soular and how, out there surrounded by nature, they'd all felt closer to Archie.

Even Wendy looked more cheerful.

After Morag had gone home, Ally loaded the washing machine and then decided the time had come to pay a visit to Finlay McKinnon's shop, known locally as Fin's Fish. Because of the similarity of their names and Queenie's bad eyesight, Ally frequently got Finlay's mail, and often wondered if he got any of hers, although he always denied it.

Finlay was a small, wiry man with a weather-beaten face and a full head of curly white hair. Every morning early, he went out on his boat with his son, Forby, and generally came back with a good haul, most of which he sold throughout the day. You could count on Fin's fish being very fresh indeed. In the summer months, they'd have sold everything by early afternoon and they'd shut up shop to take the tourists out for fishing trips on the sea loch.

Ally normally bought all her fish and seafood from Finlay, but today she was particularly interested in having a chat with Forby.

It was quite a distance from the village, beyond Ross's place, so Ally decided to take her car. She hoped it would be Forby selling in their big hut, but today it was Fin himself behind the wooden counter.

'Nice day, Mrs McKinley!' he greeted her. 'You must have known I've got some lovely sea trout!'

'Wow!' Ally exclaimed as he lifted a large trout carefully from his tray of ice. 'How much is that?'

'Special price for you!' he said, which is what he said to everyone. 'Like me to gut it for you?'

The price was reasonable, and Ally couldn't resist his offer to gut and clean the trout for her. It was a task she didn't relish doing. 'Oh, yes, please!'

As Fin took the fish behind to a bench at the rear, he yelled out, 'Forby! Can you hold the fort for a few minutes?'

Forby emerged from somewhere outside, rolling up his

sleeves as he got behind the counter. He was taller but sturdily built like his father, with a crop of black curly hair and nice brown eyes.

'Oh, hello, Mrs McKinley!' he greeted her as he pulled a striped apron over his head.

'Hi, Forby!' Ally was determined now to get off the subject of fish and onto the subject of the Locharran Games. 'Have you recovered from the games yet?'

Forby rolled his eyes. 'I keep trying to forget it, but the bloody police – excuse my language – keep coming back and asking the same old questions.'

'That's what they do,' Ally agreed.

'I keep telling them that none of us wanted that Armstrong to be there, but we're not sodding killers for goodness' sake!' Forby shook his head. 'It's only a sport, isn't it?'

'I couldn't agree more,' Ally said, wondering where he'd been standing when the shot was fired. 'I guess you were probably standing with the McConnachies?'

Forby shook his head. 'No, I was trying to edge my way out of the crowd. The caber was the last event I was involved in, and I knew damn well that Armstrong was going to win. I kept watching him, so I stopped at what the police now call the north-western edge of the field, where I'd left my motorbike. I could see the action from there, but I'd have had to be a bloody contortionist – excuse my language – to shoot the man from that position!'

'Surely the police realise that?' Ally asked.

'I hope they do. But no one was looking at *me*, and so I've no proof of where I was.' He sighed loudly. 'Surely somebody somewhere must have taken some photos, mustn't they?'

'Of course they must have done,' Ally agreed. 'Most people have phones these days and would be snapping away.'

'Yeah, but they'd all be concentrating on filming Armstrong.'

Several customers had now come into the hut, and Forby said, 'Excuse me,' and went to serve them.

In the meantime, Fin had re-emerged with the gutted and cleaned trout. 'You're going to enjoy this,' he prophesised as he wrapped it up in some newspaper and popped it into a bag.

As she got back into her car, Ally knew that she and Ross would indeed enjoy a trout supper, probably tomorrow evening.

She also reckoned, for no good reason, that Forby McKinnon was telling the truth.

After she put the trout in the fridge and unloaded the washing machine, Ally went outside to hang the washing out, and that was when she heard the raised voices – one male and one female, in the front garden. She couldn't quite make out, from here at the back, exactly who it was and what they were saying. Ally laid down a pillowcase she was about to hang up and made her way stealthily round the outside of the house to the wall which divided the utility area from the garden.

'Archie was right!' Patti was shouting. 'You shouldn't have come with us on this trip!'

'Bloody right!' Greg shouted back. 'And if it wasn't that Wendy wanted to see where her parents were born, I would not be here! I'd be back home trying to save the business that your husband was in the process of wrecking!'

'You've always been jealous of him – that's your trouble,' Patti continued, then lowered her voice. 'Anyway, shut up because I can hear the girls coming.'

'Hi!' one of them called out. 'Why were you shouting, Mom? Just wondered if the dog was here?'

Ally looked to where Flora was rolling on the grass as she tiptoed back to the washing line. *These poor girls need some sort of diversion*, she thought.

'Come on, Flora! Time to play ball!'

Back in the kitchen, she could hear Greg stomping up the stairs, going into his bedroom and slamming the door, followed shortly afterwards by Patti, heading to the sitting room and closing the door firmly. Where did that leave poor Wendy? Ally wondered as she let Flora out into the front garden, much to the delight of the girls.

'Can we take Flora for a walk, please?' Janey asked.

'You are more than welcome to take Flora for a walk,' Ally said, dreaming of sitting down with a restorative cup of tea on her own in the kitchen.

No sooner had she got the kettle on when there was a timid knock on the door, and there stood Wendy looking somewhat worried.

'I'm so sorry to bother you,' she said apologetically, 'but I wondered if it would be OK if I read my book in the dining room?'

'Well, of course you can,' Ally said, feeling sorry for the woman.

'I'd sit in the garden, but it's clouded over, and it's not too warm,' Wendy said, 'and Greg and Patti have had a bit of a row, so I'd like to keep out of their way for a bit.' She gave a wry smile. 'Are you sure you don't mind?'

'I don't mind at all,' Ally confirmed, thinking that this might be a very good opportunity to get more information. 'In fact, I was just going to make myself a cup of tea, so why don't you join me?'

Wendy hesitated for a moment. 'Well, if I'm not keeping you back...'

'You are not keeping me back,' Ally said firmly. 'I'd enjoy some company.' Which wasn't strictly true, but the opportunity to have a chat with this woman was too good to pass up.

She led Wendy into the kitchen and insisted she sat down in one of the armchairs positioned by the wood burner, which she'd lit earlier when she'd come back with the fish.

'We've got a stove similar to this back home,' Wendy said.

'It's particularly cosy in the winter,' Ally said. 'Now, how do you like your tea?'

'Black with two sugars, please.'

'Similar to myself,' Ally said.

'Have you lived here long?' Wendy asked.

'Coming up to three years,' Ally replied as she gathered the tea things and got out the biscuit tin, then went on to explain about converting the malthouse and trying to convince her family that she hadn't gone completely gaga. She wondered how to turn the conversation round to Wendy's family. 'I imagine this must be a very tense time for you all,' she said. 'It must be horrible.'

Wendy nodded as she accepted her cup of tea and took a chunk of shortbread. 'It is,' she confirmed.

Ally could see that her eyes were full of tears and began to wonder if she should have said anything at all.

Wendy wiped her eyes. 'Archie was my baby brother, and he was a good guy. And a good businessman. A *real good guy*,' she repeated.

'I'm sure he was,' Ally said.

'But he could be difficult, no denying that, when it comes to business. And, of course, he and Patti weren't all that well suited,' Wendy continued, frowning slightly. 'They were always rowing, but they kinda thrived on it – know what I mean?'

'Some couples do,' Ally agreed.

'Whereas me and Greg, we just jog along, you know?'

'Yes, my marriage was like that,' Ally said.

'Archie and Greg went into business together about five years ago,' Wendy continued, sipping her tea, 'but it's not worked out that well.'

'What went wrong?' Ally asked.

Wendy sighed loudly. 'Personality clash, I guess. Both good guys but not together.'

'Oh dear,' Ally said, hoping Wendy would tell her more.

Wendy sighed again. 'Archie was the senior partner, you see, because he'd inherited the business from our father. Our dad had set up the premises shortly after he emigrated from Mallaig. But Greg worked really hard, and he had so many ideas for increasing our output. And he always resented the fact that Archie inherited all the business, when half of it should have come to me, in his opinion, when Dad died. But I was never bothered. After all, Archie worked in the business and I never did. I think Archie might have thought Greg was trying to take over.' She gazed at the glow of the fire. 'Greg can be quite forceful but' – here she looked Ally straight in the eye – 'he did *not* kill my brother!'

'Of course not!' Ally agreed, looking at her fruity picture on the wall, still glad that she'd kept Greg at three o'clock. 'Do you have children?'

'Yes, we have a son. He's working in construction at the moment, but Greg and I were both keen to bring him into the business – another bone of contention. But I guess Greg can do that now. Joel would be a great asset to the company, but Archie was always hesitant about him. It's damned difficult when it's your own brother, and your own husband and your own son! Thing is, I suppose I've come to agree with Greg over the years because he had so many good ideas for expanding the business. But… there we are!' She sighed.

'I'm sure it must be tricky. So when did your brother begin competing?' Ally asked, by way of diversion.

'I guess he'd have been around sixteen,' Wendy replied. 'We had a lot of Scottish traditions, and he was very keen on body-building and all that kind of thing. Then he began winning competitions all across Canada – because there's lots of folk with Scottish ancestry in Canada, you know. Anyway, he became the Canadian champion about three years ago and then thought he should try his luck back here where it all began.

He's been over a couple of times and won all the prizes here too.'

'More tea?'

Wendy shook her head. 'I'd best go upstairs in a minute. Greg will have calmed down by now, and he'll be wondering where I've got to. This is my first visit to Scotland, and I'm loving it, but know what?'

Ally shook her head.

'We should have come on our own, Greg and me. It was never going to work out well with Archie and Patti.'

With that, she got to her feet, thanked Ally profusely and headed towards the stairs, leaving Ally to muse quietly in the kitchen on everything she'd just heard, and wonder if anything Wendy had just told her would be relevant to her investigation.

NINE

Ross arrived in the early evening with a bottle of champagne and a fish pie from his freezer.

'Did you make this?' Ally asked once he'd hugged her.

'I did. I wanted you to know that I am not a bad cook,' he said, grinning. 'Before you came on the scene, I'd become a dab hand at stuff like this. Not,' he added hastily, 'that I'd want to turn the clock back! Talking of clocks, how are your suspects ticking along?'

Ally rolled her eyes. 'I had Greg at the three o'clock position, but after chatting to Wendy this afternoon, I became a little more confused. I've moved him up to one o'clock.' She popped the pie into the microwave to defrost, while Ross opened the champagne. 'Are we celebrating?'

'Only that I've finally said farewell to the plumbers,' Ross said, handing her a glass. 'So, apart from Will wanting my services again at the vet clinic tomorrow morning, and an exorbitant bill for a new boiler, I'm a free man! And I just happened to find this bottle lurking in my fridge for no good reason.'

They clinked glasses.

'Thank you, Ross,' Ally said, wondering yet again what

she'd do without this lovely, caring man, not to mention his pie and champagne.

'So,' said Ross, 'tell me all.'

'Wendy came knocking on my door asking if she could read her book in the dining room because Patti and Greg had had a bit of an argument, and she didn't particularly want to be with either of them.' Ally told him about hearing their raised voices in the garden. 'So I asked her to come in for a cup of tea and she did.'

'I bet you gave her the third degree!'

'I didn't have to,' Ally explained. 'She was actually very nice. She said she felt uncomfortable at times because of the animosity between Archie and Greg. They were partners in business apparently, a business which was passed down to Archie from his father. It sounded like maybe Greg was more innovative and Archie didn't like his ideas. So maybe Greg wanted to get rid of Archie?'

'I suppose it's possible,' Ross said, looking thoughtful.

'But then she said that she and Greg wanted their son to go into the business too, but Archie wasn't having it.'

Ross sipped his drink. 'So now you think that she might have a hand in this? But why come all the way to Scotland to do it? Why not take a potshot at him back in Canada?'

'I don't know. I mean Archie was her brother, her "baby brother" she called him, and she had tears in her eyes.'

'In other words, would her filial love be greater than her fraternal love?' Ross mused.

'I've no idea, but I can't see her as any kind of Annie Oakley! My top suspects are still Greg and Patti,' Ally said as she removed the defrosted pie from the microwave. 'How long will this need in the oven?'

Ross shrugged. 'Thirty or forty minutes probably. I can't honestly remember. So, have you eliminated the other suspects then?'

'No, but they're way further down on my clock,' Ally replied.

'None of the contestants, so far as I can remember, had watertight alibis, and they'd all just been defeated by this Atlantic Warrior, so feelings were running high,' Ross said. 'It'll be interesting to hear what your friend Amir has to say about all this next time he comes calling.'

'He's always interested to know what I've found out, if anything, but he doesn't give much away about what he thinks himself,' Ally said.

'That, Ally, is why he's a good detective.'

Ally was sure that Amir probably had a great deal of information, technical or otherwise, but he wouldn't necessarily be aware of all the niggles taking place within the Armstrong family. That's where she came in...

There was a frosty atmosphere at breakfast in the morning. Patti was obviously not communicating – other than very politely – with Greg: 'Can you pass the milk, please?' – that sort of thing. As she cleared away some of the dishes, Ally was quite relieved to see the police car draw up at the front and Detective Inspector Kandahar emerging.

Amir headed straight for the kitchen. 'I'll have a word with the Armstrongs later,' he said, sitting down at the far end of the table.

'Two of them are having cooked breakfasts,' Ross said by way of greeting, 'and I've been put in charge of the sausages!'

'I'm most impressed,' Amir said with a grin. 'I'll keep out of the way until you've finished!'

A few minutes later, after the breakfasts had been delivered, Ally came back into the kitchen and put the kettle on to boil. 'We all need a cup of tea,' she said. Then, glancing at Amir: 'No arrests yet then?'

Amir shook his head sadly. 'We have quite a few suspects, not least the earl and his ghillie, plus a section of the Locharran bodybuilding youth, with a great deal of resentment and no proper alibis.'

'You've questioned the family?' Ally asked.

Amir nodded. 'I have, and I'm about to question them again. You can never tell with families, you know. Blood's supposed to be thicker than water, but I sometimes wonder.'

Ally then decided to fill him in on Patti and Greg's argument, plus her conversation with Wendy.

Amir listened attentively, nodding slowly. 'Thank you, Ally. This is the kind of conversation they're unlikely to give me.' He then made Ally repeat everything she could remember about her chat with Wendy and all she could decipher from the fight in the garden. He was plainly recording their conversation, but he was also making copious notes.

'OK, Ally,' he said, standing up. 'I'll have a chat with the Armstrongs in a minute.'

Thinking of blood being thicker than water, Ally asked, 'How are your girls, Amir?'

He smiled. 'Indira is now eighteen and wishes to become a doctor, and I am very proud of her.' Amir sighed. 'Then there is Maya, who is nearly sixteen and has no idea what she wants to do. She is more interested in boys than anything else.'

'My daughter was just like that,' Ally said, remembering how wayward Carol had been in her teens. 'But she sorted herself out and now leads a very respectable life, and I'm sure Maya will too.'

Just then, a pink-faced Morag burst into the kitchen. 'What's that *policeman* doin' here...?' She hadn't noticed Amir sitting at the far end of the table.

Completely unflustered, he replied, with a smile, 'Just doing my job, Mrs McConnachie!'

'Aye, well...' For once, Morag had run out of words.

Amir stood up. 'I need to have a little chat with your guests, Ally. Do you think they've finished eating yet?'

'I'm sure they have,' Ally said.

As the door closed behind him, Morag, who was stirring her mug of tea, said, 'He's got it in for our poor Micky!'

'Why's that?' Ross asked.

Morag shrugged. 'I know Micky talks big; he always has. And I know he was shoutin' in the bar about wishin' he'd been able to pull the trigger himself and all that. But Micky wouldn't hurt a fly!'

Ally had her doubts about that, but she nodded dutifully.

'Anyway,' said Morag, gulping her tea, 'I'd better be off. I've a lot to do today.'

'Thank you, Morag. See you tomorrow!'

'If the good Lord spares me,' she added as she set off down the lane.

'I must be off in a minute too,' Ross said. 'I'm on duty until lunchtime, I think. But let me tell you, Micky McConnachie has an evil temper and a big mouth to go with it. He's been in no end of fights. And his brother, Bobby, is no saint either. And Morag knows that perfectly well, which is why she's so edgy around the police.'

Shortly after Ross had left, Amir reappeared.

'I need to question your guests individually,' he said. 'Well, the three adults anyway. And so I'm going to take them down to the police station, such as it is.'

He referred to the temporary police station which had been set up in one of the Craigmonie's letting cottages. There was a constable on duty at the door and a banner overhead with 'Temporary Police Station' written on it, but that didn't stop tourists queueing up to ask directions to all manner of places.

'The thing is,' Amir said, 'we haven't anyone here to keep an eye on the girls while I'm talking to the adults, so I wondered...'

'If I could step in?' Ally provided.

'That would be very helpful,' Amir admitted. 'I mean they're quite grown-up, but I'd like to think someone was keeping an eye on them.'

'I'll suggest they take Flora for a walk to Loch Soular,' Ally said. 'They've done it before and enjoyed it.'

Flora was already on her feet, wagging her tail, fully fluent in dog-related language, in particular 'walk', 'dinner' and 'biscuits'.

'If you're sure?' Amir asked.

'Of course,' Ally agreed, picking up the dog's lead as she and Flora headed towards the hall. She found the two girls being reassured by Patti that no, no one was being arrested, and they'd be back soon, and there was no need to worry. Their faces lit up when they saw Flora.

'She really needs a walk,' Ally said truthfully, 'and I thought you might fancy tramping through the heather to Loch Soular again? And it's a lovely day.'

Amir interviewed Wendy first, and she got back to the malthouse shortly before the girls returned from Loch Soular. Relieved that her 'girls-sitting' duty was almost over and that she had a couple of hours to herself before Ross got back, Ally made herself a strong cup of coffee and switched on the radio to get the news before vacuuming the two downstairs rooms.

As she sat down, she heard some sort of commotion in the hall. Sighing, she set her coffee down on the table and went to investigate. And there, with her babies now asleep side by side in their Silver Cross pram, was Magda. And also there, oohing and aahing over the twins, were the Armstrong girls, newly returned from their walk with a very happy, muddy dog.

'I let myself in,' Magda explained, 'because the door was open. I was taking these two down for a walk to the shop and suddenly decided I might need some fortification before facing Queenie, so here I am!'

'Come into the kitchen, Magda,' Ally said as the girls reluctantly tore their attention away from the twins and made their way into the sitting room. 'What sort of fortification do you need?'

'Oh, coffee's fine,' Magda said, collapsing into an armchair, having positioned the pram near to the door. 'I don't need much from the shop, but these two are always happy to be on the move.'

'How are things up at the castle?' Ally asked as she filled the kettle and snatched a gulp of her own rapidly cooling coffee.

Magda sighed loudly. 'Not good. Hamish is so worried by all this, particularly as he's a suspect.' She ran a hand through her hair. '*Of course* he's a suspect, as is poor Angus and the other two ghillies, because it was certainly his rifle that fired that shot! They've found the rifle, of course, so who had it? I mean it's not something you could carry around without it being seen, is it? And, for goodness' sake, whoever stole it had to break the glass cabinet, and why would anyone at the castle have to break the glass when they have keys to open it?'

'Well they wouldn't,' Ally agreed, 'unless they were guilty and had to break in to make it look as if it wasn't them.'

This didn't seem to have occurred to Magda. 'I suppose so,' she conceded, accepting a mug of coffee. 'But I am worried about Hamish because he is so distressed by it all.'

'Poor Hamish!' Ally said sincerely. 'It's not as if he'd have given a damn as to who won any of these contests!'

'Exactly,' Magda agreed. 'He didn't much care. All he cares about is bringing tourists into Locharran and for them to spend their money here.' She raised her eyes to heaven. 'And, as you can see, he *has*! I mean the media are here, aren't they? It's on the news, and people are coming here out of curiosity. Lots of interviewers and TV people are staying at the Craigmonie and hoping to catch sight of one of the Armstrongs.'

'Locharran is certainly on the map at the moment! For all the wrong reasons though,' Ally said.

Magda shrugged again. 'And, of course, everyone will think that because he is the earl, he wouldn't do the dirty work himself but would allocate someone, like poor old Angus, to do it!' She rolled her eyes.

'You don't honestly believe that, do you?'

'No, of course I don't! But that is what the police might think,' Magda replied, accepting a chocolate biscuit.

'But the police were interviewing Angus when the shooting took place, weren't they?' Ally asked.

Magda shrugged. 'They were there in the early afternoon, so I doubt very much that he'd have had an opportunity to get to the games.'

One of the babies started crying. 'Like I told you, they're always happier on the move,' she said, standing up and replacing her mug on the table. 'I must get them to the shop and then back home. Thanks so much for the coffee, Ally.'

'You're very welcome,' Ally said, accompanying them to the door.

After they'd gone, Ally considered what Magda had said. She knew Hamish hadn't been involved, and it looked as if Angus hadn't been either. But what about the two men who now worked for him? They might well be crack shots, but surely they wouldn't be persuaded to *murder* someone for Angus?

TEN

It was mid-afternoon before Ally heard Patti and Greg returning, talking avidly and loudly.

Ally, with her ear pressed hard against the kitchen door, could only hear some of what they were saying.

'How come that detective knew about our log cabin business? That's what I want to know,' Greg was saying.

'Well, I expect your dear wife must have told him,' Patti snapped. 'Who else would know? Did you tell *her*, our hostess, about the problems we were having with the business?'

'I might have done,' Greg admitted. 'After all, I'm proud of our little business and what it's achieved.'

'Pity then you've got such a big mouth!' Patti retorted as they made their way upstairs. 'That cop seems to know an awful lot about us.'

'Well, don't start having a go at me!' Greg yelled, slamming shut his bedroom door. Then Patti slammed her bedroom door, and Ally could only feel for the two girls and their aunt, who'd closed the sitting-room door to shield them from the conversation.

. . .

Shortly afterwards, Ross arrived with a box of vegetables. 'There's enough here for a few days,' he informed Ally. 'I got this from poor old Jim Murray who hasn't got two pennies to rub together, but he does have an old collie who needed medication, so he's paid me in kind.' He laid down the box and gave Ally a hug.

'But, Ross, this was for *you*!'

'No, it's for us. I eat more meals here than I do at home, and these are beautiful home-grown vegetables that can keep us going all week. Tell you what, I'll do a veggie curry this evening – how about that?'

'That would be wonderful,' Ally agreed.

'How was your day?' Ross asked as he unloaded the box and decided which vegetables he was going to use.

Ally told him. 'Magda popped in with the twins, but the real news is that Amir has questioned all the Armstrong adults separately down at the police station.'

'Oh, has he?' said Ross. 'Incidentally, remember what Morag was saying this morning about Micky? Well, a few people today have mentioned he was drunk as a skunk in the Craigmonie Bar last night, telling anyone who'd listen what a crack shot he was, how he and his brother were cheated out of their prizes, how his daughter was a better dancer than the Armstrong girls and should have won. He added that he'd had enough of the Canadian bastard!'

'Presumably everyone knows what he's like though?' Ally said.

'They do, but poor Ivan had had enough and had to call the police because Micky was becoming drunk and disorderly. There was a group of the press in the bar last night, I believe, so they've been having a field day. He's going to get himself into serious trouble one of these days.'

'You don't really think he *could* have had anything to do with it, do you?' Ally asked.

'Frankly, I think he's all mouth,' Ross said, 'but who knows? Anyway, I must get started on this curry. Have we any rice?'

Ross stayed overnight and then had to spend the next day at his own place. There was maintenance to attend to, and he needed to show his face occasionally to his self-catering guests just to ensure that all was well and that they had no complaints. But first he was in charge of cooking the sausages, a self-appointed job which he'd taken over since the Armstrongs had arrived. He took great pride in getting them beautifully golden on all sides, and Ally, in charge of everything else, wasn't about to argue.

There was a definite frosty tension between the three adults in the dining room. Fortunately, the girls didn't seem to be aware of it, or, if they were, chose to ignore it. They ate hearty breakfasts while gazing into their phones between each forkful.

As Ally re-entered the kitchen, Morag had just arrived, was tying her pinny on as usual and then burst into noisy tears.

'Morag, whatever is the matter?' Ally asked, exchanging glances with Ross, who merely shrugged as he turned each sausage over carefully.

Morag rubbed her eyes. 'They've arrested our Micky – *that's* what's the matter!'

'Oh no!' Ally exclaimed, giving Morag a hug.

'Oh yes, they bloody well have!' shouted Morag, tearing off a piece of kitchen roll and blowing her nose.

'Why?' Ross asked.

'Just cos he was in the Craigmonie the other night and said that he'd had enough of the Armstrong bastard! Just cos he'd had a few too many! Your bloody Amir is getting desperate if you ask me!' She spat the words out as she tied her pinny round her waist.

'He is not *my* Amir,' Ally protested, 'and he must have had a reason.'

'We'd *all* had enough of the Armstrong bastard, but that didn't mean we was linin' up to kill him, did it?' Morag demanded loudly. 'And I'll tell you somethin' else – if it was our Micky firin' that gun, he'd have done a proper job and not shot the bloody caber!'

Ally drew in her breath. 'Morag, please keep your voice down. You may not have liked him, but his grieving family are all in the dining room.'

'They won't keep him in for long,' Ross assured her, 'once they realise they've got the wrong man. Where is he now?'

'They burst into his house yesterday evening and took him to Fort William,' Morag said. 'And wee Katy's been cryin' all night for her daddy! And so has Nell, Micky's poor wife. Cryin' all night!' Morag blew her nose lustily on another piece of kitchen roll. 'It was them reporters, that's who it was. They was listenin' in a corner of the bar, and they was puttin' two and two together, and makin' God only knows what!'

'They can only keep him for twenty-four hours or so,' Ross said consolingly, 'and without some sort of definite proof, they'll have to let him go. And I'm sure they have nothing else other than a few drunken words, Morag.'

'Aye, well, do they know about this next door?' Morag sniffed as she pointed towards the dining room.

'I shouldn't think so, if Micky was only arrested last night,' Ally said.

Morag braced herself. 'I'm goin' to go right in there and tell that family a thing or two! Because it wasn't our Micky that did it!'

'No, no!' Ally, alarmed, grasped Morag by the arm. 'You can't do that! They don't seem to know yet about the arrest, and since Micky's liable to be released soon, there's no reason for them to know at all – or for anyone to know for that matter!'

This seemed to pacify Morag for a moment.

'Let's get you a cup of tea before you start on the rooms.

The Armstrongs will be in the dining room for a while yet, and they usually go into the sitting room afterwards anyway.' Ally was trying to dispel visions of Morag reading out the riot act to her guests.

Morag didn't need a great deal of persuasion and flopped onto a chair while Ally was plating up the full breakfasts, assisted by Ross depositing his perfectly cooked sausages onto each plate.

This scene of domesticity did appear to calm Morag down, and finally, duster in hand, she made her way upstairs to do the bedrooms.

Later, when both Ross and Morag – still muttering to herself – had gone home, Ally walked down to the shop. On the way, she decided to see what she could find out at the temporary police station, but the constable at the door was the height of discretion.

'No, Detective Inspector Kandahar is not here today,' he said firmly.

'Any idea when he might be back?' Ally asked hopefully.

'I'm afraid not. He's questioning a suspect.'

'What, here in Locharran?' Ally asked, knowing full well that he wasn't.

'No, madam, in Fort William.' He pursed his lips and Ally knew that she'd get no more out of him, so she walked on to the shop.

As might be expected, there was a cluster of women around the counter, all talking at the same time. Queenie motioned them to be silent when she saw Ally approach.

'Ah!' she exclaimed. 'Here comes Mrs McAlly!'

'Her name's McKinley!' said Mrs Jamieson, the earl's cook, who was one of the crowd.

'I'm Ally McKinley, but Queenie got a little confused when

I suggested she use my Christian name,' Ally said by way of explanation, well aware that this was still unlikely to register with Queenie.

'Well, at least poor Angus is off the hook,' Mrs Jamieson said, going back to their conversation. 'The police were all over the place for a couple of hours after the break-in was reported, and then Angus came into the kitchen and said he was needin' a cup of tea when they were done making him fill out all that paperwork. We gave him a wee drop of whisky in it to make him feel better, and then he had a few more and fell fast asleep! We had to wake him up at six o'clock because we had to get started on the dinner.'

'We were just sayin',' said Queenie, 'that they've taken away poor Micky McConnachie and arrested him! But ye'll know that, won't you, what with Morag workin' up at the malthouse?'

'So far as I know they're just questioning him,' Ally said, picking up a box of teabags.

'Aye, but he's forever gettin' drunk and sayin' daft things,' said a woman with golden curls framing her old, wrinkled face.

'He's almost as daft as yersel' with that wig!' exclaimed a younger woman with a green beret.

'Nothin' wrong with my wig!' protested Golden Curls.

'Except that it's meant for a twenty-year-old,' said the woman with the green beret.

'Which is absolutely none of your damn business!' snapped Golden Curls. 'But we live just across the road, and we saw it *all*, so we did! Him shoutin' and screamin' and the wife and kids howlin' and cryin'...'

'How's Morag takin' it?' Mrs Jamieson asked.

'Well, she's naturally upset,' Ally admitted.

'You know what?' said Mrs Jamieson. 'Morag and Murdo McConnachie brought up a real good Christian family who knows right from wrong!'

Ally nodded, desperate to pay for her teabags and get out of there.

'Unfortunately,' continued Mrs Jamieson, 'sometimes the demon drink takes over!' She raised her eyes to heaven.

'Aye, but the French have a word for that,' said Green Beret.

'I daresay they do,' snapped Mrs Jamieson. 'They have a word for most things!'

'What about the Auld Alliance?' asked Golden Curls, apropos of nothing.

'You're probably thinking of "in vino veritas",' Ally said helpfully, 'which only means that alcohol can loosen the tongue.'

'Aye, that's right,' said Golden Curls, 'and that's no' French, that's Latin! Anyway, poor Micky'll no' be guilty.'

'But he was awful mad about Armstrong winnin' everythin',' Queenie pointed out.

'Whose bloody side are ye on then, Queenie?' asked Green Beret.

Ally placed her teabags on the counter. 'That's all I need for the moment,' she said to Queenie, desperate for escape.

'Will ye be needin' a bag?' asked Queenie, taking her money.

Ally didn't need a bag. She'd got what she needed: Angus had spent the afternoon of the gun cabinet break-in in the kitchen at the castle and, crucially, not at the Highland Games.

When Ally got home, she found the Armstrongs in a state of high excitement, as she discovered when she let herself in the door and Julie rushed out from the sitting room.

'Mrs McKinley, you'll never guess what! They've found the horrible man who killed our daddy!'

'They have?' Ally hoped she appeared suitably surprised.

'Yes,' said Julie, 'it was one of those nasty competitors, I think.'

Janey rushed out to join her. 'We should soon be able to go home!' she exclaimed.

In spite of herself, Ally was curious. 'They've actually *arrested* someone?'

At that moment, Greg emerged. 'Oh, hi! Have the girls been telling you? Sounds like they've got the right guy. We only found out on the local BBC news website, which also said that Detective Inspector Kandahar had taken some guy into custody and would be speaking to us this morning.'

'Did they give the name of the person?' Ally asked.

Greg shook his head. 'No, just some thirty-five-year-old local guy, who they have reason to keep in custody, but sounds like they've found the killer. And I sure hope they do because I need to be getting back to Nova Scotia.' He sighed. 'It's a one-man business now that Archie's no longer with us, and someone needs to explain this to our bewildered staff, to help them to move on.'

'Oh, good,' Ally said lamely.

The moment she entered the kitchen, she checked the BBC website and found that they had now published the name, and it was none other than Micky McConnachie! She sighed. Since her guests wouldn't know Morag's surname, it was unlikely there could be any friction at breakfast time. She hoped.

As she filled the kettle, Ally couldn't believe that Micky McConnachie was a killer. Big mouth, yes. Borderline drunkard, yes. But surely not even Micky could get infuriated enough to kill someone on the strength of losing the Highland Games. It was obviously a premeditated murder because the gun had been stolen the previous day, and Micky couldn't have been absolutely sure that Archie would win the caber tossing, and surely it wasn't the end of the world if he did? Or if his daughter came third instead of first in the Highland dancing? Ally was having one of her 'feelings', which Ross always teased her about, but her feelings were usually correct. And she did *not* think they'd found the killer.

An hour later, Hamish appeared. As he sat down in the kitchen, he beamed at Ally. 'I have this idea,' he said, 'because, as I'm sure you've noticed, there's an air of gloom hanging over the village at the moment. Not surprising really, I suppose, in view of recent events. Anyway, I thought I'd organise a fun run for Saturday afternoon!'

'A fun run!' Ally stared at him. 'What's that?'

'It's a kind of mini marathon. Since all the hammer throwers and caber tossers are supposedly suspects, I thought it might be a good idea to organise a race for them, from the village, up past here to Loch Soular, round the loch and then across the moors to the castle, where I could lay on a barbecue. We could mark the route out with wee flags here and there. What do you think of that?' He hesitated. 'And perhaps a prize?'

'I'm sure it would cheer everyone up, but—'

'Do you think one hundred pounds would be sufficient for the winner? I mean, it must be about ten or eleven miles, a bit less than half a marathon, so it would be quite an achievement.'

'I think it would be very generous of you, Hamish. How many would you be catering for at this barbecue?'

Hamish thought for a moment. 'Well, obviously all of the runners, and any of their friends and family who'd come up to cheer them on; yourself and Ross, of course; and the Armstrong family...'

'That would be a lot of sausages!' Ally exclaimed, laughing.

'And burgers and things,' Hamish added vaguely, knowing this would be Mrs Jamieson's headache and not his. 'Do you think it would cheer everyone up a little?'

'Hamish, do you not realise that Micky McConnachie is under arrest?'

'*What*?' Hamish looked appalled.

'It's all round the village and even been on the local BBC news,' Ally said.

'Well, it's not *him*! Good Lord, I had no idea! Whoever it was, it was *not* Micky McConnachie!'

'Really?' Ally was astounded. 'How can you say that?'

'Yes, really,' Hamish confirmed. 'I clearly remember Micky just leaving the tent at the same time as myself when we heard the shot. They've arrested the wrong man! They must release poor Micky immediately!'

'Hamish, are you absolutely sure about this?'

'Of course I'm sure! Where have they taken him?'

'Fort William, I believe,' Ally replied.

'Well,' Hamish said, getting to his feet, 'I'm going to Fort William *right now* because they can't keep that young man – silly though he is – in custody for something he damn well didn't do! And, on the plus side, he can provide an alibi for me too!'

'That's wonderful,' Ally agreed, thinking of how delighted Morag and Murdo would be, even if it probably meant that her guests were going to be under her roof for an indeterminate length of time.

Hamish refused all offers of refreshment and set off for Fort William at full speed.

Shortly after he'd left, Ally saw Greg and Wendy drawing up in their hired car. As she pulled the kitchen door behind her, she heard them talking and stood listening with the door only slightly ajar. Obviously, they had no idea whatsoever that Micky McConnachie was possibly going to be released, and Ally wondered how they'd react when they did.

'Thank God they've finally found the killer,' Greg was saying.

'I hope you're right,' Wendy said.

Ally could hear them going into the sitting room and tiptoed across the hallway, duster in hand, just in case either of them came out and spotted her.

'Thank God Patti's now agreed that the business is mine,' Greg was saying, 'so at least she won't be interfering.'

'She'll be expecting a share of the profits though,' Wendy pointed out. 'How did you manage to get her to agree to all that?'

There was silence for a moment before Greg replied, 'Let's just say that she's got her freedom now, so we'll see what she does with it...'

Nothing further was said, and Ally could only hear the rustle of newspapers, so she headed back to the kitchen.

Was what Greg said important? Should she tell Amir when next he appeared? Or was she translating what he'd said wrongly? Because it seemed to her that Greg was doing pretty well out of his brother-in-law's demise. He and Wendy could bring their son into the business, which could now be run the way Greg wanted, with no interference from Archie – or Patti either. And where *was* Greg when Archie got killed? They weren't going to be too happy at Micky's release because it didn't now seem likely that any of the family would be going anywhere any time soon.

ELEVEN

Later, when Ross got back, Ally told him about Hamish's visit.

'Is he certain that he saw Micky at the tent?' Ross asked. 'I mean he'd probably had a few drinks by then.'

'He seemed very certain, and he's bolted off to Fort William to tell the police what he saw. Fortunately, the family here have no idea about this. They just seemed delighted that *someone's* been arrested so that they can go home.' She told Ross about what she'd overheard.

'Ally, don't read too much into that,' Ross said. 'I mean his wife said to you, didn't she, that the two men didn't get on all that well business-wise, so of course Greg's going to enjoy a certain amount of freedom that he didn't have before.'

'Yes, but it was also the way he referred to Patti,' Ally said. 'She's excluded from the company altogether, apart from getting a share in the profits.'

'I expect that's how she wants it,' Ross said. 'I can't see her as much of a businesswoman, and what does that matter if she gets her share of the profits for doing nothing?'

'I suppose you're right,' Ally admitted grudgingly.

'You *want* it to be Greg, don't you?'

Ally pulled a face. 'I just don't want it to be someone from Locharran.'

'That's understandable, and I can see why you might suspect Greg. I've no doubt the inspector will be here again before long if they're releasing Micky, so let's wait to see what he thinks.'

Yet again, Ally found it difficult to get to sleep.

An elated Morag appeared next morning. 'They let our Micky go yesterday evenin',' she said, 'and thank God for that! Not that they should ever have arrested him in the first place! And, thank the good Lord, they seem to have lost interest in Bobby too.'

Ross had had to go home first thing in the morning because of a visitor problem, and so Ally was having to cope with the sausages along with everything else. 'I'm so pleased, Morag.'

'And I'll tell you why,' Morag continued. 'It was the earl himself – God bless his soul! – who remembered seein' Micky just leavin' the tent at the very moment we all heard that shot.'

'That must be such a relief,' Ally said. But all she could think of at the moment was that the family were about to appear in the dining room, and had they been told of this yet? And how would they be likely to react? Would Amir put in an appearance to inform them in person?

As she heard her guests going into the dining room, Ally took a deep breath, pasted a smile on her face and went in to greet them, as she always did.

'Good morning, Ally,' they chorused as usual.

'I hope you've all slept well,' Ally said, beginning to relax.

'Oh yes,' said Wendy, looking around at the others for confirmation. They all nodded in agreement.

'Except I heard a funny noise in our bathroom again when I woke in the night,' Julie said.

Ally's spirits plummeted. She knew she shouldn't really

believe in her wretched ghost, but it had to be said that he'd been right so far.

'I expect you were just dreaming, darling,' Patti said soothingly.

'No, I wasn't,' protested Julie. 'It sounded like some kind of wailing.'

'Probably air in the pipes,' Wendy said.

Oh, how true that is! thought Ally.

Nevertheless, she could see they were all quite upbeat, and no one seemed aware of Micky's release.

As Ally went back to cooking and Morag headed upstairs to do the rooms, Amir arrived.

'Don't let me interfere with breakfasts,' he said to Ally as she ushered him into the kitchen. 'I need to have a word with your guests, but not until they've finished eating.' He pulled out a chair and sat at the far end of the kitchen table, removing files and phones from his briefcase.

He gave a slight smile and, for the umpteenth time, Ally thought what a good-looking man he was. She plated up breakfasts and carried them next door.

'What's that police car doing out there?' Greg asked with a frown.

'Oh, I expect they want to update you on whatever's happened,' Ally said casually, making a rapid escape before he could ask anything else.

Back in the kitchen, Amir had poured himself a cup of tea from Ally's pot. 'I hope you don't mind?' he asked, pointing politely at his cup.

'Of course I don't mind! Would you like something to eat?' Ally asked.

Amir shook his head. 'No, thank you.' He took a sip of tea. 'We've had a suspect in for questioning,' he said, 'but we've had to let him go, due to the fact he now has an alibi. A witness has come forward.'

'Micky McConnachie?' Ally said.

Amir looked surprised. 'You knew?'

'Have you forgotten that his mother is my cleaning lady? And that it was on the local news?'

'Of course!' Amir shook his head. 'I should have remembered.'

'Furthermore, Hamish – the earl – called in yesterday afternoon. When I told him about Micky's arrest, he told me he'd seen Micky at the time of the shooting, and he left here immediately,' Ally said.

'So you knew before I did,' Amir said with a smile. Then he looked serious again. 'You know the earl much better than I do, and I know I've asked you this before, but would you say he was trustworthy?'

'I certainly would,' Ally replied firmly.

'Because the earl, as you know, is also a suspect, so I can't altogether rule out some sort of collusion between the two of them. The two of them were standing just outside the tent, and we've had no witnesses come forward yet to confirm this.'

'Meaning that you think the two of them could have been in this together?' Ally asked, realising that she hadn't thought of that possibility. But the whole idea was quite preposterous!

'We can rule nothing out at this stage,' Amir replied.

'The family knew that you had someone in custody,' Ally told him, 'and seemed certain that you'd got the killer and that they'd be going home.'

'I hate to disappoint them,' Amir said with a sigh, 'but that is not the case.' He studied Ally for a moment. 'Have they said anything relevant to you?'

'Only that Greg seems very keen to get back to take over the business he co-owned with Archie Armstrong.'

'That's not entirely surprising,' Amir said.

'I suppose not,' Ally admitted, feeling a little deflated. 'And I overheard him saying to his wife that he'd persuaded Patti to keep away from the business but just take a share of the profits. And when Wendy asked him how he'd managed to persuade her, he said something to the effect that Patti was glad of her new-found freedom.'

'I've a feeling that you suspect him then?' Amir asked. 'Is he top of your list?'

Ally looked at her painting of oranges, lemons and grapes on the wall. 'He's near the top of my list,' she said, aware that she had indeed placed Greg at one o'clock and Patti was at the top at twelve o'clock – always suspect the nearest and dearest, she had discovered.

Shortly afterwards, Ally could hear the chairs being pushed back next door so assumed her guests had finished breakfast. She signalled to Amir, who picked up his briefcase, made his way to the door and waylaid them all in the hallway, suggesting they had 'a wee chat in the sitting room'.

Ally could hear, from all the pleasantries being exchanged, that the family were most likely convinced that Amir had arrested the killer and that they'd be free to head for home. She could hear him talking quietly for a few minutes – followed by uproar.

'What do you mean?' Greg was shouting. 'Why have you not arrested this guy?'

'We just want to go home!' Patti wailed.

'I'm sorry,' Amir said, raising his voice. 'I've already told you that we have insufficient evidence against him and that he produced an alibi.'

'But surely we can go home?' Wendy piped up.

'I'm afraid that will not be possible,' Amir replied calmly.

'Are you suggesting we're suspects still?' Greg roared.

'I can rule no one out at this stage,' Amir said diplomatically.

'Ridiculous!' shouted Patti. 'How can you accuse me of shooting my own dear husband?'

'I'm not accusing anyone of anything,' Amir said. 'I'm only telling you that the person we took in for questioning has now been released due to lack of evidence.'

'Could we not go and stay in Inverness?' Janey asked hopefully.

'I'd prefer it if you could stay right here,' Amir replied.

'Bloody ridiculous!' Greg shouted as Amir was leaving the room.

When he came back into the kitchen, Amir rolled his eyes and said apologetically, 'I've left you with some unhappy customers, Ally, but there's nothing I can do about that. Let me know if you have any problems.'

Ally nodded. 'I will,' she said, just as Morag reappeared from upstairs.

'What's all that shoutin' goin' on?' she asked crossly, glaring at Amir as she began to make herself a mug of tea.

'I must be on my way,' Amir said hurriedly. 'Thanks for the tea, Ally. And I'm glad we were able to release your son, Mrs McConnachie.' With that, he sped towards the front door.

'Well, well,' said Morag, sitting down with her tea, 'them police never give you a straight answer, do they?'

After Morag had gone and Ally was clearing up in the dining room, she could hear raised voices and the sound of arguments emanating from the Armstrongs. She could clearly hear one of the girls asking, 'Why *can't* we go to Inverness? There's nothing to *do* here!'

That much was true. Most young people here, as in many other country areas, left to go to college or work in the nearby towns and cities. They didn't want to get away from it all – they wanted to be where the action was.

At that point, Patti emerged from the sitting room, slamming the door behind her.

'Would you believe they've *still* got no idea who killed my Archie?' she snapped.

'I'm sure they'll find the killer soon,' Ally replied.

'Well, I'm not optimistic. And he won't even let us move to *Inverness*! No offence – you've been very kind – but the girls are bored, and I so need a visit to a beauty salon and a nail bar...' She shook her head at the injustice of it all. 'I think I'll pop up to see Uncle Angus.'

Ally had mixed feelings about all this. Yes, like everyone else, she wanted the killer to be found, and she wouldn't be particularly sorry to see the back of this family. But it was autumn now, and the visitors were dwindling, and so, from a purely financial point of view, Ally was grateful for their custom.

Next out of the sitting room was Greg, looking extremely angry.

'Goddam detective!' he roared. 'That guy couldn't catch a cold!'

Ally laid down her tray on the hall table. 'Actually, Greg, I've found him to be very efficient, and these cases take time to solve, as I'm sure you'll agree. It's just over a week since Archie was killed, and they're doing their best.'

'It was definitely that McConnachie guy!' he ranted. 'Why the hell they had to let him go I'll never know.'

'He had a reliable alibi,' Ally said.

'Well, who else could it be?' Greg's face was red with fury. 'These guys were just all so jealous of Archie, so it has to be one of them! I hope you don't think it was one of us?'

'No, no,' Ally replied hastily. '*Of course* not!'

'So it's got to be the earl or one of his helpers,' Greg said. 'Who was the reliable alibi?'

'As far as I know,' Ally replied, 'the earl vouched for him because he saw him at the tent when the shot was fired.'

'The *earl*!' Greg almost spat the word out. 'Surely the earl is a suspect too? So how can he give anyone an alibi? And who's to say he's not in cahoots with McConnachie? A joint venture perhaps?'

'The earl had no reason to kill Archie,' she said defensively, 'and he'd be *very* unlikely to be colluding with any of the McConnachies.'

'Well,' Greg said with a sigh, 'I guess they're both friends of yours and so I can understand your loyalty, but, from a neutral point of view, I can see the unbiased picture.'

There's no convincing this man, Ally thought. And the last thing she wanted to do was get into an argument with one of her guests.

Greg didn't appear to be calming down though, as he stomped his way upstairs, and Ally felt sorry for poor Wendy, who would now be most likely to be at the receiving end of his rants. Not for the first time, Ally wondered why he was so keen to pinpoint the blame on anyone, however unlikely. She could, of course, understand that the man was keen to get back to his cabin building, unfettered by his brother-in-law, and was understandably frustrated by the delay in an arrest.

Ally's phone was buzzing as she returned to the kitchen. It was Linda.

'Now that the tourist season has quietened down, I was going to suggest that you and Ross join Callum and myself for a nice meal up at Seascape Saturday evening, but now he's going to have to run the bar because Ivan is off on some fun run or something. Have you any idea what *that's* all about?'

'I do,' Ally admitted. 'Hamish thought there'd been a gloomy atmosphere over the village since the murder, and that the suspects needed something to cheer them up – and keep them fit at the same time. So he's organised this fun run, a race up round Loch Soular, across the moors and ending up at the castle grounds, where Hamish will present the winner with one hundred pounds and lay on a barbecue to boot!'

'That's very generous of him, but he's scuppered my plans for Saturday,' Linda said sadly.

'Look, I'm on my own this afternoon,' Ally said, 'so why don't you come up for a cup of tea? I've made some shortbread, and I'd really appreciate your expert opinion.'

'I'll do that,' Linda said, 'and I'll bring up some cake I've just made. You can tell me if it's good enough as a base for some new desserts for the Craigmonie!'

Ally groaned inwardly at all the calories likely to be consumed, but what the hell! These were tense times.

Linda duly appeared about four o'clock with an orange and lemon cake, and it couldn't be denied that there was a definite hint of Cointreau in the recipe. It was, as always, absolutely delicious. So much so that she was secretly pleased when Linda accepted a second cup of tea and suggested another 'teeny weeny' slice of the heavenly concoction. So much for her worries about her calorie intake, but at least Linda was very enthusiastic about her shortbread.

'So, how is Callum?' Ally asked.

'Oh, he's fine, and I shouldn't begrudge Ivan doing his fun run or whatever because he hardly ever asks for an evening off.'

'I guess the prize is also quite an incentive,' Ally remarked. 'None of these lads earn a great deal of money. Hamish thinks it's about ten or eleven miles, so they're going to be pretty knackered by the time they get to the castle and the barbecue.'

'To change the subject,' Linda said with a wicked grin, 'how's the sleuthing going? Have you solved the crime yet?'

'I honestly haven't a clue,' Ally admitted. 'I can't believe it's any of the village lads, but I can't think who else could have killed Archie.'

'His family perhaps?'

'Well, I sometimes think it must be, and then I think it can't be.'

'I can't help you there I'm afraid!' Linda glanced at her watch. 'I'd best get back because I've a load of desserts to make for the Craigmonie. Glad you liked my cake!'

'I certainly did,' Ally said. 'Just don't leave it here because I've had an overdose of calories this afternoon.'

'We will get to Seascape one of these fine days,' Linda said as she put the remainder of her cake in the box and made her way to the door.

As Ally cleared the tea things away, she couldn't help thinking that the fun run might have scuppered Linda's plans for dinner at Seascape, but hopefully it would take everyone's mind off Archie's murder. She just hoped that it was as uneventful as possible.

TWELVE

Ross, having done an afternoon working at the surgery, appeared just after six o'clock, accompanied, as usual, by Ebony. 'I've just passed a group of brawny young men heading up this way,' he said.

'Ah, they've started practising for their fun run on Saturday then,' Ally said, 'because they've a long way to go before they get to their beer and barbecue – not to mention the prize!'

'Best of luck to them,' Ross said as he brought in a bag. 'And how are your guests today?'

'Well, Greg is particularly belligerent, and none of them are really happy now that no one's been arrested. And Patti and her daughters are watching something on Netflix. The girls, predictably enough, are becoming very bored. There's not a lot for them to do. And Amir wants them to stay here for the moment.'

'So, what's Greg so angry about?' Ross asked.

Ally rolled her eyes. 'He obviously wants to get back to his cabin building, and I get the impression that he doesn't much care who's arrested, as long as someone is, so he can leave. And, in his own words, he thinks the earl and Micky could have been in cahoots!'

'Always a possibility, I suppose!' said Ross cheerfully. Then, seeing Ally's face, added, 'Not likely though!' He dug in his bag and produced a carton of eggs. 'Will gave me these, so I thought we might have omelettes or something?'

'Great idea!' Ally agreed. As she spoke, she heard someone stomping around in the hall.

She exchanged glances with Ross and peeked round the corner of the door to see Greg taking off his walking boots and placing them in the cupboard under the stairs, where the shoes were kept.

'Everything OK, Greg?' Ally asked, realising that he'd seen her.

'I've just been for a walk up on the moor to try to wind down a little,' he said. 'But, damn me, no sooner had I set off than all these young guys start running past me! What's going on?'

'Well, the earl has organised a fun run for Saturday, a sort of mini marathon of ten or eleven miles. It's for the competitors in the games really because they've all been feeling very low since Archie's death, and they're obviously practising this afternoon. The earl's laying on a barbecue at the castle at the end of the race, and a prize for the first one back.'

Greg snorted. 'I suppose they're all glad that they don't have to compete against Archie because he'd be bound to win it if he was here. Doesn't it *matter* to the earl that one of these guys could be the killer?'

'Of course it matters,' Ally said sharply. 'But they can't all be killers, and they need something to boost their morale. And keep them healthy!'

He didn't look convinced.

'It would be good to go up there on Saturday to watch the

race as they come round the loch, and then we're all invited to the barbecue afterwards,' Ally added.

'Huh!' Greg shook his head. 'I guess I'll find something better to do.'

'I think the girls would like it,' Ally said. 'They're becoming very bored here, and it would be something more interesting for them. In fact, you could all do with cheering up!'

'I'll put it to the vote,' Greg said, climbing the stairs.

Ally sighed as she closed the door. 'That man is really bitter,' she said to Ross.

'Yes, he sounds it. I think it would be good if you could encourage them when they have breakfast in the morning,' Ross said.

'I will,' Ally agreed.

They all appeared, looking morose, at breakfast in the morning. Greg was uncharacteristically quiet, Wendy seemed a little more nervous than usual, and Patti and her daughters just looked bored.

As she wished them all a bright, 'Good morning!' Ally repeated what she'd told Greg about the race and the barbecue.

'Oh, cool!' enthused Julie. 'Oh, *please* can we go and watch?'

'A barbecue would be fun!' Janey exclaimed.

'It might be getting dark before they all get back for a barbecue,' Patti said, 'and you are not going *anywhere* in the dark on your own!'

'Everyone's invited,' Ally reminded her. 'It would be nice to all go together, wouldn't it?'

'*I'll* come with you, girls,' Wendy said, looking more cheerful. 'I'd like to see the runners – and the barbecue later.'

'Oh, Auntie Wendy, that would be *great*!' Julie turned to her mother. 'Why don't you come along, Mom? It's only a bit of fun, and we haven't had much of that while we've been here!'

Patti pulled a face. 'Oh, OK, I'll come.'

'I might even try to walk part of the route,' Greg said. 'I really like walking up there. Not the eleven miles, of course, but maybe two or three miles.'

'I could come with you,' Wendy said, 'and then we can go on to the barbecue, can't we?'

'I suppose so,' Greg grunted without enthusiasm.

'I'm told that the race will begin at five o'clock,' Ally said. 'Leaving from the village shop, up past here to Loch Soular, all the way round the loch and then they follow a path over the moor to where the castle grounds begin – and the barbecue.'

Both girls were now in a huddle discussing what jeans they might wear, would it be warm enough just to wear a T-shirt and had they better wash their hair?

'I think we've cheered them up a little,' Ally said with a smile as she got back into the kitchen, 'particularly the girls!'

'They're teenagers, Ally. They're going to be impressed with all that testosterone! I mean most of these guys taking part are single and in good shape,' Ross remarked.

'I hope that doesn't present any problems!' Ally said with a sigh, reminding herself that these girls hadn't had contact with any young men since their arrival at the malthouse. 'Anyway, I've told them that we'll set off late afternoon, to watch them coming round the far end of the loch and see if anyone's dropped out.'

The following day, the day of the fun run, everyone was in the hall at half past five, as planned, having watched the runners galloping past the malthouse about twenty minutes before. Patti was wearing an outfit Ally imagined more suitable for a yoga class, and the girls were wearing skintight jeans and skimpy tops, but at least they'd all taken jackets with them. Greg and Wendy, on the other hand, were clad in serious-looking sportswear, a well-known logo scrawled over their chests and a stripe down the sides of their jogging bottoms. They had a 'we-do-this-all-the-time' type look on their faces and plainly meant business as they searched in the hall cupboard for their walking boots.

As he tied his laces, Greg glowered at Wendy. 'You sure you're going to be OK with these new boots?'

'Oh, they'll be fine,' she replied. Then, turning to Ally: 'I didn't bring any with me from home, so I bought these in Glasgow, and they need to be christened! I'm kinda hoping they'll be OK.'

And so they set off, Greg and Wendy leading the way and slightly ahead, followed by Patti and the girls, with Ally and Ross bringing up the rear. Ally was beginning to feel that she and Ross were quite frumpy in their normal jeans and T-shirts, with warm sweaters tied around their waists, in readiness for the cooler temperature in the evening to come.

As they walked, Ally noticed that Wendy was limping a little and, halfway up, she stopped.

'It's no good,' she said sadly. 'These boots are killing me, specially the left one. I'm going to have to go back.'

Greg sighed. 'Well OK, but do you mind if I carry on? I really want to do this.'

Wendy nodded, looking disappointed. 'You carry on; I don't want to hold you back if I'm limping.'

'Are you OK to get back?' Ally asked her anxiously.

'I can come with you!' Patti said eagerly.

'No, I'll be OK,' Wendy said. 'I'll hobble slowly!' With that, she turned on her heel and limped back down the hill.

They watched her for a moment until she was out of sight, and then made their way towards where the flags were positioned. Someone had planted the little red flags about every hundred yards all the way up to the loch, and Ally wondered who'd been assigned to this task. Angus? Much more likely he'd sent one of his under-ghillies.

On arrival at the lochside, they could see the runners in the distance on the far side of the water's edge, but it was impossible to make out who was who or who might be in the lead. The path which eventually led to the castle was clearly marked with the flags, so there was no chance of anyone getting lost. There was a group of spectators already there, including Finlay McKinnon and Murdo McConnachie.

'No Morag?' Ally asked as she approached Murdo.

'Och, she's no' a great one for walkin',' Murdo said, 'but she'll be at the castle later and, hopefully, to see one of our lads as the winner!' He produced a couple of plastic water bottles. 'Thought I'd better have these spare in case they need it by the time they get here!'

At this point, Greg took his leave, with much waving, and set off for his walk along the flag-decked path.

'See you at the barbecue!' they yelled.

As Ally studied the distant figures on the far side of the loch, she reckoned it must be a good four or five miles to circle round, and then there was as far again to get to the castle.

Ross had had the good sense to bring his binoculars and was using them to try to decipher who was who among the runners. 'I can make out Micky and Bobby, and Ivan... and Forby and that could be Forby's younger brother...' He screwed his face up. 'And a few others whose names I don't know. Oh, and I think that's Tom, the heart-throb ghillie.'

'Oh, *he's* real cute,' Julie said as she and Janey collapsed into giggles.

'How do you know him?' Ally asked.

'Oh, it was when we went up to see Mom's Uncle Angus,' Janey replied.

Patti sniffed. 'Well,' she said, turning up the collar of her jacket, 'I hope they bloody well hurry up because it's getting cold.' She was making it clear that she was here on sufferance.

Finlay McKinnon had had the foresight to bring along a flask of whisky, which he imbibed at regular intervals. Murdo had a can of beer and politely offered a mouthful to Ally, who thanked him but refused. She was beginning to wish they'd brought a Thermos of something hot to drink because it was turning decidedly chilly.

'I think I might go back anyway,' Patti said. 'Come on, girls – there's not much to see!'

'No, we want to stay!' Julie protested. 'We want to see these guys running past here!'

'Well, you can see them at the castle,' Patti snapped.

'Can't *we* stay?' begged Janey.

'Not on your own,' Patti said firmly.

'But we've been here before, with the dog,' Julie protested.

At this point, Ross, ever the gentleman, said, 'I'll stay and keep an eye on the girls if you ladies want to go back. I'll bring them back to the malthouse, and then we can all go up to the castle together.' He looked through his binoculars again. 'They're on the east bank now, hidden by the trees, and my guess is that the runners will be here in less than half an hour.'

Ally, now feeling very chilly, decided that she too would go back.

'It's very kind of your Ross to stay with the girls,' Patti said as they set off. 'Thing is, it's getting to the stage where they've become real interested in boys, and I can see I'm going to have problems.'

'Ross will keep an eye on them,' Ally assured her.

As they arrived back, she decided she'd put on a warm jacket before they headed for the castle. The evenings were cooling rapidly.

. . .

When they got back to the malthouse, they found a note from Wendy on the table in the hallway.

> *I've treated my foot, but it's still sore, even in comfortable trainers, so I'm setting off early to the castle as I really want to be there when Greg arrives, and I don't want to hold you all back with my hobbling!*

Shortly afterwards, Ross returned with the two girls, had time for a quick hot drink, and then they all set off for the castle.

The girls raced ahead, followed by Ally and Ross, with Patti a few steps behind.

'Barbecue food is so fattening,' Patti grumbled. 'How many fry-ups can you consume in one day, for God's sake!'

Ally didn't reply, knowing full well that Patti normally breakfasted on just coffee and toast, or cereal. For what seemed like the fiftieth time, she reminded herself that this woman had just lost her husband and was entitled to be a bit erratic. But how erratic was *too* erratic? And just how quickly could she solve this mystery and get this family off her hands?

THIRTEEN

The sun had not long set and the castle was floodlit against a red-streaked sky, as it usually was on such occasions, giving it a magical Disney-like appearance. The field which abutted the castle gardens was also floodlit, with two large gas-fed barbecues already glowing alongside a mountain of mini-steaks, sausages and burgers. Standing beside the barbecue, also glowing in the heat, was the cook, Mrs Jamieson, ably abetted by the housekeeper, Mrs Fraser, both in large, striped aprons. Neither of them looked particularly thrilled to be there. The earl, however, looked extremely cheerful in his kilt and polo-necked sweater, dashing about here and there and welcoming visitors. There was already quite a crowd of the runners' families and friends, including Morag and Murdo, of course, along with Finlay and Aisla McKinnon, and about twenty others, most of whom Ally knew by sight. Excitement was in the air as everyone waited for the first runner to appear.

'Well,' said Morag, by way of greeting, 'at least that Armstrong man's no goin' to come first *this time*! I'm expectin' our Micky to win this one.'

Ally had no special fondness for Micky but knew it would

improve Morag's mood in the morning if he did win. She discovered that Finlay's younger son, Fergus, was also running, as Ross had thought, along with Forby and Tom, the much-fancied young ghillie.

It was hardly a marathon, but nevertheless it did take some stamina to run ten or eleven miles and, for the most part, over rough, uneven terrain.

Alongside the barbecue was a huge bin full of cans of beer for the thirsty. On a side table, there were also soft drinks and bottles of wine. Ross opted for a beer, while Ally poured herself a glass of red wine. She hoped the event wouldn't last too long, although, doubtless, it couldn't finish until the last contestant staggered in.

Wendy, still limping, had appeared at Ally's side. 'I'd have thought that Greg would be here by now,' she said, looking worried. 'I thought he'd be here half an hour ago.'

'He probably had to keep side-stepping to let the runners go by,' Ally pointed out.

'I expect you're right,' Wendy said, but she looked doubtful. 'I've tried phoning him, but there's no reply.'

They stood sipping their drinks for about ten minutes before the first runner came stumbling in, gasping and grinning.

It was Forby McKinnon!

There was much applause and cheering, with Finlay and Aisla whooping with delight as Forby crashed down on the grass, grabbing a much-needed proffered can of beer.

'Well, well,' said Morag, her lips tight. 'There's a surprise!'

Murdo shook his head. 'Thae lads didn't have enough time to prepare for this, that's the trouble.'

Let's hope Micky's second, for all of our sakes, Ally thought.

But he wasn't. The next runner to come staggering in was Ivan, the Craigmonie barman, and it was another good five minutes before Micky McConnachie made his appearance, coming in third, with brother Bobby just behind him, and then Tom, the ghillie.

There was much cheering and clapping, with Morag still muttering about how Forby McKinnon could possibly have beaten her two sons, when he didn't do half the bodybuilding they did? 'And,' she said to Ally, 'that Forby McKinnon's goin' home with a hundred quid in his bloody pocket, and he doesn't *need* it! Not like our lads do! Them McKinnons have got plenty of money!'

Ally, fed up of her grumbling, moved away to where Forby was being congratulated by everyone, and young Tom was being congratulated by an excited, shiny-eyed Julie.

The final few runners had now arrived in various stages of dilapidation, but there was still no sign of Greg.

Wendy was asking each of the runners if they had seen her husband, but apparently no one had. She came back to where Ally was standing. 'No one's seen Greg,' she said, 'and I'm getting really worried now. He was only doing the last three or four miles of the route, so he should have been back long before this.'

'Surely he'd have been in touch if he had a problem?' Ally said. 'I mean, he would have had his phone with him, wouldn't he?'

'He never goes out without it,' Wendy said. 'But I've called him several times now and there's still no reply.'

'Perhaps he forgot it, or it needed charging?' Ally suggested.

Ross had come back to join her and overheard the conversation. 'I think it's more likely there's no signal up there,' he said, pointing up at the moorland.

'You mean he could have fallen over and injured himself and wouldn't be able to contact anyone?' Wendy's voice had risen in panic.

'I'll tell you what I think, Wendy,' Ally said. 'I think he was hot, sweaty and exhausted, and he's made his way back to the malthouse for a bath and a rest. He'll probably appear here any minute now.'

Wendy seemed slightly relieved. 'I hadn't thought of that,' she admitted. 'Perhaps I should try phoning again.'

At this point, Hamish called for a hush and, with the help of a loudhailer, presented Forby with his winnings in an envelope, causing further cheers from his friends and family, if not the McConnachies.

An increasingly jittery Wendy reappeared, having been chatting to more of the runners.

'No one's seen him,' she said. 'I think I'll go back down to the malthouse to see if Greg's gone back there. I'm sure that's probably what he's done. And he didn't seem all that keen on coming to the barbecue anyway.'

Ross put his hand on her arm. 'Look, you've got a sore foot, so I'll pop down and check that he's there. He most likely is and has fallen asleep.'

'Isn't he a *gentleman*!' Wendy said admiringly as Ross set off.

'He is,' Ally agreed, watching Julie, who was now chatting animatedly to Tom, who appeared to be enjoying the attention. Janey was standing to one side looking decidedly sulky. Patti didn't appear to have noticed and was trying to pacify a still-agitated Wendy.

Ally filled up her glass again and watched the deserving runners all standing in line at the barbecue while the two ladies loaded up their plates. They studiously avoided all the salads which Mrs Jamieson had concocted, and which were set out on a side table. The barbecue was for everyone, but Ally decided she'd wait until Ross got back. And she'd definitely be attacking those delicious-looking salads.

Ross returned a while later, looking worried. 'He's not at the malthouse,' he murmured to Ally as Wendy approached.

'Is he *there*?' Wendy asked anxiously.

Ross shook his head. 'I'm afraid not, Wendy. I think we're going to have to go look for him.'

Wendy dissolved into tears. 'I *knew* something was wrong,' she wept.

'I'll have a word with Hamish,' Ross said, heading towards the barbecue.

Ally saw the two of them talking, with glances over at Wendy. When he came back, Ross said, 'The earl is going to get Angus to drive the Land Rover on the exact route that Greg was planning to take, and I suggest that you go with him and keep a look-out all around.'

Wendy nodded, blew her nose and, accompanied by Ross, walked over to where Hamish was standing.

'Where the hell has he got to?' Patti murmured to Ally. 'How can he just disappear?'

'I'm sure they'll find him,' Ally said, hoping she sounded more confident than she felt.

She had a bad feeling about all of this.

Angus, looking less than delighted, had been unearthed from his cottage, where he'd been dozing gently while watching the local news on TV. He glowered at Wendy as he opened the passenger door of the Land Rover for her and climbed into the driving seat. They then set off rather jerkily, along the route just completed by the runners, and leaving behind a somewhat muted celebration.

Everyone was looking at everyone else and shrugging. Who was this guy who was missing? Since all the publicity had been centred on Archie Armstrong's demise, few people were aware that he had a brother-in-law travelling with him. There was tension in the air, and some of the runners, along with their families and friends, were beginning to slope away. It was as if most of the joy had been syphoned out of the event. Nevertheless, many of the runners were still eating heartily.

The little group from the malthouse waited anxiously for the Land Rover to return, and it was about another fifteen minutes before it did. A distraught Wendy climbed out of the passenger door, and a grim-faced Angus reversed the Land Rover back up to where it was normally parked.

'No sign!' Wendy wept. 'No sign at all! Where in God's name *is* he?'

To make matters worse, it was now properly dark. Ally looked at Ross, who was gazing at his watch.

'I suggest we go back to the malthouse,' he said, 'and we'll set off with torches, and the dogs, and check the whole route again.'

Wendy nodded dumbly, and Ally, feeling sorry for her, gave her a hug. 'Never fear, Wendy,' she said, 'we will find him.'

Janey had returned and was talking to her mother.

'Oh my God!' exclaimed Patti. 'Julie's necking with that wretched boy somewhere!'

Ally smiled to herself. She'd not heard the word 'necking' used in a long time. Well, the girl was seventeen, so it wasn't exactly unusual and, from what Ally had heard, Patti had been no saint in her youth either.

'Where the hell have they gone?' Patti was now in full panic mode. She turned to Janey. 'Where did you see them last?'

Janey shrugged and muttered something.

'Well,' said Patti, 'I'm staying right here until I find her! Nobody's going to play fast and loose with my daughter! And you're staying *right here* with me until we find her, Janey!'

'We have to go,' Ross said to her. 'We'll see you later.'

As the sad little group made their way back to the malthouse,

Ross said, 'I'm sorry, perhaps we should have had something to eat before we left, but...'

'I couldn't eat a thing,' Wendy said.

'I'll make us all something later back at the malthouse when we catch up with Greg,' said Ally.

Wendy was continuing to call him on her phone, but there was no response. If he'd pulled a muscle and fallen by the roadside, Ally reckoned, he would still have to be there *somewhere*. She didn't imagine Angus had been very thorough at searching on his side of the vehicle, and Wendy was in such a state that she could well have missed a clue from the passenger seat.

'Perhaps he did forget to charge the battery before he went out,' Wendy said, her voice shaking, 'and if he had no power, he'd have no torch either. How on earth will we ever find him?'

'We will,' Ross said firmly as they got back home. 'We'll need a few minutes, and then we'll set off and do a thorough search.' He looked at Wendy. 'Are you fit enough to walk back up there? You don't *have* to come, you know.'

'It still really hurts, but I *must* come! I'd never forgive myself if he was lying injured somewhere and I wasn't there...' Her voice crumbled. 'I'll just get another sweater.'

'I think we should prepare ourselves for a long walk in the dark,' Ross murmured to Ally as Wendy made her way upstairs. 'The silly fool's got himself lost somewhere that has no phone signal, or else – like she said – he didn't charge it up before he left. Maybe he's tripped or something? Who knows?'

Ross went out to search in his car for the powerful torch which he took with him everywhere – a hangover from his days as a vet delivering lambs at midnight. Ally fetched her warm coat.

'We're taking the dogs, aren't we?' Ally asked as Ross came in with the torch. She noticed how excited both animals had become when they saw coats being produced.

'Definitely,' Ross said. 'They could be invaluable and will probably find him before we do.'

Wendy had reappeared and, after a few minutes, they all set off on the well-trodden path towards Loch Soular. It had suddenly become pitch-dark, the moon hidden behind some heavy clouds, and so they were relying on Ross's torch to see the way.

'Give me an arm each, girls!' Ross said cheerfully as he shone the torch ahead. 'Can't have either of you tripping over!'

Ally did not like walking in the dark at the best of times and, to be sure, this was not the best of times. Both she and Wendy stumbled a little as they made their way carefully along the rough path. At least the heather had been flattened over time, mainly due to Ally's walks, and again this evening by the runners.

After fifteen minutes, the clouds rolled back, and the moon appeared just as they neared the loch, producing a silver glow on the surface of the water. It was breathtakingly beautiful.

Ally had never seen this lovely wee loch by moonlight before, and she was enchanted.

'I think he was going to cut across over there somewhere...' Wendy pointed vaguely to the right.

'Then there must be a marker there,' Ross said. 'Didn't you say something about flags?'

'Oh yes,' Wendy said. 'Red flags. That's how he knew where to go.' She pointed again to the right. 'It's disorientating in the dark.'

Ross swivelled his torch around as they veered in that direction, the dogs bounding ahead.

It was Ally who spotted it. 'Look! Over *there*!' She walked ahead, trying not to stumble. Ross was now pointing the torch towards Ally, and they all saw the little red flag anchored into the ground and the path alongside.

'That's it!' Wendy exclaimed excitedly.

'OK,' Ross said, 'this is the race route, but are you sure this was the way *he* was heading?'

'I don't know,' Wendy said, her face falling. 'Greg was in charge of the map, and when I left to go back to the malthouse...' Her voice broke.

'Let's keep going then,' Ross said quickly.

At this point, Wendy began to call out, 'Greg! Greg!' But there was total silence as they shuffled on.

Ally noticed that the dogs appeared to be getting excited and sniffing everything more than usual. They'd covered about a hundred yards when both dogs, who'd been running ahead, began to bark excitedly.

'Something or someone's around,' Ross said quietly as they carried on walking more slowly, with Wendy continuing to call out, 'Greg! Greg! We're here!'

Ross shone the torch around, concentrating on the two barking dogs and said, 'Stay here!' to the two women before walking forward to where the dogs were and where there was a large rock embedded in the ground. In the moonlight, Ally could see Ross standing stock-still for a moment before bending down. 'Oh my God!' he said.

Ally and Wendy rushed across to where he was standing, then stood, rooted to the spot.

Lying on his back, clearly felled by a blow to the head, was Greg Watson.

FOURTEEN

Wendy screamed before collapsing beside the body of her husband. Ally stared in horror, wondering if she was going to be sick. Ross checked Greg's pulse and then got straight onto his phone.

'Body found on the moor, near Loch Soular,' he said calmly. 'We need urgent police and ambulance.'

All the time he was speaking, Wendy was weeping loudly. 'Who the hell would *do* this?' she shouted through her tears. '*Who*?'

Ally, feeling very shaken herself, felt there was little she could say or do because Greg was so obviously dead and, only for a moment, wondered if there was any possibility that he could have accidentally tripped, fallen on the sharp edge of the rock and split his head open. Then she noticed the torn piece of paper beside Greg's body which had probably fallen out of his hand or his pocket. Certain that it was probably just a shopping list or a receipt, she picked it up and shone the torch on it.

If you want me to keep your secret, you need to meet me... was written before the horizontal tear. Ally's blood froze. What secret? Who was he supposed to meet? And where?

Ross was still on his phone, explaining where they were as best he could, and stressing the need for urgency. When he clicked his phone off, he took Ally gently aside, leaving Wendy to grieve over her husband's body.

'This doesn't look like an accident to me,' he said, keeping his voice low.

'You mean that you think someone's killed him?' Ally asked, horrified.

'I do,' Ross confirmed. 'But then, I'm no policeman.'

The moon was throwing a ghostly, pale light across the moor, almost like something out of a horror film, before sliding behind the clouds again, leaving them with only Ross's torch to illuminate the eerie scene. The dogs, sensing something was wrong, sat down next to Ally.

'Will the helicopter be able to land?' Ally asked, looking around.

'Yes, on that flat area beside the loch,' Ross said, recalling a previous emergency. He looked at his watch. 'They're bound to be half an hour at least.' He looked at Ally. 'Let's find a comfortable boulder to sit on.' He shone the torch back at Wendy, who was sitting up but still weeping softly.

'Who would do this?' she asked over and over again. '*Someone* did it! Someone killed my brother, and now they've killed my husband! Oh God!' She was holding Greg's limp hand as she spoke.

'Try not to touch him too much,' Ross suggested, 'and for God's sake don't try to move him. The police will want to see the body exactly as we found it.'

'But I'm his *wife*!' Wendy shouted. 'Why the hell did we ever agree to come over here!'

The wind had got up now and was carrying her voice soulfully across the moors.

Ally found a little hillock and had sat down with her head between her knees to ward off the nausea that kept rising in her throat. Ross sat down next to her and took her hand in his.

'So he's been murdered,' she said in little more than a whisper.

'Almost certainly,' Ross replied, squeezing her hand. 'And there goes one of your chief suspects for Archie Armstrong's murder!'

They heard the helicopter in the distance before they saw the flashing light in the sky, coming from the south. Ally and Ross made their way back towards the loch, leaving Wendy still weeping beside her husband's body.

As the helicopter approached, its lights illuminated them and the ground, and it hovered for a few minutes before carefully landing. With the blades still rotating, the door opened and out rushed a small group of forensics and paramedics, armed with a stretcher. As if on cue, at the same time, a Land Rover came hurtling up the path, disgorging Amir Kandahar and a young constable.

'Fortunately, we were in the village overnight,' Amir said before heading towards the white-clad forensic group. They all looked around.

'I found this close to his body,' Ally said, handing the scrap of paper to Amir. 'I think it's important.'

Amir, who knew better by now than to dismiss anything Ally told him, took the note with a nod, slipping it into a small evidence bag and handing it to the young constable.

'Follow us,' Ross said, taking Ally's hand and leading them towards the red flag that heralded the beginning of the runners' route. The dogs romped ahead, and, as they walked, Ally told Amir briefly about Greg Watson going for a walk earlier, intending to meet them at the castle for the barbecue, and the three of them setting off to look for Greg when it became obvious that something had happened. Ross also explained about the fun run and that this was the route the runners would have taken.

'Meaning that most of the suspects for Armstrong's murder would also have been running along here?' Amir asked.

'I'm afraid so,' Ross replied. Then, as the rays of his torch lit up the rock: 'Over there...'

They all trundled across the heather towards the rock and the weeping Wendy, still holding Greg's lifeless hand.

'I'm sorry, Mrs Watson, but I must ask you to move away, please.' Amir spoke gently, laying his hand on her arm.

'But he's my *husband*!' she shouted.

'I know.' Amir's voice was calm. 'But we need to examine him before we move him.'

Ally moved across and took Wendy's arm. 'Come and sit with us over there.' She motioned towards the little hillock where they'd sat earlier. She found a couple of tissues in her pocket and handed them to Wendy who, very unwillingly, allowed herself to be helped to her feet.

'This is the nightmare of all nightmares,' she sobbed as she blew her nose.

The forensics were already hard at work, measuring and taking photographs, while the paramedics had laid the stretcher down by the body in readiness for its removal.

Amir was supervising the scene while talking non-stop into his phone, then turned back to where the others were sitting. 'I know it's late and it's dark,' he said, 'but I'm going to have to ask some questions right now.'

'Where are you taking him?' Wendy asked, stifling sobs.

'They'll take him to Glasgow shortly,' Amir replied. 'We need to do a post-mortem and establish the cause of death. Let's all get back to where the helicopter is.'

Leaving the forensic team and the paramedics at the scene, they slowly made their way back along the track towards the loch, Wendy supported on one side by Ross and by Ally on the other. As they walked, Amir was questioning Wendy about what time they'd set off for their walk, what time she got back and what time they'd all finally left to look for Greg.

Back at the loch, he ushered an unwilling Wendy into his Land Rover for some further questioning before returning to where Ally and Ross were standing a few minutes later. 'I'll be back to talk to you all in the morning,' he said as the slow procession appeared out of the gloom, carrying Greg's body on the stretcher. This sent Wendy off into paroxysms of grief again, and she tried to run towards them.

Amir held her back firmly. 'No, Mrs Watson,' he said. 'You can see him later. Right now, there's work to be done, and I'll be back to talk to you in the morning.' He turned to Ally and Ross. 'How can I find out how many runners might have taken part in this thing?'

'Well, your best bet would be Hamish, the earl, because he organised this. It all culminated in the barbecue up in the castle grounds,' Ally explained.

'Reckon they'll still be there?' Amir asked, consulting his watch.

Ross shrugged. 'Some of them may be.'

'Right,' Amir said to the young constable, 'that's our next stop.'

He looked at Ally. 'Can we give you a lift back down to the malthouse?'

'No thanks, we have the dogs, and we've got a good torch,' Ally replied.

Amir nodded as he rushed towards his vehicle, at the same time as the helicopter began to rise slowly into the air.

By the time Ally and Ross began to support a staggering Wendy back to the malthouse, the helicopter was just a tiny, distant, flashing light in the night sky.

FIFTEEN

The malthouse was lit up, with an anxious Patti and her daughters standing on the doorstep.

'You wouldn't believe my daughter was only kissing that boy in the bloody summerhouse, in the garden next to the barbecue!' Patti said by way of greeting. 'She is in *big* trouble!' She glared at Julie, who pulled a face. 'Where's Greg?' she asked as the dogs bounded into the hallway.

'Bad news, I'm afraid,' Ross said, glancing at the girls.

'Oh no!' Patti put her head in her hands for a moment, then stared at the tear-drenched Wendy. 'Oh my God! What's happened?'

'He's dead.' Wendy spoke flatly.

'*What*?' Patti looked from one to the other. 'How can he be dead? He *can't* be dead!'

The two girls were clinging to each other and looking at Wendy, saucer-eyed.

'We think he might have tripped and knocked his head on a sharp rock,' Ally said diplomatically, hoping to spare the girls any gory details.

'A *sharp rock*?' Patti repeated. 'How the hell could he have done that?' She appeared to be about to faint.

Ross moved swiftly across to support her.

'It's been a shock to us all,' he said, 'but I think you should sit down.' He led her into the sitting room and sat her down in an armchair.

Patti burst into floods of tears. Wendy sat on the sofa opposite, with the girls, all of them now weeping openly.

'I think drinks are needed,' Ross said, exchanging glances with Ally. 'I'll go and get them.'

He headed off towards the kitchen, and Ally wondered what on earth she could say to give a shred of comfort to this group of weeping women.

'So where is he?' Patti asked between sobs.

'The air ambulance has taken him away,' Ally explained. 'That's why we're so late.'

'Oh, Auntie Wendy!' Janey rushed towards her aunt and put her arm round her. Julie rushed to her other side, both girls weeping – which set Wendy off again.

Patti looked directly at Ross as he re-entered the room with some drinks and mixers. 'It *was* an accident?' She was shuddering uncontrollably.

'We'll know after the post-mortem,' Ross replied. 'Who needs a nightcap?'

Both Wendy and Patti shook their heads. 'I feel sick,' Patti said.

'Maybe a brandy would help?' Ross suggested.

Patti nodded, tears still streaming down her cheeks. 'I'm taking it upstairs with me.'

'I'll have one too,' Wendy said, drying her eyes. 'But I feel I want to be alone tonight.'

'Well, I think we should all at least try to get some sleep because the police will be here first thing in the morning,' Ally said.

Patti stood up, hugged her sister-in-law, took her arm and led her towards the stairs. 'I've got some sleeping tablets somewhere,' she added.

Ross followed Ally and the dogs into the kitchen, took two glasses out of the cupboards and poured out two hefty measures of Scotch.

'Oh, I need this,' Ally said, taking a sip. 'But I still don't think I'm going to be able to sleep. Did I tell you about that scrap of paper I picked up?'

'I saw you handing something to Amir.'

'Ross, it looked like it could be some sort of blackmail note or something.'

'What do you mean?' Ross asked.

'It said something like "if you want me to keep your secret..." but the paper was ripped in half. This could mean that he was planning to slip away from Wendy and go meet someone, couldn't it?'

Ross shrugged. 'I guess so. Hopefully the police will find the rest of it.'

She shuddered. 'I keep seeing him lying there, like that...'

'I know,' Ross said, taking her in his arms, 'but you must try to put it out of your mind. Let's get to bed.'

Ally found herself wide awake at five o'clock in the morning. Afraid that her tossing and turning would waken Ross, she got up. But Ross was awake too.

Ally looked out of the window at the darkness and said, 'It's too early to do anything.'

'Not too early for a cup of tea,' Ross said, getting out of bed. 'I'll go down and get the kettle on.'

As she got dressed, Ally wondered if Wendy would be able to eat any breakfast. Her guests were fast disappearing, one by one! Who might be next? Would anyone ever want to stay at

The Auld Malthouse B&B again? One of the main suspects on her board was now dead. Ally began to doubt if he really had been Archie's killer, but, if it wasn't Greg, who was it? And she knew, deep down, that someone had well and truly brained the poor man. With mixed feelings of revulsion, she now felt guilty at ever having suspected Greg at all.

Ally made her way downstairs to find Ross brewing a large pot of tea. He let both dogs out into the garden, and then poured them each a mugful. Within minutes, the dogs had come bounding in, hoping for breakfast.

'These are two clever girls!' Ross said, stroking their heads and digging some dog food out of the cupboard. 'Without you two, we might never have found the poor guy!'

I almost wish they hadn't, Ally thought, trying to dispel the vision. She wondered what Greg could possibly have done to deserve this.

Patti and the girls surfaced around eight o'clock. 'I didn't get a wink of sleep,' she said, still tearful. She looked drab this morning in a grey, high-necked jumper and black leggings. Both the girls looked utterly exhausted.

'What about Wendy?' Ally asked.

'No idea. There's no sound from her bedroom, so perhaps she took the sleeping tablets I gave her.' Patti studied Ally for a moment. 'It just seems too much of a coincidence that all the suspects for Archie's death were running around that spot at the time of Greg's death, don't you think?'

'Yes, it does seem strange,' Ally agreed.

'I'll just have fruit juice and coffee,' Patti said, 'and I'm not really sure if I can manage that.' She was looking extremely agitated.

Julie sat down close to her mother. 'I could eat some toast,' she said.

Janey nodded. 'Yeah, me too.'

Back in the kitchen, Ally thought that Patti's reaction was a little odd, to say the least. She seemed more upset than Wendy, though Greg was only her brother-in-law, not her husband, whereas when her husband *had* been killed, Patti had recovered almost immediately.

Wendy finally appeared around nine o'clock, looking gaunt, tired and swollen-eyed. She, too, could only manage coffee, so Ally produced a couple of pots and left them to it, aware that Amir had arrived and was sitting in the kitchen, waiting for her guests to finish their meagre breakfasts.

He looked up when Ally came in.

'Before I question the family,' Amir said, 'I need to be absolutely certain that neither of you two were up there when that so-called fun run first began?'

'No, we all went up there as a group around half past five or thereabouts,' Ross said. 'The runners were on the far side of the loch then.'

'So what time did you come back here?'

'Half past six probably. Wendy had hurt her foot, so she'd come back a little earlier.'

'Hmm,' said Amir. He turned to Ally. 'I have forensics looking for the other half of this note that you found, which hopefully is in his pocket or somewhere. It looks very much like he may have been blackmailed.'

'For what?' Ally asked, askance.

'That's what we need to find out,' Amir said. 'Mr Watson's death *could* have been an accident, but it's looking more and more like foul play. So, tell me what happened when you got to the castle.'

'Well, we saw the runners coming back in, and then Wendy got worried because there was no sign of Greg.'

'Didn't she try phoning him?' Amir asked.

'Yes, she'd tried several times, but there was no reply,' Ross said. 'So we wondered if he'd forgotten his phone, or not charged it up enough, or if there was no signal.' He hesitated for a moment. 'Shortly after we found the body, I tested to see if there was a signal on my phone, and there was. Of course, he would have had a different phone, and perhaps a different network, so maybe there wasn't a signal on his...'

'Did anyone make any effort to see if he'd fallen by the wayside?' Amir asked.

'The earl sent his ghillie with the Land Rover back along the path, Wendy with him. But they didn't see anything,' Ross replied. 'That was when we decided to come back here, get some torches and set off to look for him with the dogs.'

'And what time would that have been?'

'Probably around half past eight, I think,' Ally replied, looking at Ross for confirmation.

He nodded. 'Yes, about then.'

'And at what time do you reckon you found the body?'

'Probably about nine thirty,' Ross replied, 'bearing in mind it takes a good twenty minutes to get to Loch Soular, and it was dark.'

'Forensics reckon he'd been dead for two hours before they examined him. And I understand that all the runners would have passed along that route in the early evening,' Amir said.

'Surely one of the runners must have seen *something*?' Ally suggested.

Amir nodded. 'Apparently, they all set off at the same time, running round Loch Soular and then following the flags across the moor until they reached the castle. But some were fitter than others and so ran faster. By the time they got to that particular location – where Watson was found – they were probably five or ten minutes apart from each other.'

'Enough time to attack a walker and drag him down to that rock?' Ross asked.

'It's possible,' Amir said. 'Someone called Forbes McKinnon won, I believe.'

Ally pulled a face. 'Yes, he did. Morag will be here in a minute, and she's *still* going to be upset that it wasn't one of her sons that got the prize!'

'Furthermore,' Amir said, 'I've now got a note of who arrived first and who arrived last in this race, but little clue as to what might have occurred in the middle.' He sighed. 'I just wish that the earl or someone had thought to make a note of the runners and their times of arrival, so we could get some idea who was likely to be passing the murder site and at what time.' Amir consulted his watch. 'OK, I'll go and talk to your guests now before your irate cleaner arrives!' He picked up his folder and briefcase and disappeared into the dining room at the exact moment said irate cleaner came in through the back door.

'You wouldn't *believe* it,' she greeted them with a scowl as she fastened her pinny on. 'If it wasn't bad enough that Forby McKinnon won the bloody race, they've now found a *body*!'

'I think we would believe it,' Ally said calmly, 'since it was us who found the body.'

Morag gasped. 'They wouldn't tell us *who* it was.' She looked hopefully from Ally to Ross. Unable to wait for a reply, she asked, 'Who was it then?'

'It was Greg Watson,' Ally said. 'Brother-in-law of the late Archie Armstrong.'

'Oh my God!' Morag sat down heavily on a kitchen chair and wiped her brow. 'You'll have nobody left in them rooms at this rate!'

'The thought did cross my mind,' Ally admitted.

'So, what was you doin' up there on the moors anyway?' Morag asked.

'We were looking for him. He hadn't returned from a walk, and it was dark.'

Morag frowned. 'Why would he go for a walk in the dark?' She looked genuinely puzzled.

'It wasn't dark when he set out,' Ally explained patiently. 'Now, Morag, the detective is talking to the family in the dining room at the moment, so I'd have a go at the bedrooms if I were you.'

Morag heaved herself off the chair. 'I'll tell you *something else* – that Forby McKinnon shouldn't even have entered. He doesn't *need* that bloody hundred pounds!' She seemed to have forgotten that Ivan had also thoroughly beaten her sons.

'Fair's fair,' muttered Ross as he buttered himself some toast.

'No, it's *not* fair!' Morag ranted. 'Like I said to you, that Forby doesn't need that money! Himself and his dad make a bloody fortune down there with all that fishin' and tourists and everythin'.'

'They should have run faster then,' Ross said under his breath with a wink at Ally. They both knew that Morag would now launch into countless reasons why they couldn't. Ally knew for a fact that Bobby didn't appear to ever have a job, and Micky's wife had to work all hours so he had plenty of time off from plumbing to do his bodybuilding.

'I know,' she said soothingly to Morag, 'but life isn't always fair, is it? Best get these rooms done while the going's good!'

Morag, with a backward scowl at Ross, mounted the stairs.

No, life isn't fair, Ally thought, *not fair at all.* She thought of Archie and Greg both bringing their families over here but never going home again. And who on earth would want to kill them both? Now that there was the possibility of a blackmail note involved, how could she ever come close to finding this killer?

SIXTEEN

It was almost ten o'clock before Amir emerged from the dining room. He put his phone and his folder into his briefcase and snapped it shut. 'I don't think your remaining guests will set foot out of the malthouse now,' he said to Ally. 'They seem convinced that someone wants to annihilate their entire family.'

Ally nodded as she accompanied him to the door. 'It's certainly beginning to look that way,' she agreed. 'Although it doesn't really make sense, does it? I mean, Archie was an unwanted competitor, but Greg...?'

'I know,' Amir said. 'Now, if you should see or hear anything which might be relevant, would you let me know straight away? I'm up against a brick wall at the moment!'

'I will,' Ally replied, wondering if the board might help.

The only problem was that Ally didn't have a clue as to what names to write on her Post-its! If it was only Archie, she had likely culprits amongst the bodybuilding/caber tossing contestants, but what about Greg? Where did Greg come into all of this? Did he upset one of the contestants in the fun run as they raced past? And why would he do that? Did Greg think that Micky McConnachie, for example, knew something relevant? Had she got it completely wrong when she thought Greg might have killed Archie? And who could possibly have been blackmailing him?

Ally could feel a headache coming on.

Patti and Wendy appeared to have shut themselves in their respective rooms, while the girls watched TV in the sitting room. It was late morning when Julie tapped timidly on the kitchen door.

'Would it be OK if we took Flora for a walk?' she asked.

Ally was somewhat taken aback. 'Well, that's fine by me, but you must really ask your mother.' She doubted that Patti would agree because this area was now a murder scene.

Julie rolled her eyes. 'Mom's in a world of her own,' she said, just as Janey arrived at the door.

'Are you planning to go up to Loch Soular again?' Ally asked. As she spoke, the thought occurred to her that it was possible, just possible, that there was still some madman on the loose, killing people for no good reason. After all, the killer didn't *have* to be anyone from around these parts. Then she wondered if Amir had put any police on duty up there, particularly where Greg had been found.

'Look, girls, you must ask your mum because she may well want to go with you.' *Not,* Ally thought, *that Patti would be a tower of strength should any madman decide to pounce.*

'I'll go upstairs and ask her,' Janey said.

'No, I'll go,' said Julie. 'You go get the dog.' With that, she made her way upstairs.

'I hope Mom agrees,' Janey said, 'but otherwise I guess we'll just have to play with Flora in the garden.'

After a couple of minutes, Julie reappeared. 'Mom says it's OK, so let's go!'

Ally was a little surprised, particularly as Amir had said

something to the effect that the women were convinced that someone wanted to annihilate the whole family.

Later that morning, the doorbell rang. When Ally opened the door, she found herself facing a horde of cameras and a microphone being pushed towards her face.

'Mrs McKinley?' asked a tall, red-haired man with a beard. 'Just wondered if you could give us a minute?'

Totally unprepared for this, Ally looked round in confusion. 'Why do you want to talk to me?'

'We understand that two of your guests have been murdered, and we wondered how you, and the grieving family, are coping?'

'We are all coping,' Ally replied briefly, backing into the hallway.

'But you have two widows and two fatherless girls in there, I believe?' the red-haired man persisted.

'Yes, but I think it's highly unlikely that any of them will want to talk to you,' Ally said, about to close the door.

The reporter wasn't about to be fobbed off. 'Perhaps you could ask *them*?'

Ally nodded, closed the door and went to the foot of the staircase. 'Anyone want to talk to the media?' she yelled upstairs.

'No!' shouted Wendy. 'Tell them to sod off!'

'Give me a minute,' said Patti.

Ally returned to the front door to face the mob, which appeared to have grown in the few minutes since she'd seen them last. She then turned to see an immaculately made-up Patti behind her, wearing a classy cashmere sweater and straight-legged jeans. Switching on a smile, she walked towards the door to face the barrage of cameras and microphones.

'Ah!' said the red-haired reporter. 'Mrs Armstrong, I believe?'

'Yes,' Patti replied confidently. 'We have to remain here until the killer is found. I heard what you were asking Mrs McKinley, and she was right – we're all coping as best we can.'

'So you have no plans to return to Canada any time soon?'

'I already told you that we have to remain here.' Patti smiled sadly. 'Will that be all?'

'Um, just one more thing, Mrs Armstrong,' one of the other reporters shouted. 'Have you any idea who might have done these killings? Do you think it was one person or two?'

'I have no idea,' Patti shouted, 'but perhaps you should be asking the police instead of harassing innocent, grieving women. Thank you.' With that, she backed into the hallway, having closed the door firmly. 'You have to know how to deal with these people,' she informed Ally, who was standing behind her.

Ally really didn't know what to make of Patti. Was she really grieving either man? Or was this confidence, this put-together appearance, just a coping mechanism?

Then, as she began to make her way upstairs again, Patti suddenly paused. 'Where are the girls?'

'They've taken Flora for a walk, if you remember,' Ally replied.

'*What*?' Patti rotated and began to descend the stairs again. 'Did you say they'd gone for a *walk*?'

'Yes, an hour or so ago. Julie went upstairs to ask your permission – don't you remember?'

'She did *not*!' A furious Patti rounded on Ally. 'You're lying!'

'I am not lying!' Ally shouted back. 'They asked my permission, and I told them it was OK as far as I was concerned, but they had to ask you. I saw Julie going upstairs!'

Patti narrowed her eyes and took a deep breath. 'She did *not* ask for my permission. And I certainly would not have agreed. Not with someone clearly out to murder my family!'

At that very moment, Janey appeared with the dog.

'Where the hell have you been?' Patti yelled. 'And where is your sister?'

Janey looked around guiltily. 'She'll be back in a moment, Mom.'

'Why is she not with you?' Patti asked.

'Well, she wanted to stay on for a while,' Janey said, looking at the floor.

'*She wanted to stay on for a while*!' Patti exclaimed in fury. 'And where, exactly, did she want to stay on for a while?'

'The castle,' Janey muttered.

'The *castle*!' Patti glared at her. 'What the hell were you doing at the castle?'

'We fancied a change from Loch Soular,' Janey said. 'We thought it would be nice to see Uncle Angus.'

'You've never shown the slightest interest in Uncle Angus,' Patti said through her teeth. 'I don't suppose for one minute that it was anything to do with that over-sexed young ghillie, was it?'

'We just bumped into him...' Janey began.

'I'm going right up there *now*!' She turned to Ally, who'd just shut Flora in the kitchen. 'I'd like you to drive me up there, please.' She hesitated. 'If you wouldn't mind?'

Ally nodded. 'OK,' she said.

Patti got herself ready very noisily, while instructing Wendy, at the top of her voice, to take Janey into the sitting room and neither of them were to move one inch until she got back with the errant Julie.

She was still breathing heavily when Ally directed her to the car, leaving by the back door, just in case any of the press might still be hanging around.

'I'm sorry to drag you into all of this,' Patti muttered as they drove upwards, 'but speed is of the essence. Just wait until I find that daughter of mine!'

Ally tried hard to think of something reassuring to say. 'She's seventeen, Patti, and so it's hardly unusual for her to be interested in the opposite sex – particularly as she's been more or less incarcerated in the malthouse since you all arrived here.' She wondered if she should add something about the problems she'd had with Carol years ago.

Patti snorted. 'I don't know anything about this guy, and I hold Uncle Angus entirely responsible because he must know what goes on with his staff.'

Ally sighed loudly. 'Angus is an old man, and he can't be *everywhere*. Not only that, there's an absolute warren of outbuildings up there, and he can't be checking them all every five minutes. Besides, this boy might be a good-looker, but he seems decent enough, and I'm sure he wouldn't take advantage of Julie.'

'But she could be leading *him* on,' Patti said.

When they approached the building which contained Angus's office, Ally parked the car, and Patti marched inside and out again. 'No one in there!' she hollered.

That isn't altogether surprising, Ally thought, *as you'd hardly have a little love-in in the main office,* although such liaisons did exist, of course, in all manner of public spots.

'We need to find Angus,' Ally said, 'so let's try the kennels.'

'It's not *Angus* that's worrying me,' Patti snapped.

Ally bristled for a moment. 'Angus will know the likeliest places that Tom might use to woo his girlfriends,' she replied tersely.

'Sorry, I wasn't getting at you,' Patti said with a hint of contrition. 'I'm just worried.'

They'd glanced into several other buildings and sheds before they finally located Angus. He was having a cup of tea with Gordon Soutar, on a bench outside of Gordon's front door.

'What you lookin' for?' Angus growled.

'I'm looking for my daughter and that young Lothario that you're supposed to be overseeing,' Patti said loudly.

Angus took a slurp of tea and wiped his mouth with the back of his hand. 'Why's that?' he asked. Then he grinned. 'Are ye lonely already?'

'Don't be so bloody offensive!' Patti exploded. 'That boy is cavorting around here somewhere with *my daughter*!'

'Ah, yer daughter,' said Angus. He still had a smirk on his face. 'So what? She obviously takes after her mother.' He cackled with laughter.

Ally had to replace a restraining hand on Patti's arm because she could see that Patti was ready to do damage, her face reddening in fury.

'We just want to find her,' Ally interjected quickly.

Angus turned to Gordon. 'Where was it ye found him *last time*?'

'At the back of the wee barn, just up the hill there,' Gordon replied, pointing upwards vaguely. 'That's very likely where he'll be!'

Ally knew that there was a big barn and a wee barn, but, to her anyway, they seemed to be similar in size, although she'd never had reason to venture into either of them. Now, in spite of Patti shouting at the top of her voice, there was no sign of them in the first barn.

'Julie Armstrong, where *are* you?' Patti thundered.

As they entered the second barn, Ally was aware of a solitary figure among the hay bales piled up at the rear and, the next thing they knew, Julie was emerging alone and sobbing.

'Where is he?' shouted Patti, looking around.

'I don't know,' wept Julie. 'He left suddenly a few minutes ago because—'

'Because of *what*?' Patti yelled, looking behind the bales. 'Because he'd had his wicked way with you?'

Julie turned on her mother. 'Of course he bloody well didn't! It was just something he *said*.'

'Do you expect me to believe that?' Patti ranted.

Ally knew she had to mediate somehow or other. 'Look,' she said, 'we all need to calm down, go back home, have a cup of tea, and then you two can sort yourselves out!'

'Thanks, Ally,' said Julie. Then, turning to glare again at her mother: 'Thank God *someone's* being reasonable!'

Ally could only hope that Patti's still-burning fury might lessen as they made their way back down the rough path to Ally's car in total silence. She could still recall similar scenes with her own errant daughter in the past. But, when they got back, Patti stomped straight upstairs to her bedroom and slammed the door, leaving both Ally and Julie open-mouthed in the hall.

'Typical of her,' Julie said witheringly. 'Thank God for Auntie Wendy.'

Ally felt desperately sorry for the girl. 'Look,' she said, 'would it help if you came into the kitchen with Flora and myself? I can offer you a Coke?'

Julie smiled through her tears. 'Thanks, Ally, I'd like that.'

It helped, of course, that Flora made a great fuss of Julie as she lowered herself into one of Ally's comfortable armchairs.

'Your mum just needs time to calm down,' Ally said. 'It was only because she was so worried about you, and she'll soon come round, I'm sure.'

Julie shook her head. 'You don't know Mom! She's been real peculiar since Dad was killed, and I can understand that. He was my dad, and I loved him dearly.' She looked around for a tissue, which Ally supplied from a box on the table.

'Had Tom upset you in some way?' Ally asked casually as she made herself some coffee.

Julie shook her head. 'He's real cute, and I enjoyed kissing him, but then...'

'But then what?' Ally prompted.

'He said that I was so lovely that he couldn't believe I had a mother "like that".'

'Like *what*?' Ally was agog.

'I'm too ashamed to tell you!' The girl was becoming almost incoherent again. 'Just said it was something to do with my dad. And that he'd overheard her talking with Uncle Angus.'

Ally could scarcely believe what she was hearing. 'Julie,' she said gently, 'you don't need to tell me, but you need to tell this to the police! It could be important!'

'He said, "I shouldn't have told you that," and said I wasn't to tell anyone,' Julie muttered.

Ally shook her head in despair. 'You must tell the police! Would you like me to call Detective Inspector Kandahar right now?'

Julie shrugged. 'I don't want to get Tom, or Mom, into trouble,' she muttered.

'You don't want to get Tom into *trouble*?' Ally exclaimed. 'Are you serious, Julie? This guy might well have withheld information from the police.'

'I guess so,' Julie admitted sadly. 'But it was a lie. I know it was a lie!'

'I'm phoning right now,' Ally said, picking up her phone. 'And please don't tell your mother what you've just told me!'

'I can't...' Julie stood up, looking very dejected as she made her way towards the door.

'*Promise* that you make no mention of this to anyone until you talk to the detective?' Ally called out. '*Promise*?'

Julie shrugged. 'OK, OK, if you think it's important.'

'I think it's *very* important,' Ally said.

SEVENTEEN

'I'm back in Glasgow,' Amir said, 'but I can be there in the morning, around ten o'clock. How's that?'

'That's fine,' Ally replied. 'I don't think any of them are going anywhere.'

'And you can't tell me what you've discovered?'

'Julie won't tell me,' Ally said. 'But I think it could be important.'

'I'll be with you in the morning,' he said.

Ally poured a glass of wine. Then she worried whether she'd overreacted. After all, Tom might well have just overheard Angus referring to Patti's misspent youth, which had nothing at all to do with this case. She wished Ross was here.

Ross had gone home to cut the grass and reply to emails, and he returned at around six o'clock. He'd run out of petrol for the mower, the guests in the barn had spied a rat scuttling past the kitchen door and he'd had a cancelled booking. Ross was not a particularly happy man.

'How was your day?' he asked gloomily as Ally poured him a glass of wine.

'You would not believe,' she said.

'Try me,' he said.

So she told him about the events of the afternoon.

'Dear Lord!' he exclaimed. 'Whatever next? Where are they all?'

'They're all in the sitting room now, except Patti. She's still up in her room.'

'Your friend Amir needs to be doing some interrogating tomorrow. Do you think she'll keep her promise not to tell her mother?'

'I hope so. I mean, Tom might just have overheard something quite trivial, and I'm going to feel like an idiot.'

'Yes, but it was a front-page story, and the police were questioning everyone, so why didn't he come forward if he'd overheard something relevant?' Ross scratched his head.

'Which might prove it couldn't be anything important,' Ally concluded sadly.

Amir arrived at five minutes past ten with his briefcase and his phone. As usual, he was persuaded to have a cup of tea while the guests finished breakfast next door.

'I'm sorry if I've alerted you unnecessarily,' Ally said as she passed him his tea. 'I've been worrying all night that I might have overreacted, but it just *might* be important, you know.'

Amir nodded and took a sip of his tea. 'Ally, you *know* that I asked you to tell me about anything that might be relevant because any one of them would be a whole lot more likely to confide in you than in me. I'd much prefer a false alarm than missing a vital clue.' He laid down his mug. 'In fact, I'd like you to sit in while I question this lass – what's her name?'

'Julie.'

'How old is she?' he asked.

'She's just seventeen,' Ally replied.

'I'd like an adult present while I chat with her, and I

certainly don't want any of her relatives around,' Amir said. 'This could be quite a delicate matter.'

Ross stood up. 'Now that my sausage cooking is no longer required, I feel the urge to tackle your garden, Ally.' And, with a grin, he made his way to the back door.

'That man should get a medal for diplomacy,' Amir exclaimed. Then, looking serious, he asked, 'How has the mother been since you contacted me yesterday?'

'To be honest, she shut herself in her room when we got back, and there's been no sight or sound of her until breakfast this morning, and I think it's fair to say that the atmosphere in there is somewhat tense.'

'So not exactly the reaction you'd expect from someone worried about her daughter?' Amir said.

'No,' Ally replied. 'It's almost as if she wanted to avoid Julie.'

'Now I need to get Julie to open up to me as much as possible. Do you think they've finished eating?' Amir asked.

'I'll go get her,' Ally said.

There was definitely a strained atmosphere in the dining room. Julie and Janey had taken their breakfasts at the little table in front of the window, leaving Patti and Wendy sitting silently at the main table and studiously avoiding looking at each other.

They looked up expectantly as Ally came into the room. 'Would you come with me, Julie,' she said, 'so the detective can ask you a few questions?'

At this, Patti rose from the table. 'If he's going to talk to my daughter,' she said, 'then I should be there.'

'I'm sorry, Patti, but the detective has asked for me to be present, rather than a family member, and I've promised to ensure that the questioning is impartial,' Ally said.

'I'm her mother!' Patti exploded. 'It's my place to be there!'

It was Julie herself who saved the situation. 'Mom, I'm

happy for Ally to do this, and if there's anything bothering me, I promise to call you straight away. OK?' Without waiting for a reply, she stood up and followed Ally into the kitchen.

Amir questioned her gently. 'You're Julie Armstrong?'

The girl nodded.

'And how old are you?'

'I'm seventeen. And a half!'

'Good, good. Now, you're a pretty young lady, so I can see why that young man was attracted to you.'

Julie gave a nervous little smile.

'I believe he's a trainee ghillie – is that what you'd call him?' Amir asked.

'I guess,' said Julie.

'And he's in the employ of the earl but training under your mother's uncle Angus – is that right?'

Julie nodded.

'So the obvious place for a bit of privacy would be in a nice, quiet corner of a barn?'

Julie nodded again. 'We were only kissing...'

'I believe you,' Amir said. 'I can remember how difficult it was to find somewhere out of the way when I was dating at your age.' He hesitated. 'But did Tom upset you in some way?'

'It was just something he said,' Julie muttered. 'Something about overhearing Mom and Uncle Angus talking the day before the games, but I promised him I'd tell no one what it was.'

'Perhaps they'd had a row?' Amir suggested.

Julie shrugged. 'Mom argues a lot with people, so I wouldn't have been surprised. I asked Tom about that but, at first, he shut up like a clam and said he wished he'd never opened his mouth.'

Amir nodded slowly. 'Trouble is,' he said, 'once you've said something, you can't unsay it – know what I mean? But he obviously upset you, and, honestly, Julie, I do need to know what he said.'

'It was something real bad, and I can't believe it.' Julie looked at him imploringly.

'Would you like Ally to leave the room for a moment?' Amir nodded at Ally.

'No, it's fine. It's just that it can't be true. It *can't*!'

'Tell me, Julie. No matter how bad it was, we only have his word for it. Remember that.'

Julie lowered her head and stared at the floor. 'He said that he overheard Mom and Uncle Angus talking, and that Mom asked Uncle Angus for a gun.'

Amir stared at her. 'This was the day *before* the games?'

'Yeah, just after we got here. She asked him for a *gun*!'

'Did Angus ask her what she wanted it for?'

Julie shook her head. 'And there's more! She even said that he should break into the cabinet because otherwise everyone would know it was him because he has a key.'

'And your friend, Tom, overheard all this?'

'Yes.' Julie was weeping again.

'And you haven't told your mum what it was he told you?' Amir probed gently.

'No because Ally said I shouldn't tell anyone until I'd spoken to you!' Julie blew her nose. 'I honestly wish I'd never set eyes on that Tom!'

'One way or the other, he doesn't sound very admirable,' Amir agreed. 'I'll have a little chat with him later. Off you go now and give your mum a hug! But, Julie, do *not* tell her what you've just told me. Promise?'

Julie stood up. 'I won't. Can I go now?'

'Yes, you can,' Amir said. 'After you've promised to say nothing to anyone, including your mum, about what Tom told you. I think there's a fair chance he was lying, and there's no need for her to get herself upset.'

'I promise,' Julie said.

Then, after the door had closed behind her, Amir said, 'You can guess where I'm heading now.'

Ally spent most of the day on tenterhooks, wondering if Amir would be able to work out if Tom had been telling the truth. Then she thought about Rigby, his predecessor, now retired due to heart problems. Rigby would probably have had a different approach: more direct; straight to the point; yes or no; did you or didn't you? She had a feeling that Amir wasn't like that. He would probe gently to gain someone's confidence, be almost sympathetic. Then she wondered if Amir would tell her anything anyway because, after all, it wasn't really her business. Unless... unless it was something to do with her guests. And, let's face it, she had been extremely useful to him.

Amir phoned in the early afternoon. 'I'm coming to question Mrs Armstrong,' he said. 'So I want to make sure that she's still there and not out somewhere?'

'I haven't heard her go out,' Ally replied. 'Give me a minute and I'll double-check for you.'

'If you wouldn't mind.'

She did so, confirming that Patti was still in her room, then relayed this information to Amir.

'I'm on my way,' Amir said.

Ross was at the surgery this afternoon, helping his son, Will, with an overload of appointments. Ally wished that he was there as she tried desperately to think of any way in which she could overhear what Amir was going to be asking Patti. Perhaps she could be 'gardening' and might hear something through the window, or could she just listen at the door? A few years ago, she wouldn't have dreamed of eavesdropping on anyone, but times had changed, and she was now desperate to know what Amir had found out and wanted to talk to Patti about. Would he question Patti in the dining room, well away from the others? In which case, she could try that old trick of putting her ear to a glass pushed against the wall. Not that that worked particularly well.

Amir arrived via the back door, and the first thing he asked Ally was, 'Where can I talk to this woman alone?'

'Well, there's the dining room, or the garden I suppose,' Ally replied.

'I don't want any of the others to overhear this conversation,' he said, looking serious.

'The garden might be best,' Ally suggested. 'It's a nice, sunny afternoon, and it's very sheltered out there.'

Amir nodded. 'That might be best so long as no one can hear from inside.'

'Not from inside,' Ally confirmed, already planning to listen in at the high wall which separated the main garden from the utility area.

'I'll go ahead then,' Amir said, heading towards the sitting room, where she heard him say, 'Mrs Armstrong, could I have a word with you alone, please?'

'Alone?' Patti snorted. 'I've got nothing to say that can't be heard by anyone here.'

'*Alone,*' Amir repeated.

'Why?' asked Patti.

'Because I'm asking you to,' Amir replied firmly. 'I think the garden might be best.'

There was much murmuring in the background and grumbling from Patti. She got to her feet with a great deal of sighing before following the inspector out of the front door and into the garden at the side.

Ally wasted no time in dashing out of the back door, rushing past the washing lines and tiptoeing towards the wall. She could hear Patti still mumbling about being 'singled out', as she put it.

'Please sit down,' Amir said, obviously indicating the garden seat. Ally wondered if he, too, was sitting on the other end of the seat or if he'd remained standing.

'I understand that you visited your uncle on the Monday and the Tuesday, having arrived in Locharran on the Sunday evening?'

'Yes.'

Amir cleared his throat. 'You were overheard asking your uncle to provide you with a gun.'

There was silence for a moment before Patti exclaimed, 'What nonsense!'

'No, it doesn't appear to be nonsense,' Amir said calmly. 'You were also overheard suggesting that Angus faked a break-in, so no one would suspect him.'

'Who told you this rubbish?' Patti asked, her voice shrill.

'Are you denying this?' Amir asked.

'Of course I'm denying this! Why on earth would I want a bloody gun?'

'Perhaps to kill your husband?' Amir suggested.

'Don't be so bloody ridiculous! Why the hell would I want to kill my husband?' Patti shrieked.

'You tell me. Apparently, not only did Angus consider breaking in to get the gun, but he also told you the best place to hide it in the woods above the field where the games were due to take place the following day.'

'Such bloody nonsense! Who on earth told you this?' Patti's voice had risen an octave or two.

'You were overheard,' Amir repeated.

'By whom?'

'I can't tell you that,' Amir said.

'*Why* can't you tell me?' Patti shouted. 'I've a right to know who's accusing me, but I'm betting it's that wretched Tom whatever-his-name-is who fancied my daughter! He's obviously the killer and has fed you this ridiculous story to draw attention away from himself.'

Ally heard Amir sigh. 'He insists that he's telling the truth. But *someone's* lying. In the meantime, I ask that you do not leave this house. I don't want to make any arrests yet, but I will if I have to. I'm thinking only of your daughters and how it could affect them if their mother was taken into custody.'

'This is so damned unfair!' Patti shouted. 'This is all a heap of lies! I want to go home to Canada! I cannot believe that so many ghastly events have taken place since I set foot again in this country – the country of my *birth*!'

'That'll be all for now,' Amir said calmly. 'I'd prefer not to position a policeman at the door, but I will, unless you promise to stay right here in the malthouse. Or the garden,' he added hurriedly.

There followed a great deal of shuffling as they obviously made their way back inside.

Amir tapped on the kitchen door just as Ally had hurriedly tiptoed back into the kitchen. She realised she must have been looking a little guilty because Amir said, 'I've no doubt whatsoever that you managed to hear that conversation, in which case you'll have heard me tell Mrs Armstrong to remain within these four walls.' He gave a wry smile. 'I really don't want to have to post a constable outside your door unless absolutely necessary. And if you suspect that she might try to leave, please ring the police immediately. There's always someone on duty, and I shall fill them in on what's transpired.'

Ally nodded. 'I will.'

How did he *know* that she'd been eavesdropping?

EIGHTEEN

After Amir had gone, Ally sat down at the kitchen table and removed the still-life picture from the wall. Turning it over, she stared at her Post-its around Archie's name, wondering where on earth to start. She realised that she'd never got round to removing Greg from the one o'clock position, and he was hardly likely to be a main suspect now – in fact, she should probably start a new 'clock' for him too. So, could Archie's murderer be Patti? Or Angus? Or could it even be Tom? Tom was already positioned at ten o'clock, so perhaps she should push him up to eleven? And definitely remove Greg from one, but who to replace him with? Should she leave Patti at twelve o'clock and also place Angus at twelve, the chief suspects? Or was it someone else altogether? Ally had rarely felt as confused as she did now.

Someone was tapping at the door, so Ally hurriedly replaced the picture on the wall, ensuring that there were no Post-its peeking out from behind the oranges, lemons and grapes.

'Can I come in for a minute?' An anxious-looking Wendy was standing there.

Ally noted how drawn and exhausted looking she was. 'Of course!'

'Thank you.' Wendy slumped into a chair. 'I honestly don't know which way to turn,' she said.

'Tea? Coffee? Something stronger?' Ally asked.

'Tea would be lovely,' Wendy replied. 'Black, two sugars with a slice of lemon, please.'

'You've had a ghastly time, Wendy,' Ally said as she handed over a cup of tea.

'It's been a nightmare,' Wendy admitted. 'I can't get my head round the fact that both my brother and my husband are gone. It's too much!' Her voice wobbled, and her eyes filled up. 'And now the detective is questioning Patti. *Patti!* What's going on, Ally?'

'I don't know,' Ally replied.

'I shouldn't burden you with my woes,' Wendy continued, 'but I don't know where else to turn! My son, Joel, will be here soon. He flew here overnight, and he's picking up a car at the airport, so should be here by late afternoon or early evening. You've no idea how pleased and relieved I'll be to see him.'

'I can believe that. And he should bring some comfort,' Ally said.

'Yes, but what's really worrying me right now is the girls. I mean, they're only teenagers, and they're caught up in all this awful business, and they've been so brave.' Wendy sipped her tea. 'As for their mother, well...' Words seemed to fail her for a moment. 'She's been no comfort to them because she's so wrapped up in herself. We're all in this nightmare, and the police don't seem to be getting any closer to finding the killer. I mean some person seems set on killing this whole family!'

'I sincerely hope not,' said Ally, looking at her in horror.

'We're all too scared to go out, and Patti's shut herself in her bedroom, and I don't know what the hell to do!' Wendy burst into tears.

Ally felt desperately sorry for the woman. She squeezed Wendy's hand. 'I really don't know what to say, other than if there's anything I can do...' She thought for a moment. 'Don't forget that you and the girls are free to go out, so perhaps you could have a stroll down to the Craigmonie and wait for your son to arrive, have a late lunch or something?' Then another thought struck her. 'But what about Patti? She's not allowed to leave the malthouse under any circumstances, so we're going to have to organise some food for her.'

'Oh, Patti doesn't eat much – she's always on some diet or other. I guess your wonderful breakfast would last her all day.'

The trouble was Patti wasn't eating her wonderful breakfasts but surviving on toast or cereal. Of course, having both your husband and brother-in-law killed within days of each other wouldn't necessarily improve one's appetite.

At that point, Flora, who'd been asleep, woke up and put her head on Wendy's knee.

'Your dog is a tonic,' Wendy said. 'The girls love her and adore taking her for walks but' – she drew breath between her teeth – 'I wonder if it's safe? I mean the killer could be lurking around anywhere, couldn't he?'

'You think there's only one killer?' Ally asked.

'Yeah, because there's got to be a connection, hasn't there?' She stared at Ally for a moment. 'Do the police think it's Patti? Is that why that detective was questioning her?'

Ally knew she had to choose her words carefully. 'I think it's possible they might think she could be a suspect, but she's not the only one.'

'Does the detective confide in you then?'

'No, but he did stress that Patti must not leave the house because she's one of several suspects.'

Wendy nodded. 'I don't know what went on between Archie and Patti, but if he hurt her as badly as Patti claims, I suppose I can understand her wanting to get rid of her own husband, but why *mine*?'

'I've no idea.'

'Don't get me wrong because I really am quite fond of Patti, but I know their marriage was in trouble. And although Archie was my brother, I realise he could be difficult at times, and even violent, but to actually kill him... I'd never forgive her if she laid a finger on him!' She blew her nose. 'I'm telling you, it's a nightmare.'

'I'm as keen as you are to find out who committed these terrible murders.' As she spoke, Ally worried for a minute if Julie had told her aunt about the incident in the barn and what Tom had overheard, but Wendy didn't appear to know, and Ally decided not to ask. And Julie had promised not to say anything.

'Any time you want a cuppa and a chat, I'm here,' she said, 'but, hopefully, this nightmare won't last much longer. And at least your son is on his way.'

'Yes, he should arrive soon. And he's booked in at the Craigmonie, and I'll go down to welcome him, of course, but as far as accommodation is concerned, I'll stay on up here for the sake of the girls, if that's OK?'

'Yes, of course it's OK,' Ally replied, wondering if she should charge less for one-person occupancy of the room now that Wendy was widowed. The same applied to Patti, of course, and it would be the decent thing to do.

'Thank you, Ally, and thank you too for the tea and sympathy!' Wendy said as she got up to go.

She'd only just got into the hallway when there was a knock on the back door, and in marched Hamish. 'What the hell's going on, Alison?' he asked by way of greeting.

Ally, feeling a little weary by now, could only shrug. 'I've no idea, Hamish. I only wish I knew!'

He sat down on the chair recently vacated by Wendy. 'The

police have been roaming around for hours, and they've really upset poor Angus. *Angus*, for God's sake!'

Ally nodded. 'I thought they'd be questioning him – and Tom.' She lifted up a bottle of Locharran's finest. 'Whisky?'

'Oh, go on then! Just a wee one!' He sighed. 'Neither Angus nor Tom are allowed to leave the castle grounds, and Kandahar has even posted a constable up there to make sure they don't. Angus isn't talking, but Tom certainly is, and has been telling me about this supposed conversation he overheard between Angus and Pat. I've never *heard* such nonsense!' He accepted the glass of whisky and knocked it back in one gulp. 'Mind you, I wouldn't put it past Pat, you know. She wouldn't be the first to want to bump off her husband, but Angus would never have anything to do with that.'

Ally picked up the bottle to refill his Scotch, but he hastily placed his hand over the glass. 'Better not have any more,' he said, 'as my dear wife tells me I've been drinking too much of late – but is it any wonder?'

'All I know,' Ally said, 'is that someone is lying. Is it Patti, or Angus, or is it Tom?'

'It has to be Tom,' Hamish said. 'It's not that I wouldn't doubt Pat, but I certainly wouldn't doubt Angus – *never*! This is the most ridiculous accusation, but how are we going to find out?'

Ally shook her head. 'You must remember that blood is thicker than water, supposedly so anyway, and as a result Angus might have been sympathetic to his niece, particularly if he didn't much care for her husband. Just a *thought*,' she added hastily.

'But Angus knows how flighty she is. He'd never agree to such a thing.'

'Hopefully the police will find out,' Ally said, smothering a yawn and longing for a few quiet moments with a cup of tea.

'The sooner the better,' agreed Hamish, 'and we can be rid of this family. Where is Pat by the way?'

'She's rarely moved out of her room,' Ally said, 'but Wendy, her sister-in-law, has been very good with the girls. She's just been in here and is plainly more concerned with finding out who killed *her* husband. Don't forget that Greg Watson has been killed as well.'

'I daresay she is,' Hamish said with a sigh. 'What's she like, this Watson wife?'

'She's a sensible type of woman, but just now seems permanently worried and anxious, which I suppose is hardly surprising. But her son is arriving this afternoon, so that might help. Apparently, he's booked himself in at the Craigmonie, but I've no idea how long he plans to stay.'

'I have a feeling,' Hamish said, 'that you'll be very relieved when they all go back to Canada.'

'You are so right,' Ally agreed.

'Well, I must be on my way because I'm supposed to be going to the shop. But you will let me know, won't you, if you see or hear anything relevant? Anything that might exonerate Angus?'

'Of course I will.'

Hamish stood up and, as he got to the back door, he added, 'Well, do you know, I've completely forgotten what it was I was supposed to be going to the shop for? Do you think it might have been milk?'

Ally smiled as she closed the door behind him.

When Ross appeared about five o'clock, he asked, 'Have you had a nice, quiet day?'

'You would not *believe*!' Ally replied. 'Where shall I begin?' She then related the events of the day.

'I think we should have dinner at the Craigmonie tonight,' said Ross.

'That would be great. Any special reason?'

'Firstly, you're tired. Secondly, we might get some idea of what this son of Greg Watson is like, if he's arrived by then. And, thirdly, the food's good!'

Ally also hoped that they might catch sight of the Watson son and couldn't believe her luck when, as they walked into reception later, there was Wendy with a younger, larger replica of the late Greg Watson. And, as she caught sight of them, Wendy called out, 'Hey, you two, come and meet Joel!'

There were introductions all round and murmurs of sympathy from Ally and Ross on the awful deaths of his father and uncle.

Joel nodded. 'I couldn't have Mom dealing with all this on her own,' he boomed. 'And I ain't gonna be leaving until I find out who killed my dad and Uncle Archie.'

He was well over six feet tall, barrel-chested and loud-spoken. He wore jeans, a T-shirt and a plaid jacket, all looking somewhat crumpled after his long journey. 'You just show me the likely suspects and *I'll* get a confession out of them!' he added ominously. 'I just got the key to my room' – he dangled this in the air – 'and I'm gonna have some room service and then hit the sack cos I've been travelling nigh on twenty-four hours. I'm gonna escort Mom back to your place though because I'm not taking any chances on all these killers round here. And I'm going to need my strength to sort out that detective tomorrow.'

Wendy nodded mutely and followed him to the elevator.

'"*Sort out that detective*,"' Ally exclaimed when they were out of earshot. 'I'm not too sure that Amir will appreciate being "sorted out"!'

'Hmm,' Ross agreed. 'This Joel comes across as a tad dogmatic.' He steered Ally towards the bar. 'Shall we treat ourselves to a little aperitif before dinner?'

. . .

The following morning, Patti joined the rest of the family for breakfast, and there was a general feel of optimism around the dining-room table.

Wendy was positively cock-a-hoop because Joel was coming up after his breakfast and they were going to help the detective to 'get a move on' with finding the killer or killers.

'I don't think Amir is going to be particularly thrilled at being told how to do his job,' Ally remarked to Ross as she re-entered the kitchen with a tray-load of dirty plates. 'Apparently, Joel wants a list of all the suspects and *he's* going to sort it all out.'

'I told you he was dogmatic,' Ross reminded her, 'and he's unlikely to be winning any popularity contests round here.'

'It'll certainly set the cat among the pigeons,' Ally said.

'He'll probably be asleep now anyway because of the jet lag,' Ross added.

But Joel wasn't asleep. Joel was at the front door at precisely nine thirty, and after embracing his mother, his aunt and his cousins, they all settled themselves in the sitting room because, apparently, Joel had a lot to say.

In the meantime, Morag had arrived.

'Who's *that*?' she asked when she heard a man's voice booming from the sitting room.

'It's Joel, Wendy and Greg's son,' Ally explained. 'He arrived last night from Canada.' She thought it politic not to mention Joel's intentions as Morag would have a lot to say on the subject of her precious sons.

'Ach well, the poor man's lost his dad and his uncle,' Morag said sadly, shaking her head, 'so it'll be a comfort for his poor mother.'

. . .

It was well after Morag had done the bedrooms, had her tea and headed for home before the family emerged from the sitting room. Ally had just finished vacuuming the dining room, and they all coincided in the hallway.

Wendy looked positively animated. 'Joel's taken over,' she said cheerfully to Ally, 'and we've made a plan. We're making a list of the suspects, and we're now going to see Detective Inspector Kandahar.' She inched a little closer to Ally and murmured, 'Sometimes you just have to take matters into your own hands.'

'Oh, quite,' Ally said.

'We're sure that Patti will be exonerated by the end of the day, but of course she'll have to sit tight for the moment. Oh, I'm so glad Joel's here!' Wendy beamed.

Ally wondered if Amir might not be quite so delighted with their input, but this newfound confidence they were all displaying did make her wonder if indeed they might have something important to say.

In the meantime, Ross was keen to keep working in the malthouse garden and tidy up before the frosts set in, so he was going to be around for most of the day. And Patti remained alone in the sitting room with the door tightly shut.

It was just before lunchtime before the others returned. Ally wondered what they'd been up to but decided it was wisest not to ask. And then Wendy was knocking on the kitchen door again.

'I'm really sorry to bother you again, Ally, but we need the addresses of all the suspects for these murders, and we wondered if you could help us?'

Ally was quite taken aback. 'Wendy, I don't *have* their addresses.' *And if I did,* she thought, *I wouldn't be giving them to you.*

'You must ask the police,' she added.

'The police haven't been particularly helpful,' Wendy said

sadly. 'They just said that they had the matter in hand. But Joel thinks they're dragging their feet, and he wants to get things moving. And, let's face it, we all want to get things moving so we can go *home*.'

'I'm sorry, Wendy,' Ally said, 'but I really can't help you.'

Not for the first time, Ally felt sorry for Amir. She doubted he would receive these new amateur sleuths with open arms.

NINETEEN

While she and Ross were eating sandwiches at lunchtime, Ally told him about her conversation with Wendy. 'What I don't understand is why this Joel thinks he can solve the case when the police can't, and when he doesn't know anyone in the village. But even Patti seems to think he's going to get things moving because she's finally left her bedroom and is sitting in there waiting for something to happen.'

'Just as well he doesn't know that if he goes into the Craigmonie Bar most nights of the week, he'll find all the suspects commiserating with each other over pints of beer,' Ross said with a grin.

But Joel was just getting started and, according to Wendy – who was admiring Ross's spadework in the garden – they were now heading for the castle because Joel was convinced that the Earl of Locharran must surely know what was going on. Ally wondered if she should phone Hamish to warn him, but then decided she'd like to know how he'd act spontaneously and, doubtless, very politely.

Leaving the girls with their mother, Wendy and Joel set off

for the castle and, shortly after they left, Amir appeared at the back door, having driven up in an unmarked car.

'I didn't want to draw attention to myself,' he told Ally and Ross, 'in case they started questioning me again.' He grinned, and Ally, as usual, delighted in his beautiful smile. 'I've had quite a morning with this son of the victim. He's upset the constable on the door, he's shouted at me for being inefficient and I believe he's going to have a go at the earl next.' He emitted a loud sigh.

'I think you need a cup of tea, Amir,' Ally said.

'That's very kind. Is he staying here?'

'No, he's at the Craigmonie. We ate down there last night and met him shortly after he got here,' Ally said.

'Would you believe he wanted a list of the suspects?' Amir asked. 'He's actually planning to interrogate each of them and come up with an answer.'

'I hardly dare to ask,' Ross said, 'but are you any further on with the investigation?'

Amir nodded. 'A little. We're concentrating on Angus at the moment, but I can't tell you more than that. I'm just hoping Joel won't come across Angus. Not that Angus would give him the time of day!' He accepted the mug of tea from Ally. 'But if he's not staying here, then there's no point in my asking you to ask him to keep his nose out of this investigation.' He paused. 'But, to be fair to the man, we are talking about his father and his uncle, so we can hardly blame him for wanting to get justice done quickly.'

'I could perhaps have a word with Wendy,' Ally said. 'She's been very brave and is holding this family together at the moment.'

'Yes, maybe you could encourage her to dampen down her son's enthusiasm a little for solving the case. I can assure you, and her, that we're doing every damn thing we can to bring this to a close, and I think we're getting there, albeit slowly.' Amir replaced his mug on the table. 'I must go. I'll let you know as much as I'm allowed to in due course.'

After he'd gone, Ally realised that her supply of coffee was rapidly running out. 'I'm going to have to pop down to the shop,' she said.

'And I've got one more flower bed to do,' Ross said.

Queenie was, as usual, gossiping with a little clique of four local women as Ally entered the shop, and they stopped chattering when they noticed her arrival.

'Ye'll no' be needin' much now with half yer guests bumped off!' Queenie greeted her cheerfully.

Ally ignored the remark. 'I've just come for some coffee,' she said.

'Ye'll have another visitor now though,' Queenie continued. 'The son, isn't he?'

'He's not staying with me; he's at the Craigmonie,' Ally said, wondering how on earth they already knew about Joel. She picked some tomatoes out of the display. 'I'll have these as well, Queenie.'

'Aye, that'll be why he was in here askin' questions this mornin',' Queenie said.

'What, he's been in here *already*?' Ally was amazed. 'What sort of questions?'

'Well, he was lookin' for addresses of the caber tossers and the runners in the earl's running competition, or whatever it was.'

'I hope you didn't give him any addresses,' Ally said.

'Aye, well, he was awful nice and polite, so I gave him one or two, didn't I, Bessie?'

Bessie, who'd suddenly appeared from the storeroom, nodded. 'Aye, ye did that.'

Ally sighed. 'You shouldn't have. He's out to cause trouble

and seems to think he's more qualified than the police to solve these killings.'

'Well, the police aren't doin' much,' Queenie snapped.

'They're needin' a kick up the arse,' remarked the tiniest of the women, which was followed by nods of agreement from the others.

'And I told him that what he was needin' to do was to go into the Craigmonie Bar any night of the week, and most of the folk he was after would be there,' Queenie added. 'It'd save him knockin' on all them doors, wouldn't it?'

Which is exactly what Ross said, Ally thought, *and would well and truly set the cat among the pigeons.* She placed the tomatoes on the counter, along with a bag of coffee, and got out her purse.

'Yes,' she replied, 'I daresay it would save him knocking on doors.'

As she walked home, Ally wondered if she should have asked Queenie whose addresses she'd actually given to Joel. Since Queenie ran the post office as well, she did, of course, have everyone's addresses, and Ally could only hope that it wasn't the McConnachie brothers' ones that she'd handed over.

She had a bad feeling about it, which proved to be right because she'd hardly opened the door and put the kettle on when a grim-faced Morag came barging in through the back door. She came straight to the point. 'Did *you* give that bloody Canadian our address?'

'No, I did not,' Ally replied. 'I would never do that without your permission. Looks like you might be in need of some tea?'

Morag nodded as she sat down heavily in one of the armchairs. 'Somebody gave that man our address, Ally, and if it wasn't you, then who was it?'

'Perhaps it could be the person who *does* know everyone's addresses?' Ally supplied hopefully.

Morag narrowed her eyes and gave it some thought. 'Well now, that would be Queenie McDougall,' she said after a moment.

'Exactly right,' Ally confirmed. 'Apparently, he was in the shop looking for addresses for all the competitors in the games, and of the runners too.'

'I'll never speak to that Queenie again! *Never*! Why would she do that? I bet she gave him directions as well!' Morag accepted a mug of tea from Ally and, after a large gulp, continued, 'He comes bangin' on our door a couple of hours ago wantin' to speak to Bobby McConnachie, if you please! Our Bobby was very busy upstairs with his video games and that, so I knew he wouldn't want to be disturbed, and I told the Canadian that Bobby wasn't in. And then I asked what was it he was wantin' anyway. And the Canadian said that he had reason to believe that Bobby knew somethin' about who killed his father and his uncle and that he'd come back later. Bloody nerve!'

'Well, I don't suppose you can blame him for wanting to ensure that the killers are arrested. He seems to think that the police are dragging their feet and that *he* can do better. So I think he's upsetting a few people, Morag, not just you.'

'Aye, that's as may be,' said Morag, 'but my lads will no' put up with bein' accused of somethin' they didn't do, and by someone who wasn't even *here* when it happened!' Morag's voice had risen to a crescendo. 'Have you any of them chocolate digestives left?'

Ally got out the biscuit tin and placed it, open, on the table alongside Morag's chair. Morag took out a biscuit and dipped it into her tea, then got it into her mouth a split second before it was about to disintegrate into her mug. This was a feat which must have taken Morag years to perfect because she loved these biscuits, and Ally had never seen her drop one crumb into her tea yet.

'Well,' said Morag, 'I'm goin' right down to give that Queenie a piece of my mind! And I'm goin' to tell her that I'll be takin' my custom elsewhere.'

Ally raised her eyebrows. 'Like where?'

'I'll just have to go a bit further afield, but that woman's not gettin' another penny of my hard-earned cash, let me tell you.' Morag helped herself to another biscuit and repeated the whole ritual. 'Wait until I tell Murdo,' she muttered through the crumbs. 'He'll go mad!'

Ally couldn't quite see mild-mannered Murdo getting particularly excited about this. She wondered for a moment if she should warn Morag that Joel Watson might well be in the Craigmonie Bar this evening, but then decided not to. Let things run their course.

By the time Morag had digested the second biscuit and drained her tea, she'd calmed down considerably. And as she stood up to go, she said, 'Aye, well, you can see why I was annoyed, can't you? I'm off now to have a few words with that Queenie McDougall. See you in the mornin'!'

'I've just seen the Watson woman going down the road,' Ross said as he came in from the garden. 'I expect she's going to join up with her son at the Craigmonie.'

'He's certainly causing a few ripples,' Ally said as she continued to cook supper. 'I'm betting he'll be in the bar this evening, as both you and Queenie predicted. I've just had a visit from Morag; did you see her come in?'

'I did,' Ross admitted with a grin, 'and I took one look at her face and decided to stay out until she'd gone!'

'Apparently, Joel has already been knocking on her door, having got some addresses from Queenie, and she is not pleased,' Ally said, rolling her eyes. 'She's off now to have a go at Queenie and, in her own words, take her custom elsewhere!'

'That won't last long,' Ross said. 'It must be twenty miles to the nearest grocer, and she doesn't drive. Poor old Murdo!'

'All because he dared to ask to speak to Bobby,' Ally told him. 'And Bobby was in, but would have been annoyed to be disturbed when he was playing with his video games, according to Morag, so she said he wasn't in. She really spoils that son of hers.'

'You're right. He's the youngest, of course, but the rest of his siblings are all doing OK. I mean Micky's no saint, but at least he does some plumbing and has a wife and daughter and a mortgage. And then there's Debbie, whose husband Sam is a waiter in the Craigmonie dining room, you know? And Gordon very sensibly left the McConnachie household and went off to work on the oil rigs and lives in Aberdeen with his wife and kids.' Ross scratched his head. 'Oh, and I almost forgot Geordie – he must be the oldest of the brood. I'm trying to remember where he went – I think it was Australia.'

'So she's hanging on to her youngest,' Ally said. 'I suppose it's kind of natural...?'

Ross sniffed. 'I'm not sure I agree. Never mind, after supper I fancy a nice quiet evening watching a film or something. Let them all get on with it! What do you think?'

'I think it's a wonderful idea,' Ally agreed, 'if we can.'

Ally knew she was probably tempting fate because just as they'd settled down after supper to watch some old episodes of *Friends*, there was a kerfuffle in the hall.

'I'll go,' Ross volunteered. 'I'll be back in five minutes. Pause the TV for a moment!'

Five minutes passed, and then another five minutes, and then Ally switched off the TV and went out into the hallway to see what was going on. And there stood a tear-stained, exhausted-looking Wendy and an exasperated-looking Ross leading her into the kitchen.

He sighed loudly as he spotted Ally. 'I think we might need something to drink. Wendy has had a bad experience.'

Still sobbing, Wendy was led into the kitchen and sat down in the chair which seemed to have been occupied all day with people with problems.

'What would you like to drink?' Ally asked Wendy. 'Brandy?' Ally glanced at Ross, who'd opened the door of the drinks' cupboard.

'Yeah, great,' Wendy replied.

'Whatever's the matter, Wendy?' Ally asked solicitously as Ross handed her a drink.

'It's Joel – I've had to leave him in his bedroom with swollen eyes and bags of ice. He asked me to go home because he didn't want a fuss. *Fuss*! Can you begin to imagine how it feels to have a gang of drinkers attack *your son*?'

'Someone attacked Joel?' Ally asked.

'No, not someone; there must have been five of them. *Five*! What kind of country is this, Ally?'

'Tell us what happened,' Ally said, glancing at Ross.

'Joel only asked some very reasonable questions,' said Wendy. 'Like, why were they so jealous that Archie won all the contests, and why were they all there or thereabouts when his own dear father was just having a walk, minding his own business, and had never upset any of them? All *very* reasonable questions, don't you think?'

'So what happened then?' Ally asked cautiously.

'Well, they all denied having anything to do with it,' said Wendy. She took a few deep breaths. 'And then, I guess, maybe Joel lost it a bit...'

'Lost it?' Ross asked, frowning.

'Yeah, well, it had to be one of them, didn't it? And you can understand how frustrated poor Joel was. One of the big guys was goading him, really goading him, copying his actions, his mannerisms, everything...'

'And?'

'Poor Joel was annoyed – and upset. I mean he's probably still suffering from jet lag, for God's sake. Anyway, he took a swipe at the big guy who was goading him, which sent him reeling. I mean, you can't blame Joel for *that* now, can you?'

Neither Ally nor Ross uttered a word.

'And then the others all joined in!'

'What exactly do you mean?' Ross asked.

'Well, because he'd punched the big guy, they all seemed to have a go at him,' Wendy said sadly, 'and they almost knocked him senseless. My poor Joel. They were *barbaric*!'

'What happened then?' Ally asked.

'Well, the bartender was no damned use because he'd joined the others,' Wendy exclaimed. 'So I got hold of the manager, and the manager called the police.'

'What did the police say?' Ross asked.

Ally couldn't begin to imagine Amir's reaction – if he was there.

'The police said that Joel should go to his room and everyone else should calm down, and if there was any further trouble, every single one of them would end up in the police station accused of being drunk and disorderly. Can you imagine? Drunk and disorderly – *my son*!'

With that, she snorted angrily, finished her drink, said goodnight and marched upstairs to her bedroom.

'Fancy watching some more of *Friends*?' Ally asked as she heard Wendy's door slam.

'Oh, why not?' Ross replied. 'We need cheering up!'

But Ally couldn't really concentrate on the programme. Joel had certainly stirred things up in the short time he'd been here, and she could only hope that he wasn't next on the killer's list.

TWENTY

Morag was strangely quiet the following morning, other than muttering, 'That bloody Canadian boy got his just deserts!'

Ally's guests appeared for breakfast and picked at cereals and coffee, but not much else. It was Julie who asked, 'Is it OK if I go out in the garden for a while?' as she drained her coffee. 'I just need some fresh air.'

It wasn't a particularly warm day, so Ally was a little mystified, and it wasn't until she was hanging out washing that she became aware of voices in the garden – one male, one female.

Immediately alert and, by now, well practised in eavesdropping, Ally made her way silently to the dividing wall.

'Tom!' she heard Julie exclaiming. 'What are you doing over there?' She was obviously referring to the wall that sheltered the back of the garden.

'I can't be seen,' he said, 'because I'm not supposed to go anywhere, but I wanted to see you.'

'Well, I got your message...'

'I wanted to ask you why the hell you told that detective about what I told you.'

'Because he kept asking me...' Julie protested.

'You promised not to tell anyone,' said Tom. 'Why did you tell them *anything*, for God's sake? I'm not allowed to go anywhere now, and neither is Angus – not that Angus goes anywhere anyway,' he whined.

'Well, that's too bad!' Julie sounded increasingly exasperated. 'And because of what you said, my mom isn't allowed to go anywhere either!'

There was silence for a minute.

'It's that cop,' Tom said eventually. 'He worms stuff out of you. I shouldn't have told you – or him.'

'So, if you're not allowed to go anywhere, what are you doing here?' Julie asked.

'I told you – I sneaked out cos I wanted to see you, Julie.'

'Why?'

'Because I like you, and I'm really sorry about the other day in the barn.'

'So am I, but there it is,' said Julie. 'And I really don't want to see you again!'

'Well fine, I'm off!' Tom was obviously moving away, and just before Ally returned to her washing line, she heard him mutter to himself, 'Plenty more fish in the sea!'

By late morning, Joel had appeared in a smart little Jeep and ensconced himself in the sitting room with his mother and Patti. The girls had escaped to their bedroom, and Ally could only hope that Julie hadn't been cajoled into telling her younger sister what Tom had said.

Ross had gone home for a few hours, and Ally was just about to make herself a cup of coffee when Desdemona arrived.

Desdemona wasn't exactly a neighbour because she lived a good five miles away, but their paths had crossed on several occasions, and a vague sort of friendship had taken place. She lived, with an assortment of dogs, in an old stone house beside Loch Trioch, a couple of miles from the nearest point of civilisation, The Bothy Inn. Rumour had it that her father, a professor of English, and his actress wife had arrived out of the blue from London many years ago, with their two young daughters, Desdemona and Ophelia. They'd taken themselves to this remote spot where the father had built a walled garden, into which he planted all manner of flora, many types which would not normally survive this far north. Her parents and sibling now gone, Desdemona carried on the gardening tradition, as well as being a talented artist. It was her beautiful watercolours which really provided her with a living. She had also been the earl's lover for years, or so Ally had been told, and her younger sister, Ophelia, had been the earl's first wife.

Desdemona, around seventy, was still a colourful character. She parked her ancient mud-splattered Land Rover outside and strode in, wearing a couple of mismatched jumpers under an emerald-green kaftan and black leggings. This whole outfit was further adorned with some red wooden beads which rattled as she walked.

'Oh, glad you're in,' she said to Ally as she plonked herself in an armchair in the kitchen, 'because I've brought you some apples. I've just been selling some fruit and vegetables to the Craigmonie so thought I'd drop in.'

'Oh, thank you. Have you time for a coffee?' Ally asked.

'I shall make time for a coffee.' Desdemona sighed loudly. 'There's a load of media people down there, milling around. Ugh! Is it any wonder I wouldn't want to live in Locharran!'

'They're becoming part of the furniture round here,' Ally agreed.

'I understand that someone out there is killing off your Canadians,' Desdemona said.

Ally brought her up to date with the latest events without going into too much detail.

'I guess you'll be glad to see the back of them all,' Desdemona said. 'It's been an eventful year one way or the other.'

'It certainly has,' Ally said, passing her a mug of coffee.

Desdemona refused the offer of shortbread and knocked the coffee back quickly. 'I've got to be on my way because I've got this new puppy, and I've had to shut him in the barn because he's not house-trained yet. Dear little fellow!' She stood up.

'Thank you for these lovely apples,' Ally said as she accompanied her visitor to the front door – at the exact time that Wendy and Joel came out of the sitting room. She introduced them to each other. 'Desdemona,' she said, 'is a wonderful painter. She painted the beautiful landscapes hanging on the bedroom walls, and some in the dining room. She's a lady of many talents because she's also an ardent gardener.'

Desdemona smiled modestly. 'I'm really sorry about your loss.' She paused. 'Losses.'

'Thank you,' they both murmured.

'You been in a fight?' Desdemona asked, studying Joel's swollen eye.

'Oh, just a little misunderstanding,' Joel said dismissively.

'Looks like the other guy won,' Desdemona said cheerfully.

Then Wendy asked, 'So you're a gardener? I guess it must be difficult to get things growing in this climate?'

'Not at all,' Desdemona replied airily, 'if you know what you're doing.'

'I love gardening,' Wendy said, 'and I'm longing to get home to my own little patch and get it all tidied up before the winter. But I'd so *love* to see your garden! I guess our climates are very similar, and I'd really like to see what you're able to grow.'

'Well, I live right off the beaten track,' Desdemona said, heading rapidly towards the door. 'But if you happen to be passing, do pop in!'

Then, with a wave, she was off, confident in her isolation.

'Where exactly does she live?' Wendy asked Ally as they waved her off.

'Oh, a couple of miles further on from The Bothy Inn,' Ally replied. 'Have you eaten there yet?'

Wendy shook her head. 'Is it good?'

'Yes, very good,' Ally confirmed.

'You hear that, Joel?' Wendy shouted to her son, who had stayed in the hallway. 'We must try this restaurant tomorrow. Maybe take Patti and the girls? And then we can go on to have a look at Ally's friend's garden.'

'I have to warn you that it's a rough old track from the inn onwards,' Ally said, 'so you don't want to be in a low-slung car.'

'Just as well I've got the Jeep then,' Joel said cheerfully. 'It'll do us good to get away from here for a while. Let's do lunch at this place and go on from there to see your new friend. I thought she was interesting – if a little eccentric perhaps.'

Ally was trying to imagine Desdemona's reaction if Wendy and Joel turned up out of the blue and smiled to herself.

'We'll go tomorrow,' Joel said firmly, 'after I've had another chat with that detective. I swear he knows something he hasn't told me...'

When Ross returned in the early evening, he brought with him two rump steaks. 'I thought maybe jacket potatoes and a salad?' he suggested as he laid them on the kitchen table.

'Wonderful,' Ally replied. 'And I've made an apple crumble to follow.'

'Did you actually manage to coax a couple of apples from that ancient tree in the garden?' Ross asked.

'No, I had a visit from Desdemona.'

Ross's eyes widened. 'To what do you owe that honour?'

'She was just being nice. She'd flogged some stuff down at

the Craigmonie and called in on her way back, so we had coffee and a brief chat.'

'So what's she been up to?' Ross asked. 'Not that there's a great deal to get up to where she lives!'

'She seems to be living a quiet life at the moment and has a new puppy of some sort. But just as she was leaving, who should come out of the sitting room but Wendy and Joel.'

'Oh yes. How's his eye?'

'Still very swollen. When I introduced them to each other, Wendy said how much she adored gardening and that she'd love to see Desdemona's garden because the Nova Scotia climate is very similar to the Scottish one. I was a little put out, to tell the truth, because she's never shown the slightest interest in the garden here. Anyway, Joel is now going to take his mother to eat at The Bothy tomorrow lunchtime, and then they're going to visit Desdemona.'

Ross pulled a face. 'Is Desdemona aware of this?'

'I doubt it, but Joel seems determined to go anyway, and he does have a Jeep, so I expect that'll cope with the bumpy track. I'd just love to see Desdemona's face when they arrive on her doorstep!'

'Oh well, at least he won't be bothering anyone in Locharran if he's up there studying horticulture,' Ross exclaimed.

'Let's hope he doesn't get another black eye from Desdemona.'

'I wouldn't put it past her,' Ross said, laughing. 'What's the atmosphere been like here today?'

'The girls keep to themselves, and God only knows what Patti does because, as you know, she's housebound,' Ally said, suddenly aware of raised voices in the hall.

'I *told* you I didn't want to see him again after the lies he told me about you!' Julie was shouting. 'I only wanted to go out to get you something to eat. I wasn't planning on bloody eloping!'

'Watch your language!' Patti shouted back. 'I'm sorry I doubted you, darling, but I don't trust that boy, not after what he said.'

'Well, we know he's a liar,' Janey piped in.

'He certainly is,' said Patti, 'and the sooner that can be proved, the better, and the sooner we're out of here.'

'Where have Auntie Wendy and Joel gone?' Julie asked.

'They've gone to complain to the manager of that Craigmonie Hotel about Joel's treatment last night, and they're going to bring back some sandwiches and a bottle of wine, thank God!'

There was then a slamming of doors, followed by silence.

'Did you hear that?' Ally asked Ross.

'I did. Do you think this Joel is determined to get himself another black eye?'

'Probably, but it's Callum I feel sorry for,' Ally said.

They didn't hear Wendy come back later, but Ally was given a full account at breakfast the next morning when Wendy was in full flow.

'This village,' she informed Ally, 'is unbelievable. Un-be-*lieve*-able! No one takes responsibility for anything. I don't feel safe here, and Joel insisted I took a taxi back last night because this is a lawless society with a useless police force and downright aggression to visitors.'

Ally placed a basket of croissants on the table. 'I've never known any aggression to visitors,' she said firmly. 'We welcome visitors from all over the world.'

'They've been saving their aggression up for my dear son then.' Wendy sniffed loudly and dabbed her nose. 'Even the hotel manager dismissed the incident in the bar as a "misunderstanding". A *misunderstanding* when a gang of drinkers set about my son!'

'Calm down,' said Patti, 'or you'll give yourself a heart attack.'

'I will not calm down,' ranted Wendy. 'The manager actually suggested that Joel was some sort of troublemaker! Joel! There never was a more peace-loving guy. You know that, don't you, Patti?'

Patti refrained from commenting but concentrated on buttering a slice of toast.

Wendy hadn't finished yet. 'And to arrest poor Patti here – what are the police *thinking* of?'

'They haven't arrested me,' Patti muttered.

'Same thing. House arrest. They suspect you. And' – Wendy turned to Ally – 'I've just bumped into your grim-faced cleaner, who wouldn't even say "good morning" to me!'

Ally took a deep breath. 'Thing is, Wendy, your Joel landed on her doorstep yesterday and began asking questions about her son, and to be honest, I don't think she was well pleased.'

Wendy frowned. 'But she's a mother, and I'm a mother, so I'd expect her to understand, don't you think?'

Keen to avoid an argument, Ally said, 'I'll have a word with her. Now it's today you're lunching at The Bothy, isn't it?'

Momentarily diverted, Wendy smiled broadly while helping herself to muesli. 'And then we're going to visit your gardening friend.'

When Ally got back into the kitchen, she found Morag, having finished the rooms, now filling the kettle. 'Wendy Watson's a little upset because you didn't look too pleased to see her this morning,' Ally said casually as she loaded some plates into the dishwasher.

'That's because I wasn't,' Morag replied.

'Well, she's my guest, Morag, so try not to let your personal feelings come into this. And don't forget she's grieving for her husband and so she's naturally very sensitive.'

Morag grunted and continued making a pot of tea. Ally opened her mouth to say more and thought better of it. Best not to rock the boat, especially where Joel Watson's new investigation was concerned.

TWENTY-ONE

It was almost four o'clock before Wendy and Joel returned from their visit to The Bothy and Loch Trioch. Ally was brushing up some leaves in the garden when the Jeep pulled up outside.

'Oh, Ally!' Wendy exclaimed as she climbed out of the passenger seat. 'We had such a lovely lunch. Thank you so much for recommending The Bothy.'

'I'm glad,' Ally replied, leaning her rake against the wall. 'And did you visit Desdemona?'

Wendy rolled her eyes in ecstasy. 'Yes, we did, and, my goodness, isn't that place in the middle of nowhere! Furthermore, there must have been at least half a dozen dogs of all shapes and sizes, barking, jumping up and even growling. We were quite nervous, weren't we, Joel?'

Joel, walking just behind her, nodded. 'She wasn't exactly welcoming,' he muttered.

'But she showed us her garden and, my goodness, we were really impressed!' Wendy said. 'She has some amazing plants in there – sub-tropical ones – and as for all her herbs and spices, well...! And she was kind enough to let me take some seeds for my own garden.'

'She tried to sell us some of her paintings,' Joel added. 'They were nice, but I couldn't see us getting them back to Halifax without a lot of hassle. If we *ever* get back to Halifax!' he added gloomily.

'She's certainly a one-off,' Wendy concluded as she made her way indoors.

Joel had gone back to his Jeep. 'I want a word with the earl,' he said. 'Do you think he's likely to be in? He wasn't the other day.'

'I really don't know,' Ally replied truthfully. If he was at home, he'd doubtless be scoffing Mrs Jamieson's sandwiches and scones at this particular time and might not necessarily be in the right frame of mind to welcome this rather belligerent man. However, it was best to let Joel find out for himself.

'Well,' said Joel, 'I'm gonna try.'

He got back into the driving seat and off he went.

The outcome of Joel's visit to the castle did not become apparent until Hamish came barging in the back door at half past six, just as Ross had poured out some pre-dinner drinks for Ally and himself.

'You will not *believe* what's happened!' he ranted. 'And yes, I would have a wee drop of Scotch – if you're offering it.'

Ross poured a generous measure of the whisky and handed it to Hamish. 'So what's happened then?' he asked.

'That man, that son, that what's-his-name Watson...' Hamish began, taking a large glug of his drink.

'Joel,' Ally supplied helpfully.

'He comes barging into the castle, demanding to see me, while Magda and I are having *our afternoon tea*!' Hamish was plainly horrified at the intrusion to this ritual. 'He wants to know what I plan to do about all the murders. The cheek of the man! "What am I supposed to do about all the murders?" I ask him. I also mention that we've only had these murders since his family arrived in Locharran, which isn't strictly true, of course, but I wasn't about to tell him that.' He stopped for breath and more whisky.

'I bet you felt like punching him on the nose,' Ross said.

'I'm not a violent man, but I must admit I did feel like it. But I told him that the police were doing their best and it was *them* he should be talking to, not me.' Hamish gave a heavy sigh.

'Did he leave then?' Ally asked.

'No, he damn well didn't. He gave me a long spiel about the stories Tom told him about Angus and Pat's conversation, and how crazy it was that his poor Aunt Patti was under house arrest because of these lies. Well.' Hamish shook his head and gulped some more whisky. 'I very stupidly told him that he should be talking to Angus and not to me. Oh Lord, why ever did I say that?'

'Did he go to talk to Angus then?' Ross asked.

'He did. I followed him, a discreet distance behind, down the drive to Angus's cottage and watched him rap on the door. Angus came to the door, closed it behind him and faced Watson. "Why are you here?" he asked.'

Ally was agog now. 'And then...?'

'And then I could hear Angus asking grumpily, "What do you want?" You know how gruff he can be. And then Watson ranted on about Tom supposedly hearing this conversation, and did he know that his poor niece was now under house arrest for something she didn't say? Then he demanded that Angus tell him where he could find Tom because it was time "that lad got sorted out", and Angus said, like I did, that it was none of Watson's business and, if he'd got something to say, he should say it to the police.'

'Poor old Angus,' Ross said. 'This bloody Joel's upsetting everyone.'

'Well, Angus stood his ground, and so did Watson, and the

argument got more and more heated until…' Here Hamish drained his glass, and Ross hastily replenished it. Hamish gave him a nod of thanks and then continued with his story. 'Angus told him to sod off, but Watson stayed put, still sounding off, and it was then that Angus punched him, hard. Really hard! Flattened Watson, who now has a bloody nose to go with his swollen eye!'

'Oh my God!' Ally stared at him in disbelief. 'Tell me you're joking!'

'I'm not joking, and that's not all. When Watson had recovered sufficiently to locate his phone, he called the police, said he'd been assaulted. The police arrive, big fuss; a Canadian visitor has been attacked and has a bleeding nose, a split lip, bruises coming up everywhere.' Hamish sighed in exasperation. 'Angus, of course, is totally unrepentant, and I don't blame him. But poor Angus has been *arrested*!'

There was a horrified silence for a moment before, in unison, Ally and Ross both repeated, 'Angus? *Arrested*?'

'Angus, for God's sake! Angus would never raise his fists normally!' Hamish took another large gulp. 'This man has only been in Scotland for a couple of days and he's already managed to get himself one black eye and, for sure, he's going to have two of them before the day is out. And possibly a broken nose.'

'And what about Tom while all this is going on?' Ally asked. 'After all, it was Tom who started all this by hearing the so-called conversation.'

Hamish shook his head. 'He never got round to having a go at Tom, which is probably just as well. In the meantime, poor Angus is in custody tonight for only doing what any red-blooded male would do when provoked like that.'

'Was it Kandahar who arrested him?' Ross asked.

'No, he's in Glasgow apparently. It was two young, enthusiastic constables. They came racing up the drive with lights on, sirens blazing. God only knows what the village thought!'

'Somebody's got to gag that Joel,' Ally said with feeling.

'He's certainly a troublemaker,' Hamish agreed, 'but it's poor Angus I'm worried about! Angus in jail – unbelievable! I shall get straight on to Kandahar about having him released on bail. I cannot run my estate without Angus, and that's all there is to it!' He drained his glass.

'Would you like another of these?' Ally indicated the Scotch bottle.

'Oh, just a wee one then, if you insist,' Hamish said. 'But only because Magda says I'm drinking far too much, but, my God, I need a drink today! I'll bring a couple of bottles of my best, to boost your supplies, next time I pop in.'

'This is the one you brought last time,' Ally said. She and Ross usually drank gin or wine. 'So where is Joel now?'

Hamish shrugged. 'I think he's gone back to the hotel, and one of the police has gone with him. I don't know what happens now, but I've been on to Kandahar and he'll be here in the morning.'

Poor Amir, Ally thought. This village must give him more work than all the rest of the area put together.

'Alison is a wonderful friend,' Hamish said, turning to Ross with a wink. 'When she resisted my charms and said she only wanted friendship, I really didn't think it was possible to just be friends with such an attractive lady. But I was wrong, and I deeply value our friendship, Alison!' He turned to her and raised his glass.

'Thank you, Hamish,' Ally said, hoping she wasn't blushing at her great age. 'I really value our friendship too.'

'Hope I'm not intruding on this mutual admiration society,' Ross said with a grin, raising his own glass.

Morag was almost rendered speechless when she arrived in the morning.

'There's this rumour goin' round,' she said, 'that Angus Morrison has been arrested. *Angus*! You couldn't make it up.'

'It's true,' Ally said, spooning coffee grounds into a cafetière.

'I can't believe it! What the hell could Angus have to do with any of this?' Morag demanded as she fastened on her pinny.

'I believe he had a difference of opinion with your friend Joel Watson,' Ally replied.

'He's no friend of mine! *A difference of opinion*! Is that what you call it? That Watson got back to the Craigmonie with a *policeman* and a bloody nose, Murdo says. But it couldn't be Angus; Angus is only interested in huntin', fishin' and mindin' his own business.'

'Apparently, even Angus has a limit to his patience,' Ally said.

As if to verify this state of affairs, there was a gentle knock on the kitchen door, and there stood Wendy.

'I just wanted to tell you that I won't be breakfasting here this morning,' she said, 'because poor Joel's been in a spot of bother, and I feel I should go down there straight away.'

'Thank you for letting me know,' Ally said, hoping to avoid further conversation on the subject.

'Because he was *attacked* last night!' Wendy went on.

'I'm sorry to hear that, Wendy,' Ally said, backing slowly into the kitchen. 'I hope he's OK.'

As she closed the door, she heard Morag mutter, 'She seems quite a nice woman, so how come she's got a son like that?'

'He's probably been spoiled and likes to get his own way,' Ally said. *Just like your Bobby,* she thought.

Morag gave a disapproving sniff as she set off upstairs.

Ross had gone home for twenty-four hours because he was having a bed delivered for one of his cottages, and he also had visitors leaving very early the next morning. Ally was rather looking forward to having a quiet day on her own and getting a few outstanding chores done. She could hear the others in the dining room now, but only three for breakfast.

The girls, as usual, wanted cooked breakfasts and Patti, also as usual, did not.

'We hear cousin Joel's in trouble,' said Janey conversationally.

'He always *was* a pain in the arse,' Patti said as she helped herself to cereal.

'Somebody punched him yesterday evening,' Julie said, 'but we don't know who.'

And I'm not about to tell you, Ally thought.

Breakfast passed without incident or any phone calls, the girls asked if they could play with Flora in the garden, and Morag – still tut-tutting and shaking her head – made herself her usual mug of tea when she was done with the cleaning.

When Murdo arrived with the mail at half past ten, he was quite excited. 'It's all happenin' up at the castle,' he said. 'There's two police cars, and the boss man himsel' is there.'

'Do you mean Kandahar?' Ally asked.

'Looked mighty like him,' said Murdo. 'Tall and dark.'

'Any sign of Angus?' Ally asked.

Murdo shook his head. 'Didn't see him at all.' He looked around. 'Any tea on the go?'

Morag drained her mug. 'I'll make you one,' she said, standing up. 'Have you been down to the Craigmonie yet?'

'No, but I'm bettin' one of their residents has got a right sore head this mornin',' Murdo replied gleefully.

'Aye, well his ma's given up her breakfast so she can go down there and hold his hand,' said Morag, handing him a mug.

'Good old Angus gave him a right bashin',' Murdo said with approval. 'And he likely deserved it, cos I've seen him at close range after the other night in the bar, and he's lookin' for trouble, that one.'

'Aye, well, there's always troublemakers around,' Morag added sagely. 'Anyway, I'm headin' for home now.'

Murdo drained his tea. 'I'd better be off too.'

'See you in the mornin' if the Lord spares us,' Morag said as she took off her pinny and donned her purple anorak.

After Morag and Murdo had left, and Ally had cleared the dining room, Amir Kandahar appeared.

'I'm sorry to trouble you,' he said to Ally, 'but I wonder if I could have a quick word?'

'Yes, of course,' said Ally, leading him into the kitchen, where he sat down but declined the offer of tea.

'I've just had one at the castle,' he said.

'You've been talking to the earl then?'

Amir sighed. 'Indeed I have. Did you know that we had to arrest Angus Morrison, the earl's ghillie?'

'Yes, Hamish called in yesterday evening and told us what had happened,' Ally replied.

'He wants us to release Morrison immediately, but we're keeping him in custody for a further twenty-four hours.'

'Can I ask why?' Ally enquired. 'I know he punched Joel Watson, but he was extremely provoked. And Joel is really belligerent, you know. He's upset a lot of people since he arrived here.'

'We don't exactly approve of what he did,' Amir said, 'but that's not why we're keeping Angus Morrison in. We have reason to believe that there could be some truth in what the argument was all about.' He pointed towards the door. 'I trust Mrs Armstrong hasn't made any attempt to leave?'

Ally, astounded, shook her head. 'Do you mean that Patti Armstrong *did* ask Angus to get a gun?'

'I can't rule that out at this stage. Morrison is not exactly a talkative man, so I need a further twenty-four hours to get through to him. And I will,' Amir said firmly. 'The earl is adamant, of course, that Morrison would do no such thing, and he's not at all happy that we're keeping him in custody. But I don't want Morrison back here until I've questioned him further. I just wanted to keep you in the picture and to ensure that Mrs Armstrong remains within these four walls.' He hesitated. 'I've told you this in confidence, Ally, so please keep it to yourself for the moment. Now I must go.' He smiled at her as he stood up. 'I think we'll all be very glad to see the back of this family. Hopefully, they shouldn't be here for much longer.'

After he'd gone, Ally wondered if he was just being optimistic or if he was about to make a breakthrough. And did he *really* think there was any truth in what Tom had overheard Patti asking Angus?

When Ross phoned later, Ally told him only that Angus was still in custody, and that Amir had called in but was giving nothing away apart from asking her to ensure that Patti wasn't planning to escape.

'That sounds ominous to me,' Ross said. 'In fact, I was wondering if these two widows were still talking to each other, after one's uncle flattened the other's son.'

It was very obvious next morning that the two women were indeed not talking to each other. Patti came downstairs early, at half past seven, wanting only coffee and toast before disappearing into the sitting room to watch the breakfast programmes on TV. Julie and Janey appeared at nine o'clock for cooked breakfasts or, more correctly, for scrambled eggs on toast, which thankfully did not necessitate any sous-chef to assist with sausages. They ate quickly, then joined their mother shortly before Wendy made an appearance.

Ally felt sorry for the lonely figure sitting at the small table by the window in solitary state. Wendy seemed to be staring into space as opposed to enjoying the view.

'Good morning!' Ally said brightly. 'What can I get you this morning?'

'Nothing, nothing.' Wendy sounded sad. 'Just coffee, please. I've got little appetite at the moment. I'll just help myself to fruit juice and cereal.'

Ally nodded. 'How's Joel? Has he recovered?'

Wendy shook her head wearily. 'He's spending most of the time in his room because he still looks pretty bad. His nose isn't broken, thank God, but it's very swollen and bruised, and then his eye is also quite swollen…' She glanced towards the door and lowered her voice. 'Interesting that they're keeping his assailant in custody, don't you think? I'm hoping he's going to be jailed for assaulting an innocent man. Patti, of course, thinks the sun shines out of her uncle's you-know-what, and all she talks about is that boy – Tom, is it? – and what a liar he is.'

'This is a very tense time for all of you after what you've been through,' Ally said diplomatically. *Understatement of the year,* she thought.

Wendy made her way towards the sideboard and helped herself to some cereal, and when Ally returned with the coffee, she said, 'It's the girls I feel sorry for. Naturally they love their mom, but Patti's turned in on herself. She's very self-obsessed, you know. Always has been.'

Ally didn't feel she could say anything other than to offer a further platitude. 'I do hope this nightmare ends soon,' she said truthfully, 'and that you'll all be able to go home.'

But the nightmare was not about to end.

TWENTY-TWO

Ally had always admired Amir's powers of persuasion, and never more so than when Hamish rang up just as she got back into the kitchen. To say that he sounded agitated would be an understatement.

'I just wanted to warn you, Ally,' he said, 'that Pat Armstrong is about to be arrested. Apparently, she *did* ask Angus to get her a gun, but he refused. He's admitted this to Kandahar.'

Ally had to sit down, the shock of what she'd just heard slowly sinking in. Surely it couldn't be true that Patti Armstrong had shot her husband? Then her thoughts turned to her two poor girls; to have your mother guilty of killing your father and then, doubtless, having your mother incarcerated for years and years! It didn't bear thinking about. Could there be any mitigating circumstances? This could hardly be described as a crime of passion when it had so obviously been pre-planned.

Amir was likely to arrive at any minute. She needed Ross badly, and just as she picked up her phone to call him, in he walked.

Taking one look at her stricken face, Ross asked, 'Whatever's the matter, Ally?'

Ally told him about the earl's call.

Ross put his arms round her. 'Oh my God!' Then, after a moment, he added, 'Those poor girls!'

'I should think Amir will appear at any moment,' Ally said. 'I suppose I should check that Patti's still in the sitting room.'

As she stood up, Ross raised his arm to hold her back. 'I'll go,' he said.

A minute later, he was back. 'Yes, she's in there, painting her nails, with the two girls, watching TV. She's obviously unaware of Angus's confession.'

Ally made coffee, and they both sat and waited, but it was almost an hour later before Amir, accompanied by one female and one male constable, walked in through the front door. 'We've come to arrest Mrs Patricia Armstrong,' he said formally to Ally in the hallway before they entered the sitting room.

Ally nodded. 'Yes, the earl rang me a short time ago.' She stood, rooted to the spot in the hallway, aware that Ross was standing right behind her and that Wendy had appeared from upstairs.

'What's going on?' she asked Ally.

'Patti is being arrested because Angus has admitted that she'd asked him to get her a gun,' Ally replied.

Wendy put her hand to her mouth. 'Oh *no*! How could Patti have done that? What about the poor girls?'

Ally thought it was interesting that everyone's concerns seemed to centre on the girls rather than whether Patti could be innocent or not.

There was a commotion then as Patti, handcuffed, was led out to the police car, her daughters trying to hang on to her and weeping. Wendy, in the meantime, had sprung into action and was trying to restrain them both. Janey, in particular, was hysterical. 'You can't take our mommy away – she hasn't done anything!' she shouted at the police. Julie stood back as if frozen, silent tears rolling down her cheeks. Somehow or other the media had found out about this, and there was a host of reporters and cameramen at the gate.

Patti put up no resistance, but she called out as she got into the back of the car with the police officer, 'I'm not guilty, my darlings; I did not kill your daddy!'

The reporters were all shouting questions: 'Did you kill your husband, Mrs Armstrong?'

'And your brother-in-law as well?'

'Why did you kill two men?'

The cameras were whirring.

The other officer sat in the front passenger seat, and Amir drove away with a brief wave, leaving Patti's two distraught daughters embracing each other and sobbing uncontrollably. Wendy put her arms round them both and said gently, 'Come inside,' before shepherding them back into the sitting room and away from the probing eyes of the press. Most of the media had followed the police car, but a couple of reporters remained at the gate.

As Ally was trying to work out what on earth to do or to say, Ross said cheerfully, 'The refreshment team are on duty here. Hot drinks, cold drinks, alcoholic drinks, some dog therapy perhaps?'

Julie dried her eyes, her arm still around her sobbing sister, and asked, 'Could we have some tea, please – and a dog or two?' She gave a teary smile.

Ross saluted. 'Your wish is my command, and I shall have a word with the Labradors!' With that, he turned around and opened the kitchen door, and both dogs came bounding out, tails wagging and heading straight for the girls.

'Tea is on the way,' Ally said, trying to sound equally cheerful.

'This has to be a complete nightmare for these teenagers,' Ross commented as he filled the kettle.

'It's so difficult to know what on earth to say to them,' Ally said. 'Let's face it, they're in a foreign country and their mother has just been arrested for shooting their father! Can you honestly think of anything worse?'

'Not much,' Ross agreed. 'I wonder if we should ask the girls in here for dinner tonight? I'm happy to cook a roast or something.'

'Do you think they'll *want* to eat?' Ally asked as she set up a tray to transport the tea things.

Ross shrugged. 'No idea. They may have recovered a little by the afternoon and, let's face it, they're growing girls and need their food.' He sighed. 'What a bloody mess!'

'I just can't believe that Angus could ever have agreed to get the gun for her, far less to break into the cabinet to divert the blame away from himself,' Ally said. 'So why has he been arrested?'

'Well, he hasn't admitted to it, has he? He's denied it, I believe.' Ross picked up the tray. 'I'll carry this through because it's heavy.'

As he made his way across the hall, Ally wondered, as always, what she'd do without this kind, decent man in her life. She followed him as he laid the tray down on the coffee table in front of Wendy. The girls were sitting either side of their aunt, each fondling a dog and drying their eyes.

'Thank you so much,' Wendy said.

'And thank goodness that Auntie Wendy is here!' Julie exclaimed, leaning closer to her aunt.

'If there's anything we can do, you only have to ask,' Ally said.

'Joel must be wondering where I am,' Wendy said. 'Should I ask him to come up here?'

'Of course,' Ally replied, hoping Joel wouldn't make things worse, as he was inclined to do.

When they were back in the kitchen, Ross asked, 'Would it be a good idea if I suggested I accompany them on a walk, with the dogs, across the moor to Loch Soular for instance. The sun's shining, and the dogs would be happy.'

'Great idea,' Ally said, 'and then, hopefully, Wendy will join Joel at the Craigmonie.'

Ross wandered back into the sitting room where his suggestion was greeted with some muted enthusiasm, and the girls went to find their coats and boots. Ally opted to stay behind and, if necessary, fend off any reporters.

'I don't really want to go up there again,' Wendy admitted, 'so it's probably better if I join Joel down at the hotel as usual. I feel so responsible for my two nieces now, but I'm torn in every direction.' She hesitated for a moment, then lowered her voice to little more than a whisper. 'Do you suppose Patti could have killed my Greg as well?'

'I don't see how she could because she was watching TV most of the afternoon, and we had to persuade her to walk up to the loch with us to see the fun run,' Ally replied.

Wendy nodded as she got out her phone. 'Joel's just not gonna *believe* this!'

Ally had several reporters ringing the doorbell before Ross and the two girls got back.

'I can tell you nothing,' she repeated time and time again. 'You'll have to ask the police.'

One of them was particularly persistent and kept asking, 'Who's looking after her two daughters?' Ally could see that this question was going to be asked on a regular basis from now on so thought she'd better have an answer ready.

A few minutes later, Wendy was tapping on the door again.

'Joel and I thought we might take the girls out for lunch,' she said. 'They might not feel like eating much, but they need to get away from here for a couple of hours.'

'Where did you plan to go?' Ally asked.

'We can't go to the village because the media are still all stationed halfway down the road, so we thought we might take them to The Bothy. And we don't plan to visit Desdemona this time!'

After they'd gone, Ally said to Ross, 'Looks like you won't need to do that roast tonight after all.'

Ross nodded. 'I've been thinking; maybe Patti did kill Archie, but who on earth killed Greg Watson?'

Ally shrugged. 'I hate to say it, but I wonder if it could be Angus? And could he really be capable of supplying Patti with a gun, knowing what she intended to do with it? And if that's the case, would he be equally capable of clobbering someone over the head?'

Locharran came into its own that afternoon. There was a succession of gifts from kind villagers – flowers, sweets, newly baked scones, some teen magazines – all brought up and laid on the doorstep, some with messages saying "Thinking of you girls" or similar.

The family returned from The Bothy looking marginally more cheerful than when they'd left, and Ally decided it was probably best to leave them alone for now. Joel had departed, but Wendy was still around somewhere. Once she knew where they'd taken Patti, Ally decided she'd accompany the girls to visit their mother. She only hoped it would be somewhere nearer than Glasgow: Fort William or Inverness, say.

In the meantime, Ross had taken both dogs for a short walk, and Ally thought she should take the board off the wall again because she'd had Greg at one o'clock at one time, and it was unlikely to have been him who'd killed Archie.

Was it Patti?

Patti had always been a suspect, positioned at the top, and she must now place Angus up there for sure too. Patti was still at twelve, and Angus at eleven now. But what about Tom? Was he in on this too? Ally didn't know what to make of him but moved him from ten o'clock to one o'clock. And it was possible that Greg might have killed his brother-in-law. He couldn't be excluded, even posthumously. But then who'd killed Greg? She moved Greg down to two o'clock. She knew she should make a new 'clock' for Greg's murder, but, at that moment, she couldn't think of any possible suspects. Perhaps it made more sense that it was one of the runners who'd come across Greg as they'd raced along. But what possible motive could any of them have? All Ally could think of was that perhaps one of them had witnessed Greg shooting at Archie. And what did the note she'd found near Greg's body mean? Was the note *for* Greg or *from* him?

Ally sighed and placed the painting back on the wall.

Amir arrived, alone, in the evening, looking exhausted.

'We've charged Mrs Armstrong and taken her to Inverness for the moment,' he told Ally and Ross, 'but she'll most likely be moved down to Glasgow prior to the trial.' He paused. 'Whenever that is. How are the daughters coping?'

'Well, they're devastated obviously,' Ally replied, 'but at least they have their aunt and their cousin here, who took them out to lunch today.'

'Ah yes, the cousin!' Amir rolled his eyes. 'Enough said. Now, we can provide a counsellor, you know, in cases like this, someone who can help them through what must be a hellish time.'

'That might be helpful,' Ally agreed. 'I'll ask Wendy because she's been very supportive. In the meantime, I thought I might offer to take the girls to see their mother, although I expect Wendy and Joel will want to do that. I trust she's allowed visitors?'

Amir nodded. 'In this case, of course. It looks like I'm going to be stationed here for some time the way things are going. I've got to find out if Watson's death is in any way connected to Armstrong's.'

'Has Patti now admitted to killing her husband?' Ally asked.

'No. She keeps protesting her innocence, but I think she'll open up some more. I shall find out,' Amir said confidently.

Ally believed him. He obviously had a way of extracting information with what seemed like gentle probing.

'I just wanted to put you in the picture, and thought I'd also have a chat with the two young ladies and their aunt, to offer them counselling if necessary. As the father of two girls, my heart really bleeds for them.'

'They're all in the sitting room I think,' Ally said, leading the way through and leaving him to it. This whole episode had taken its toll on her too, and she was feeling absolutely exhausted, drained and emotional. Was it too early to go to bed at eight o'clock? She knew Ross would be watching a big football match later in the evening.

Yes, early supper, then bed.

Morag had, of course, a lot to say in the morning. 'So his missus has been arrested for tryin' to kill her old man! She wouldnae the first! And now maybe they'll stop pesterin' our boys. But I canna believe that Angus would have given her a leg-up, so to speak! You know what I mean?'

'He hasn't admitted to it,' Ally reminded her. 'All he

admitted to is that Patti Armstrong asked him to get her a gun, which is why she has been arrested.'

'Aye, well, she is his niece,' Morag said, 'so maybe she fed him some sob story or somethin'. Poor Angus!'

As she was speaking, the three remaining guests came down together to breakfast, looking exhausted. Julie and Janey couldn't even face their usual scrambled eggs.

'Just cereal and coffee, please,' Julie said.

'We've been offered counselling,' Wendy said, 'but we've turned it down.'

'Because we *know* that Mom did not do this,' Julie said firmly, 'and we're waiting for her to be released.'

'So we don't need any counselling,' Janey added.

Ally hoped they were right, but it was becoming harder and harder to see how Patti could *not* be involved.

TWENTY-THREE

Their cousin, Joel, however was still hell-bent on finding out who had killed his father. Although Ally could hardly criticise him for that, it was the way he went about it that got everyone's backs up.

Apparently, as Ally found out when she went to buy some trout, he'd taken himself down to Fin's Fish and given Forby a grilling. He'd also upset Forby's brother, Fergus, which had incurred the wrath of Finlay McKinnon himself, who had threatened to call the police.

'He seemed to think that one, or both, of my lads were hidin' information and that they must've seen somethin' when they were runnin' round. Let me tell you this: they were that knackered by the time they'd run round the loch that they hardly had the energy to keep goin' and wouldn't have noticed if there was an invading army comin' up the moor! Stupid bugger!' Finlay was still furious.

'We know Mom didn't do it,' Julie said confidently to Ally later, 'and we are going to be visiting Mom because the policeman said that would be OK. And they've let Uncle Angus out already.'

This was news to Ally, although she wasn't surprised, knowing how determined Hamish had been to see him out of custody. She thought it would be a good idea to call Hamish to get his reaction.

'I just wondered if you'd managed to persuade them to release Angus on bail?' Ally asked when Hamish answered. He was having a barn re-roofed and apologised for the hammering in the background.

'I did, I did! Thank God!' She could hear the relief in his voice. 'Just a minute,' he continued, 'while I park my bottom on a crate here, so I can keep an eye on what these bloody roofers are doing. Do you know it's taken me months to get the roofing company to do this, and now they've upped the price because they say everything's gone up in the meantime? And don't I *know* it!' He ranted on for a few minutes before he asked, 'And how are you?'

'I'm fine. I wondered how Angus was?'

'Oh, Angus!' Hamish sighed audibly. 'Well, he's adamant that he did not break into the cabinet, but he has admitted that Pat asked him to get her a gun. He seems to think that Pat got Greg to break in, but he refuses point-blank to talk about anything else. I do try to be understanding, Alison, but at times I feel like I'm knocking my head against a brick wall. I really do! All he's said is that he was concerned about the way Pat was being treated by her husband and that she should never have married him in the first place.'

'Did he tell you how Patti was supposedly treated?' Ally asked.

'No, he did not. He shakes his head whenever I ask him anything on the subject.'

'Will he be charged for withholding evidence?'

'Probably,' Hamish replied. 'I doubt he'll spend time in

prison, but he's likely to get a bloody great fine – which, doubtless, I'll end up having to pay. He obviously turned a blind eye to what his niece was planning to do. How could he have been so damn stupid to be persuaded to do something like that?'

'Well, we're back to the business of blood being thicker than water,' Ally remarked. 'To change the subject – how are Magda and the babes?'

Ally could almost see Hamish smiling. 'Magda's well, and my wee boys are wonderful! They're both getting bigger and bigger, they smile and giggle when they see me, and they're sitting up and rolling over. I bet they'll soon be on the move.'

'You'll need eyes in the back of your head when they do,' Ally told him cheerfully.

After she'd ended the call, Ally thought about what Angus had said. Had Patti been maltreated by Archie? He had been a big, strong man, and Wendy had mentioned something about him being difficult, even violent. Scrawny, skinny Patti would not have stood much chance with self-defence, if necessary. She was known to have been a good shot once; after all, it was Angus who'd taught her, and Angus was a superb marksman. Even though the bullet had hit the caber and not her husband, the end result had been the same. Would shooting with intent to kill warrant the same degree of punishment as actually shooting him directly?

'That's an interesting point of law,' Ross said later when Ally had told him of her conversation with Hamish, 'to which I do not have an answer. I suppose it could knock a few years off her sentence. You must ask Amir when next you see him.'

'I'm looking forward to that,' Ally said, 'because I think he has a special gift for worming information out of people. He probes very gently, but he seems to get their trust or something, and they open up to him.'

'Well, Patti Armstrong's a tough cookie, so he'll have his work cut out to get much joy out of her,' Ross said rather disparagingly.

But Ross was to be proved wrong. Amir appeared at nine o'clock next morning, just as Wendy and the girls came down to breakfast. As usual, since Patti's arrest, they only wanted coffee and toast.

'I'll have a quick word with them all to make sure they're OK,' Amir said to Ally, 'and then I'd love a cup of tea.'

'Of course you can have a cup of tea,' Ally said, 'but why not have a full breakfast? I have a mountain of bacon and eggs to use up because, unsurprisingly, our guests have lost their appetites.'

He hesitated for a moment. 'Oh, I couldn't put you to so much trouble,' he said, and Ally wondered if he was eating properly at all at the moment. If he was sleeping at the temporary police quarters in Locharran, he'd be lucky to get anything other than a cup of tea.

'I insist,' Ally said firmly, noticing how tired and drawn he looked. 'While you're chatting to them next door, I'll have it cooked.'

'You are very kind,' he said and gave her one of his lovely smiles.

Ally didn't want him to feel self-conscious so she cooked for the three of them, knowing that Ross would most likely be having his usual bacon sandwich when he came in after taking the dogs for their early morning walk.

He came in just as she was laying the table for three people. 'I saw the police car outside,' he said.

'I feel sorry for him,' Ally said. 'He's on his own, miles away from his own daughters, and I don't think he's eating properly – probably rubbish food while he's on the move. So I offered to cook him breakfast.'

'And he might just give us some information?' Ross

suggested with a grin. 'I'll even cook some sausages in his honour!'

When Amir returned a while later and Ally indicated where he should sit, he said, 'This looks wonderful. You really are spoiling me.'

'You deserve it,' Ally said, 'because you must be so stressed with all this going on.'

'The two daughters seem fairly positive,' Amir said as he attacked his breakfast with gusto, 'and I think it helped when I told them that they'd soon be able to visit their mother.'

'They're convinced she's innocent,' Ally remarked.

'Hmm,' he demurred.

No more was said on the subject until they'd all finished breakfast. When they were sitting back with mugs of tea, Amir said, 'She's going to plead not guilty.'

Ally couldn't help herself. 'Do you think she *is* guilty?'

Amir sighed as he sipped his tea. 'It's possible. Did you know that Angus Morrison has been released?'

Ally nodded. 'Yes, the earl told me. But it's not as if Angus gave her the gun, is it?'

'Well, no, but he may have turned a blind eye to her getting one. Apparently, Patricia Armstrong convinced him that her husband was controlling and abusive, and that she couldn't take it any longer. This is what she told Angus Morrison. What she *didn't* tell Angus Morrison, but has told me, is that she had been having an affair with Greg Watson for some time, and that it was he who planned all this. She claims it was he who broke in, stole the gun and also pulled the trigger.'

Ally and Ross exchanged glances as they let this information sink in.

'So she's saying that it was *Greg Watson* who killed her husband, via the caber?' Ross asked.

'That's what she's saying,' Amir confirmed.

This was beginning to make sense to Ally, who had been

surprised at Patti's grief when Greg was killed. 'So will Patti be released now?' she asked.

Amir shook his head. 'It's all very well to put the blame on a dead man, who can't defend himself. We need proof.'

'How are you going to get that?' Ross asked.

'I don't know. Mrs Armstrong swears she was visiting the toilet at the exact moment the shot was fired and that a "nice woman" was coming out just as she was going in and held the door open for her. She said they both jumped at the noise and the woman said, "What the hell was *that*?"'

'Who was this woman?' Ally asked. 'Surely she could verify the story?'

'Perhaps she could,' Amir replied, 'if we could only find her. I've put a notice out asking her to come forward, if she exists, which I'm beginning to doubt.'

'For what it's worth,' Ally said, 'I should tell you that Patti Armstrong was a great deal more distressed when Greg Watson was killed than she was when her own husband was, so it could well be that they *were* having an affair.'

'It's possible,' Amir agreed, 'but that still doesn't mean that he did the shooting. As I said before, it's all very convenient to blame a dead man. Now I have the unenviable task of talking to Wendy Watson and trying to find out if she had any knowledge of the fact that her husband was having an affair with Patricia.'

'They've probably just finished breakfast,' Ally said, 'so you want to catch her before she goes anywhere.'

'Thank you,' said Amir, 'I will. On her own, so can you divert the two daughters somewhere?'

In fact, Julie and Janey had already returned to their room as Ally ushered Amir into the dining room, where Wendy was still lingering over a coffee, and shut the door firmly behind him.

'I wonder how Wendy's going to take this information,' Ally said to Ross when she returned to the kitchen.

'Perhaps she knew?' Ross suggested. 'If she didn't, then there's going to be hell to pay.'

There was a low murmur of voices which could be heard through the wall, although Ally had no idea what was being said and didn't really want to know. And then there was shouting by a female voice and a door slamming.

Amir came into the kitchen and said, 'Mrs Watson is not happy. I really don't think she knew about the affair, but she does now. I fear that the atmosphere in this house is going to be very tense, Ally, if ever Patti Armstrong comes back here. Hopefully, they'll all fly home as quickly as possible.'

'I hope you're right,' Ally said. 'She's taken it badly then?'

'I'm afraid so. I'm sorry I have to leave you now, but at the moment she's inconsolable, so you'll probably be on the receiving end. I've finished questioning her for now, but if she says anything of further interest, perhaps you could let me know?'

After Amir had left and Ally wandered into the dining room to clear away the breakfast things, she found Wendy standing and staring out of the window, her body racked with sobs.

'All this must be unbelievably stressful for you, Wendy,' Ally said, noticing the dark circles under the woman's eyes as she turned around.

Wendy sobbed and blew her nose. 'Do you know what that detective has just told me?'

'No,' Ally lied.

'Patti was having an affair with my husband! With my *Greg*! Under my very nose! How *could* he? How could she?'

'You had no idea?'

'I certainly had no idea! Now I know why Patti was so insistent that we all holidayed here together.'

'I'm so sorry.'

'I'm not sleeping well,' Wendy continued, 'because there are so many worries on my mind. I'm finding it hard to believe that Patti had an affair with my Greg. Mind you, Archie could be a bit of a bastard, and I know he had affairs. Is *that* why she killed my brother?' Wendy blew her nose lustily. 'Now she's telling the inspector that it was Greg who fired the gun, meaning she's callous enough to blame a dead man to get herself off the hook!'

'This must be a complete nightmare from which there's no escape at present,' Ally said.

'That's exactly it. And what if Patti *is* found guilty – what happens then? Do you know I was actually intending to take Julie and Janey to see their mother today? I don't think I can face it now.'

'But she may not, of course, be found guilty of Archie's murder,' Ally suggested, realising that Wendy was actually shaking uncontrollably. She felt desperately sorry for the woman.

'Why then did she ask her uncle to get her a gun? She had to be planning *something*, for God's sake! And isn't it some coincidence that the very next day Archie is killed?'

Ally cleared her throat. 'You really had no idea that Greg might have been having an affair with Patti?'

Wendy shook her head. 'I just can't believe it. This could be a story she's made up to get herself off the hook, I suppose. Julie and Janey are convinced, of course, that their mother is innocent. But that's what they *want* to believe, isn't it?' Wendy lowered her voice a little. 'How must it feel to know that your mother killed your father? And if she is guilty, she'll go to jail for a very long time, and will that be in Scotland? So the girls can't even visit her? I just thank God that Joel got here because I cannot cope any longer with all this on my own.' Tears ran unchecked down her cheeks.

'Do you want to come into the kitchen with us?' Ally asked.

'Thank you, but no. I want to lock myself away for a bit and phone Joel. God only knows what he's going to say!' Wendy blew her nose again.

Ally gave her a long hug. 'I honestly don't know what to say that will bring you any comfort,' she said.

Wendy dried her eyes. 'You've been great, Ally. Thank God we're staying here and not at the Craigmonie! Joel hates leaving his room because everyone stares, and because they know who he is, the media hound him.'

'Well, let's hope that you'll soon be able to go home,' Ally said. 'And at least we know for sure that Patti didn't kill Greg because she came back here with us and didn't go out again until we all set off for the barbecue.'

There was silence for a few minutes while Ally loaded the breakfast plates onto her tray.

Wendy showed no sign of leaving. 'But what happens when she *is* found guilty of Archie's murder?' she asked. 'I mean, we all need to go home whether she's guilty or not. And who's responsible for these two girls? Will *I* be responsible for them? Do we have to come back for the trial, whenever that may be? And when will they release Archie and Greg's bodies so we can accompany them back home? How long is it likely we'll have to stay here until they do?'

'Wendy, you need to ask Detective Inspector Kandahar about all this,' Ally said. 'He really is a very nice man, and I'm certain he'll be able to reassure you on most of these points. And maybe you should see a doctor to prescribe you something to soothe your shattered nerves.'

'Perhaps I should,' Wendy agreed. 'And thank you so much for listening to all my moans and groans!'

Ally nodded, wondering how on earth they would all cope if Patti *did* turn out to be guilty.

TWENTY-FOUR

The conversation with Wendy had unsettled Ally greatly. Wendy badly needed expert advice or she was likely to have a breakdown. Ally couldn't begin to imagine how it must feel to find out that your husband, your late husband, had been having an affair with your sister-in-law. And that the latter had probably killed her own husband, Wendy's brother. What a hellish mess!

Joel arrived about half an hour later and thumped on the kitchen door.

Startled, Ally looked up from her coffee and her newspaper.

'Joel!' she exclaimed as she opened the door.

'I need to have a word with you, Ally,' he said. 'You know how upset my mom is?'

'I do, and I'm not surprised,' Ally said.

'I cannot believe this "affair" business. I cannot think that my father would have an affair with *anyone*, far less Patti Armstrong! I do believe Patti was quite capable of killing Uncle Archie for her own selfish desires, but who then killed my father? One thing's for sure, we can't face taking the girls to Inverness today to see their mother.'

'I can understand that, but the girls are entitled to see their mother, and I'm happy to take them to Inverness,' Ally said, already thinking that this would give her an opportunity to have a word with Patti on her own.

'That would be wonderful because neither Mom nor I want to face Patti at the moment.'

'Please be very careful what you say within earshot of the girls,' Ally reminded him. 'Whatever you think of their mother, these girls are innocent, missing their mum and must be worried sick.'

'She's never been much of a mother,' Joel snapped and turned back into the hallway at the exact moment that Wendy got to the foot of the stairs. 'She's always been far too obsessed with herself.'

Mother and son disappeared out of the door, and shortly afterwards, Ally heard the sound of Joel's Jeep driving away. She wondered where they might be going and how was she supposed to tell the girls that it was she herself who would be taking them to visit their mother? And how was she to explain how their aunt and cousin couldn't – or wouldn't?

Ross had taken Ebony down to the surgery for some medicine because the dog had eaten something which had caused her to be sick during the night. Ally sat down with a cup of tea and tried to work out how to tell the girls, and she'd just drained her cup when there was a timid knock on the door.

'Ally, we wondered if you might know where Auntie Wendy and Joel have gone?' Julie asked. 'You see the inspector said we could visit Mom today, and we're booked for two o'clock this afternoon, so it seems strange that—'

'I'm taking you,' Ally interrupted quickly. 'They've probably forgotten.'

'How *could* they forget?' Janey wailed from where she was standing just behind her sister.

Julie pulled a face. 'I've got a feeling Auntie Wendy's avoiding us for some reason because it seems weird that she didn't knock on our door before she left with Joel, knowing that we have this appointment.'

'Well, never mind,' Ally said. 'I'm not doing anything today, and I'm happy to take you.'

'You're so kind!' Julie exclaimed, giving Ally a big hug.

Ally was close to tears. 'Could you be ready to leave in half an hour or so?' she asked them. 'I have to wait for Ross to get back and look after the dogs while we're away.'

'Thank you! Thank you!' they both chorused. 'We'll go right now and get ready.'

Ross and Ebony got back about fifteen minutes later. He'd given Ebony her medicine, and she seemed a little better, if a little more sad-eyed than usual.

'I should be taking them there,' he said when Ally had relayed the earlier conversations, 'but I'm still a teeny bit worried about Ebony. Would you like to take my car?'

'No,' Ally said firmly. 'I've got a full tank of fuel in the Golf, and it could do with a nice, long run. And I'd be so relieved to know that you were here with the dogs.'

She could see that Ross wasn't altogether convinced, so she added, 'And it might give me an opportunity to have a word with Patti on her own, which you probably wouldn't be allowed to do.'

Thirty minutes later, Ally brought her car round to the front where Julie and Janey were ready and waiting. Julie bagged the front passenger seat, while Janey sprawled in the back. Off they went with Ross waving from the door.

'Your Ross is a really nice guy,' Julie informed her, waving back.

'Yes, he is,' Ally agreed.

'And he loves dogs,' Janey piped up from the rear. 'Daddy didn't much care for dogs and wouldn't let us have one.'

'Maybe Mom will let us have one when we get home,' Julie said as she gazed out of the car window at the golds and bronzes of the autumn leaves on the trees mirrored in the lochs with the mountains behind. 'This is quite a spectacular drive, isn't it? Reminds me a little of a trip we did to BC and Alberta a few years back, which was fantastic.'

'We're not quite in the same league as the Rockies,' Ally agreed, 'but it is beautiful.'

She was relieved that the girls seemed relaxed and quite chatty, and wondered how long that would last.

It lasted until they got to Loch Ness. Ally could almost feel the tension rising as both girls became quiet, chewing their gum more lustily than usual.

'Little chance of seeing any monster today,' Ally said, looking at the rough surface of the temperamental loch.

'I guess there are more monsters roaming around Locharran than Loch Ness,' Janey remarked. 'Like the one who killed our dad and uncle.'

They lapsed into silence again.

'I've brought her perfume,' Julie said, holding up a bottle of J'adore. 'Mum loves her perfume, and I guess she wouldn't have had time to bring it when they arrested her.'

'Will they let us bring it in?' Janey asked anxiously.

'I guess we'll find out,' said Julie.

They arrived at the detention centre at twenty minutes to two and left as much as possible locked in the car because Ally was aware that there would be a great deal of security. There was a visitors' area with some chairs and machines which dispensed hot and cold drinks and all manner of chocolate bars. Everyone, including Ally, was now feeling understandably nervous. This was a new experience for her too.

Then, at precisely five minutes to two, a uniformed policewoman appeared and asked, 'Are you the Armstrong family?'

'Yes!' the girls replied in unison, while Ally explained that she was accompanying them in the absence of any relatives.

The policewoman nodded. 'OK, you may accompany them to see their mother,' she said, leading them along a corridor to a security point, similar to an airport, where she checked their bodies and their bags. 'What's this?' she asked, withdrawing J'adore from Julie's pocket.

'Oh, please!' Julie begged. 'I want to take it to Mom because she loves perfume.'

'And I've got her some chocolate,' Janey added, removing a large bar from her pocket.

The policewoman tested the spray in the air, wrinkling her nose. 'OK, OK, I'll overlook the rules this time.' She gave a faint smile before leading them to the cell, which she opened up with much clicking and clunking and ushered them in with many reminders that she'd be back in half an hour – not one minute later – to let them out.

The cell was probably about ten feet square, with an inbuilt narrow bed, on which a pale, wan Patti was sitting, legs outstretched, staring at the stainless-steel toilet on the wall opposite. She was wearing a regulation sweatshirt and jogging bottoms provided by her current accommodation, her hair was lank and her face was make-up-free.

'Oh, thank God!' she muttered as she jumped up to embrace her two daughters, all three of them now in tears.

Ally stood back close to the door, feeling very aware that she shouldn't really be there. 'I'm sorry, Patti,' she said, 'but I had to accompany them.'

'No need to apologise, and thanks for getting them here.' Patti sat down with a girl on each side of her, arms entwined.

'Auntie Wendy and Joel were supposed to bring us, but they disappeared,' Janey explained.

'Oh, did they indeed?' Patti raised an eyebrow.

Ally remained by the door, relieved that the three of them were now chatting normally, the words tumbling out as they remembered things to tell each other, oblivious to her presence. No, Patti told them, the bed was not particularly comfortable, but then this wasn't exactly The Ritz and, furthermore, she did not intend to be in this place for much longer. 'Just believe me, I did not kill your daddy,' she must have said half a dozen times during the visit. The half hour flew by.

'I'm going to be out of here real soon,' she said, 'but, for now, I'd like five minutes with Ally if that's OK, girls, because our time is nearly up.' She pressed a switch, and the policewoman was back at the door. Ally wondered if she'd been there all the time. The door was opened sufficiently to let the girls out after a good few minutes of goodbyes, hugs and tears.

'I'll be with you in five minutes,' Ally assured them, glancing at her watch.

Patti sighed as the door clunked shut behind them. 'Has Kandahar spoken to Wendy?' she asked.

Ally nodded.

'So she knows about Greg and me?'

'I'm afraid so,' Ally replied. 'She was very upset. That's the reason she couldn't face bringing the girls here today.'

'I'm only sorry you're having to take the brunt of all this,' Patti said. 'I just want you to know that I did not kill Archie. That was Greg, along with the caber, of course.' Her voice wobbled. 'I loved him, you know. Archie and I hadn't really got on for years, and when Greg suggested this as a way for us to be together, well...' She paused. 'But I never thought he'd really do it.'

Ally decided she might as well be truthful. 'Actually, I'm quite friendly with Amir Kandahar, and he told me about trying to find some woman who saw you at the toilets, but no luck so far, I'm afraid.'

'Please, Ally, if you do nothing else, could you try to find this woman?'

As she spoke, the policewoman's voice boomed, 'Time's up!'

Back in the car, both Julie and Janey appeared more cheerful and relaxed, seemingly confident that their mother would soon be released.

Ally wasn't nearly so confident. Perhaps the woman who held the toilet door open for Patti that day at the games would never be found; perhaps she wasn't even a local but had just been visiting for the day. In any case, Patti was bound to be charged with conspiracy to commit a murder at the very least. She'd suggest to Amir that perhaps he should get Patti's photograph printed in the newspapers and put on the TV, to ask this woman to come forward. Surely there must be some other way to prove Patti's innocence – if she was innocent. Since Greg was no longer around, her story could never be verified.

And doubtless Julie and Janey would want to visit Patti again if their mother remained in custody. Perhaps she would let Ross take them next time because, in addition to the recent killings and family revelations, this was taking its toll, and Ally was beginning to feel extremely stressed.

Ally was glad to get home and offload the girls, who went straight up to their bedroom. There was no sign of Wendy. And Ross was very pleased to see her and to inform her that Ebony was now much better.

'How did the visit go?' he asked Ally.

Ally gave him a blow-by-blow account of their visit to the detention centre. 'Patti seemed convinced that she'd be released once we found this woman who supposedly held the door open for her, but I doubt that we'll find her, and how else could she prove her innocence?'

'If she's innocent,' Ross reminded her.

Ally thought for a moment. 'You know what? She's really done nothing to help herself, but somehow, I have a strange feeling that she is.'

Ally was glad of a quiet evening and an early night. She felt much better in the morning but worried about any scenes at breakfast time. However, Wendy came downstairs early and had gone, presumably down to the Craigmonie, before the girls emerged at half past nine. Wendy only asked, 'How did the visit go yesterday?' and nodded when Ally said, 'OK.'

Ross was going home for twenty-four hours to oversee guests' comings and goings and to check on the cleaning company he employed to service the accommodation. As he kissed her goodbye, he said to Ally, 'Be sure to call me if you have any problems whatsoever and I'll be back like a shot!'

Even Morag was amenable this morning, although she complained, as usual, about the state of Julie and Janey's bedroom. 'They've never been taught to hang up their clothes,' she moaned, 'or to pick their wet towels up from the bathroom floor!' She then, also as usual, tut-tutted a little and took an enormous gulp of tea. She was particularly pleased that Patti was in prison because that was one less room to do. 'How could she not be guilty,' she asked Ally, 'when she asked poor Angus to get her a gun?'

After she'd gone and Ally had tidied up downstairs, she took Flora for a walk to Loch Soular. She saw no one, and there didn't seem to be any police presence in the area either. Fortunately, the media had never bothered to venture this far but appeared to be concentrating on the road between the malthouse, the castle and the village.

After she made a lunchtime sandwich, she rang Linda.

'Ally, come down and have a glass of wine and tell me everything that's going on,' Linda said. 'I've just made a carrot-and-ginger cake that needs to be tested!'

'Put like that, how could I refuse?' Ally asked.

She took Flora with her because Linda always gave her a home-made cheese biscuit, which the dog loved.

After Flora had devoured her biscuit and Ally had sat down, Linda produced a bottle of Cabernet Sauvignon and poured out two very generous measures. 'You look like you need this,' she said as she sliced the carrot-and-ginger cake.

'Believe me, I do!' Ally agreed as she clinked glasses with her friend.

'Tell me all,' Linda said, 'although I did hear that the Armstrong wife had been arrested.'

Ally updated her and said how concerned she was about Wendy. 'I mean the poor woman's lost her brother and her husband, been told that her husband was having an affair with Patti, and is now probably going to be responsible for the two girls.'

'Do you think then that this Patti *did* kill her husband?' Linda asked.

'I honestly don't know,' Ally admitted, 'but I feel pretty sure that she didn't kill her brother-in-law.'

'So there could be another killer on the loose then?'

'I suppose it's *possible*,' Ally said. 'The thing is that I can't imagine who would want to kill poor old Greg, who wasn't even a competitor! Not that I think any of the competitors had much to do with any of this.'

'What about Angus Morrison?' Linda asked, handing a plate with a large slice of cake on it to Ally.

'If it wasn't Patti, then I suppose it had to be Angus. Perhaps he offered to do it to save her life – I mean he's nearing the end of his, and he has no children to worry about,' Ally suggested.

'Oh, wow, this cake is just delicious! How am I ever going to lose weight with you around?'

'Ally, I think you have lost weight, probably due to all this. Have you weighed yourself recently?'

Ally shook her head. 'I honestly haven't had time.'

'Well, you look slimmer, so get that cake down you and let me fill up your wine glass!'

Ally succumbed happily.

'So you've no idea if she's guilty or not?' Linda asked as she topped up the glasses.

Ally sighed and shrugged. 'Honestly, I haven't a damn clue. But Amir, the detective inspector, told me that Patti said her husband, Archie, had been very abusive and controlling. She was afraid of him, and she planned to kill him. She even asked Angus to make the gun cabinet look as if it had been broken into, and to leave the gun in some appointed place in the woods above the field.'

'So she presumably stole the gun herself and took a potshot at her husband?'

'She claimed that was Greg, her brother-in-law, who fired the gun. What she hadn't told her uncle, but did tell Amir, was that she'd been having an affair with Greg and they planned this whole thing together. And, naturally, Amir is sceptical about all this because how can a dead man prove his innocence?'

'Oh my God! So how will she ever be able to prove this?' Linda asked.

'She told Amir that she was queueing up for the loo at the time of the shooting, and she was actually entering the cubicle at the exact moment that the shot was fired. The woman coming out held the door open for her and said something like, "What the hell was that?"'

Linda frowned. 'Did she have a description of this woman then?'

Ally shook her head. 'Just that she was "nice". Amir's put a notice up outside the police station in the hope of finding this woman, but no response as yet.'

'Could you describe what this Patti looked like or what she was wearing?' Linda asked, taking a large gulp of her wine.

'Well, she's blonde and very slim, very stylish and she's usually a bit heavy on the make-up,' Ally replied.

'I think,' Linda said slowly, 'that this woman they're looking for is me.'

TWENTY-FIVE

Half an hour later, Ally and Linda walked along to the temporary police station in the vague hope that Detective Inspector Amir Kandahar might actually be there. He wasn't, of course, but the policeman on duty called him, and Amir said that he'd be there in a couple of hours or so, and he'd go straight to The Bistro.

As they left, Linda once again studied the notice she'd been handed at the police station, appealing for witnesses who could corroborate Patti's story. 'That's definitely her, Ally. She's got quite a distinctive face and, although we only saw each other for a moment, I'd swear that it was her. I'll go crazy waiting back at The Bistro on my own. Please, can you stay with me for a bit?'

With no one requiring her assistance back at the malthouse, Ally was happy to oblige.

'I *know* it was her,' Linda said again. 'I thought for sure that she didn't look like a local resident, and when she thanked me for holding the door open, I thought I could detect a faint American or Canadian accent.'

'So long as you're absolutely sure,' Ally reminded her each time, 'because the woman's future may well depend on it.'

Linda had no bookings for her bistro that evening, so they were watching *The Greatest Showman* when they saw Amir's car draw up outside. Ally said she was going to go home because Amir would want to question Linda on her own.

'What on earth have I let myself in for?' Linda asked as she accompanied Ally to the front door.

'Amir Kandahar is a really nice man,' Ally assured her, 'and he'll listen carefully to what you have to say. Just tell him exactly what you told me, OK? And don't forget how important this is because it could save a woman a lifetime in prison.'

'I know, I know!' Linda still sounded anxious. 'But you know, there must have been other people in the queue behind her, so why haven't *they* come forward?'

'Probably because, like you, they didn't read the notice outside the police station,' Ally replied.

'I'll phone you later to let you know how it goes,' Linda said as they parted company on the doorstep.

Ally couldn't settle to do anything. She desperately wanted to be the bearer of glad tidings to the teenagers, but it would be folly to do so yet, just in case... She phoned Ross and told him about her visit to Linda and Linda's revelation; she phoned her son, Jamie, in Edinburgh, and her daughter, Carol, in Wiltshire; she cleared all the emails in her inbox, and she swept up all the leaves in the garden – anything to occupy her mind. She was just considering pouring herself a glass of wine when her phone rang.

'Whew!' said Linda. 'That was certainly an in-depth interview! But he did appear convinced that I was telling the truth. I'm really glad I was able to help because I keep thinking about those two daughters...'

'Yes,' agreed Ally. 'I think everyone's been concerned about them.'

Later, she heard Wendy come in, while Joel remained in the Jeep, engine running, before she reappeared with the two girls and they all drove off together, presumably to eat somewhere.

Ally cooked herself a pasta supper from the freezer, had a glass of wine and had another early night.

Wendy, Julie and Janey all appeared together for breakfast at nine o'clock the following morning. Both girls wanted scrambled eggs on toast again, and Wendy wanted a cheese omelette. Their appetites were on the up again, and Ally wondered if they had some inkling about Patti.

It was half past ten, while Ally was clearing away the empty plates, that Amir appeared. He settled himself at the kitchen table and got out his now bulging file.

'As you know,' he said, 'Mrs Armstrong has been given an alibi.' He accepted a cup of tea from Ally. 'Your friend Linda was very definite and has sworn her statement to be true, so we are now obliged to release Mrs Armstrong on bail, for the moment anyway. She'll still have to face charges of conspiracy to commit murder.' He paused. 'I must stress that officially she should remain under house arrest, but I've been lenient and told her that she cannot leave the village – no trips to Inverness or Fort William or anywhere like that, but she is free to go in and around the village.'

'If Patti didn't fire the shot, then that takes us back to square one, does it not?'

'I'm afraid so,' Amir replied rather wearily.

'Would you like some breakfast?' Ally asked.

Amir shook his head. 'That's very kind of you, but I have to get this show on the road. I shall shortly set off for Inverness. Have you said anything at all to the daughters?'

'No, I didn't want to give them false hope,' Ally replied.

'Good. Let's keep it that way. And thanks for the tea!'

. . .

Patti Armstrong was released from the detention centre at noon, then transported in a police car to The Auld Malthouse, and was given strict instructions as to where she could go and where she couldn't go. Any breaking of the rules and she'd be straight back in that cell, the accompanying policewoman told her sternly.

Wendy appeared to have accepted the situation, once more telling Ally that she was aware that her brother could be violent and adding that she herself had been afraid of him at times.

Julie and Janey were beside themselves with delight. After hugs and kisses all round, all Patti wanted to do was to have a very hot shower, lie down on her comfortable bed and catch up on sleep.

With that, she headed up to her room and shut the door firmly behind her. The girls had looked a little dejected but cheered up when Wendy suggested that later, after Patti had had her nap, they could all go down to Concetti's for some Italian food.

Ross had come back and spent most of the afternoon washing and valeting both his and Ally's cars – a job which was not one of Ally's favourites.

Two sparkling cars later, Ross came into the kitchen, wiping his brow exaggeratedly. 'Your friend Wendy,' he said to Ally, 'keeps coming outside and chatting to me.'

'Perhaps she fancies you?' Ally suggested. 'After all, she's a widow now too!'

'But not a merry widow,' Ross emphasised. 'She was full of complaints – she wants to go home; she's bored; the two girls are bored; they haven't brought winter clothes and it's getting cold now; the police don't seem to be any further on with their enquiries, the press are getting on her nerves, etcetera, etcetera, etcetera.'

'I suppose,' Ally said, 'that if you look at it from her point of view, having lost her brother and her husband, not to mention the affair she's only just learned of, she has quite a lot to moan about!'

'Funnily enough,' said Ross, 'neither the husband nor the brother were referred to at all. It was mainly all about what it was costing.'

Ally sighed. 'I'm beginning to wonder if we'll ever see the back of Patti. After all, she did conspire with Greg to commit murder, even if she didn't actually do the deed. It's a serious offence whichever way you look at it.'

'Well, if she ends up back in jail, at least you'll get your room back,' Ross joked.

Nevertheless, Ally was having doubts about ever getting rid of this family. Wendy was right – the days were dragging on and the killer – or killers – had still not been found.

It later transpired that Patti did not want to go out to eat Italian or anything else. She did, however, ask Wendy to bring her back a ciabatta sandwich filled with sundried tomatoes, Parmesan and basil. This information was imparted to Ally by Janey, who'd been chasing the dogs around in the garden. 'I guess Mom's really tired,' she said in a resigned voice.

Later, when she and Ross were watching a Netflix thriller, Ally heard them all coming back and tramping upstairs. She imagined Patti sitting up in bed eating her ciabatta sandwich and hoped she wouldn't drop too many crumbs. She had enough on her plate without having to deal with a furious Morag too.

TWENTY-SIX

Wendy and the two girls came down for breakfast at nine o'clock again the next morning, but there was no sign of Patti.

'She's not feeling too good,' Julie explained. 'She's been having tummy pains, so she's staying in her room.'

'I've got some tummy-settlers and painkillers, if that would help?' Ally offered.

'I gave her a painkiller earlier,' Wendy said. 'My guess is that she's just exhausted with being in prison. I've got a bowl of muesli for her – she thinks she could manage that.'

'Shall I take it up to her?' Ally asked, keen to see how Patti was.

'Yes, please,' Wendy replied.

'I think she's just worn out with losing our daddy and everything that's gone on since,' Julie remarked.

Ally could well understand that. Not only had Patti lost her husband, but there was so much that had gone on since – not least losing her lover and ending up in jail.

She climbed the stairs and knocked gently on the door. 'I've brought some muesli up for you,' she called out.

'Come in,' Patti said. She was sitting up in bed, looking rather pale and frail. 'Thanks so much, Ally. I'm sorry to be such a nuisance.'

'Of course you're not a nuisance,' Ally exclaimed. 'How are you feeling?'

Patti rolled her eyes. 'Just under the weather generally. Let's face it, I've been under a hell of a lot of stress, so I suppose it has to come out somehow. I'll try to eat some of this because I know I should eat something.'

'Well, I'll be around if you need me,' Ally said. 'I'll pop in later.'

Joel arrived as usual and, having ascertained that Patti was OK, the others all set off for a trip to Fort William. They hoped the clouds might lift to reveal the summit of Ben Nevis. They'd have lunch there and they might drive down through Glencoe.

'Patti will be fine,' Wendy said to Ally as she handed back the empty cereal bowl when they left. 'She just needs a quiet day in bed to catch up with herself. I've made her a sandwich from some of your breakfast leftovers, just in case she feels hungry.'

'I think you're being very understanding, considering all that's gone on,' Ally said.

'Well, she is suffering, and we have the girls to consider,' Wendy replied. 'I've been giving it a lot of thought and, let's face it, Greg couldn't have been innocent, could he?'

Ally refrained from commenting.

A little later, while Ally was loading the dishwasher and Ross was bringing in armfuls of logs for the stove, she said, 'I'm concerned about Patti, you know. She's very much under the weather, and I feel sorry for her being stuck upstairs on her own all day.'

'Well, bear in mind that she wouldn't have been able to go with them anyway,' Ross reminded her, 'because she's under "village arrest", is she not? Maybe that's one reason why she opted to stay in bed.'

Later, Ally tiptoed upstairs to see if Patti was all right, but there was a Do Not Disturb on her door handle, so she tiptoed back downstairs again.

'If Patti doesn't feel better by tomorrow morning,' Ally said to Ross, 'I think we should call the doctor.'

Privately, Ally wondered if Patti had lost the will to live after everything that had happened. Perhaps she'd descended into some form of depression?

'Yes, best wait until the morning,' Ross agreed.

But Patti did not appear in the morning.

'We're getting quite worried about Mom,' Julie said. 'She doesn't seem at all well.'

'I think we should call the doctor,' Ally said.

Wendy sighed loudly. 'We really don't want to make a fuss,' she said.

'She's been unwell for two days now,' Julie put in, 'so I think Ally's right.'

'She did have some muesli,' Wendy reminded her, 'so she's obviously got a tiny appetite.'

'I *still* think we should call the doctor,' Julie said.

Doctor Ian Baxter was comparatively new in the area, having finally been selected to succeed the retired Doctor Hayward, and Ally had not yet met him. Fortunately, he was one of those GPs who chose to work on Saturdays, to ease the burden on the NHS. But first she had to get past Edith Calder, who'd been the receptionist at the surgery for at least fifty years, and who devoted her life to interrogating every detail of some-one's symptoms before grudgingly granting them an appointment. After much cajoling and after Miss Calder had aired her opinions on foreigners using 'our National Health Service', the receptionist finally conceded that Doctor Baxter might just be able to fit in a short visit around lunchtime.

In fact, Doctor Baxter appeared at twenty minutes after one. He was a short, stocky, red-haired man with crinkly blue eyes and probably in his thirties, Ally reckoned.

Both girls had been hovering around all morning, but Wendy was very much in charge.

'She says she's fine, Doctor,' she said, 'but Mrs McKinley insisted we call you out.' She led the way upstairs.

Twenty minutes later, the doctor emerged, followed by Wendy, who was still fussing about wasting the doctor's time.

'No, you have not wasted my time,' Doctor Baxter said. 'It's always best to be safe.'

Ally waylaid him in the hallway.

He shook his head and frowned. 'Bit of a mystery this, Mrs McKinley,' he said, 'and I can only assume she might be allergic to something perhaps or caught some nasty bug. I understand Mrs Armstrong's been through some great trauma, so this may well be a delayed reaction. I've left a prescription with her daughter, but be sure to get in touch if you become worried about her condition again.'

After he'd gone, Ally asked the girls to see if their mother wanted anything because Morag hadn't got in there for a couple of days and she might need fresh towels and bedding. Or goodies for the tea tray.

As Julie took herself upstairs to find out, Janey said, 'We're both really worried about Mom, but Auntie Wendy's gone to the chemist to get the prescription so hopefully that'll do the trick.'

Ally sincerely hoped that it would and could only hope that tomorrow would bring a noticeable improvement.

It didn't.

. . .

Later, Ally would always remember the next day as The Day from Hell.

First of all, there was panic at breakfast time with both girls in tears because their mother now seemed to be semi-conscious.

On top of that, there was no sign of Morag. Then the phone rang. 'I'm sorry, Ally, but I'm feelin' bloody awful – all shivery like – and I'm thinkin' I might have the flu or somethin' because it's goin' round at the moment...'

'I'm so sorry, Morag. Just take it easy and get well.'

Ally sighed as she came off the phone. For a brief moment, she didn't know which way to turn, until Ross took matters into his own hands.

'Don't worry,' he said. 'Let me phone Amir first and ask if we should get an ambulance or what the system is when a suspect is ill. Then I'll tidy up down here if you concentrate on the bedrooms.'

It was on days like this that Ally loved Ross more than ever because he never lost his cool.

She went into the dining room to see if anyone wanted anything and found only the two girls in there. 'Where's Wendy?' she asked.

'Oh, she and Joel have gone off somewhere,' Julie replied, 'but we wanted to stay with Mom.'

'I think your mum should probably be in hospital,' Ally said, 'but we'll see how she is as the day goes on. So try not to worry too much. I shall be doing the bedrooms this morning because Morag's not well.'

'We've tried to keep our room tidy,' Janey said, rolling her eyes at her sister.

'Let me worry about that,' Ally replied.

Back in the kitchen, Ross had phoned Amir, who'd said to

contact him immediately if they thought it was necessary to call an ambulance. And so she set off to do the bedrooms.

Aware that the girls were in the sitting room downstairs, she decided to clean their room first. It wasn't nearly as messy as she'd feared, and apart from wiping the shower and replacing towels, she was soon finished. She was finding it all exhausting though, no doubt down to her age, and she sincerely hoped Morag's flu wouldn't last long.

Wendy's room was neat and orderly, and Ally got it done fairly quickly.

As Ally dusted down the bedside cabinet, she noticed the top drawer wouldn't close properly. She opened it to see what was causing the obstruction and discovered it was a toiletry bag. She tried to adjust it so that the drawer would close, but there was a small plastic box in the way. Intrigued, Ally picked up the box and took off the lid. It contained some sort of seeds.

Ally stared at it all for several minutes, trying to work out why it all seemed strangely familiar. Then she remembered.

Back in the days when she'd been a TV researcher, one of her jobs had been to work out which poisons might be used to kill off the protagonist in a crime drama. She'd had to study all manner of poisons to come up with some answer for what, in the programme, was to be revealed in the coroner's report.

Ally remembered these. They were laburnum seeds, highly poisonous and easily available. There were no laburnums in the malthouse garden, but there were several in Desdemona's. Could Wendy possibly have taken them from Desdemona's garden?

As she put the box back into the drawer, her fingers brushed a crumpled, torn scrap of paper. There was something vaguely familiar about it as Ally unravelled it.

...at the Borgue Boulder, the big rock half a mile from Loch Soular on the path to Locharran Castle.

Ally read the note three times before she realised what it was. This had to be the other half of the note she'd found by Greg's body and given to Amir. Why was it in Wendy's possession? Could she have possibly been blackmailing her own husband? And did *he* know he was being blackmailed by *her*? Surely he had no idea, or he wouldn't have set off for that particular rendezvous when he could sort it all out with her face to face in this very room.

Ally froze for a minute. Then she carefully replaced the lid on the box of seeds, but, on second thoughts, she took a small handful and popped them into her pocket. She was beginning to feel sick.

Wendy?

Wendy, who didn't want to bother with getting a doctor. Wendy, who'd spooned out Patti's muesli – and who would notice a few extra seeds in their muesli, for goodness' sake! Wendy, whose husband had been having an affair with Patti. Greg could only have been killed by Wendy, couldn't he? Had he thought he was going to meet some blackmailer from the village perhaps?

Ally closed the door and made her way shakily downstairs, wondering what to do first. Then she decided: she'd phone Desdemona, who would probably remember the Watsons' impromptu arrival but not necessarily what they'd got up to. Nevertheless, it was worth a try.

Desdemona, in her usual abrupt manner, said, 'Of course I remember them. Tall, scrawny woman and her big, ungainly son. Poking around and asking daft questions. Not as if they wanted to buy anything!'

'What I wondered was, did they show any interest in your garden?' Ally asked.

'No, only that the silly woman wanted a handful of seeds to see if she could get them to grow in Nova Scotia or something.'

'I remember she said at the time that you'd let her take some seeds.' Ally's heart was thumping again. 'But can you recall what sort of seeds they were?'

'Yes, they were laburnum seeds. Why? What's she done? Tried to poison someone?' Desdemona laughed at the very idea.

Ally hoped she sounded more casual than she felt. 'Thanks, Desdemona, that's all I wanted to know.'

If her suspicions were correct, there was no time to waste. She rushed up to Patti's room and, without knocking, went in.

'Patti?'

Patti was lying under the covers, motionless and grey-skinned. Ally rocked her gently, but the woman was comatose. She took her phone out of her pocket and phoned 999. Then she needed to talk with the girls downstairs.

'I've sent for an ambulance for your mum,' Ally said as she opened the sitting-room door. 'She's not at all well.'

'We wanted to do that earlier,' Julie said, 'but Auntie Wendy said we shouldn't make a fuss.'

'I think the time has come to make a fuss,' Ally said firmly, at which Janey burst into tears.

'I'm sure she'll be fine,' Ally added hastily.

Then she headed back into the kitchen, grabbed her phone and called Amir. Miraculously, he was actually close to Locharran for once. 'I've called an ambulance for Patti, and I've found the other half of that note I gave you,' she said, 'and something else. I need to see you urgently.'

'I'll be up as soon as I can,' he said.

Ally raced back to the girls, who were now in panic mode. 'The ambulance will be here shortly,' she assured them, 'and she'll be well taken care of. Try not to worry.'

Janey was in tears again, but Julie was more composed. 'We're going with her,' she said firmly.

'I'm not sure if that's allowed,' Ally said doubtfully, 'but we can ask.'

'How would we get back?' Janey asked tremulously.

'Don't worry about that,' Ally said, 'because Ross or I can come to collect you if necessary.'

Everything happened quickly then. Within about fifteen minutes, the ambulance arrived. As she opened the door, Ally noticed a policewoman sitting in the front, while two paramedics came rushing in.

As they carried her out, Ally was appalled again at Patti's appearance: grey skin, heavy-lidded eyes and barely able to move.

Julie and Janey were beside themselves, rushing backward and forward, shouting, 'Hurry! Hurry! Get her to the hospital!'

Julie turned to Ally. 'We're going with her, Ally. We must!'

Ally turned to the policewoman as the paramedics hoisted the stretcher into the ambulance. 'Look, her two daughters are distraught. They're visiting from Canada, and have already lost their father and uncle in the last few days, so please, *please,* can they go with her?'

The policewoman nodded. 'But we cannot be responsible for them,' she told Ally. 'They can come, under the circumstances, but someone will have to come to collect them from the hospital later.'

'I will,' Ally said firmly. 'Where are you taking her?'

'Inverness,' one of the paramedics shouted over his shoulder, climbing into the ambulance.

'Just a moment.' Ally fumbled in her pocket. She had put a few of the seeds into an envelope because, if this did turn out to be any type of poisoning, these could be the answer. 'Would you make sure to hand these to the medical staff?'

The paramedic studied them for a moment. 'What are they?'

'I believe they're laburnum seeds,' Ally told him. 'I think this is what has been poisoning her.'

The ambulance sped away.

Ally went into the kitchen to find a text from Ross:

So sorry, Ally, but I've had an urgent call from Will and have to do a couple of hours at the surgery. Will see you later. xx

Ally, her heart racing, tried to calm down with a cup of tea, but her mind wouldn't switch off. What to do first? Perhaps she should clean Patti's room before she did anything else, just in case Patti might be allowed back later? No, *of course* she wouldn't be allowed back later! They'd keep her in for observation, wouldn't they – if she survived? What if she didn't survive – who would look after Julie and Janey? Joel? Oh God!

She hoped that Amir would be there soon so she could tell him about Wendy. Ally suddenly realised that she hadn't seen her at all that morning. Where *was* the woman? Amir would want to know when he got there. She thought quickly and decided that the best thing to do would be to leave a message with the receptionist at the Craigmonie because she didn't have her number.

'I did see Mrs Watson in here earlier,' the receptionist said when she phoned, 'but I haven't seen her for hours.'

As Ally came off the phone, she hoped she'd done everything she should have done. She felt quite exhausted with the events of the morning, but now the house was empty, the bedrooms were all cleaned and she had the afternoon to herself. She knew what she'd do – she'd make a steak pie for supper. Ross loved her steak pies, and Ally found cooking relaxing when she was stressed. She got out all her ingredients and her rolling pin for the pastry when Flora started barking at something she'd heard outside, so Ally went to let her out into the garden. It was a lovely, still late September afternoon, the sky clear, and the air just a little crisp. As she came back in through the rear porch, Ally had a strange feeling that someone was in the kitchen.

Then she saw who it was.

Wendy.

Wendy was smiling in a strange way, and she also had the rolling pin in her hand.

TWENTY-SEVEN

'Where is everybody?' Wendy's voice sounded different somehow, and Ally's stomach did a complete somersault. Why was the woman looking at her like that?

Ally took a deep breath. 'Patti appeared to be in a coma, so I called for an ambulance.' She'd managed to pick up her phone from the kitchen table, and when Wendy was distracted for a moment at Flora barking at birds in the garden, she clicked 'Reply' on Ross's message from earlier and sent him a new text:

HELP!

Wendy turned back towards her, and there was a moment's uncomfortable silence.

'You *did*? Did you not think to contact *me* first, as her *family*?' Wendy asked.

'You didn't seem to think it was necessary,' Ally replied. 'But I did. And the girls have gone with her. Can I have my rolling pin, please?' Ally held out her hand, but Wendy completely ignored her.

'How *dare* you make decisions for my family?' Wendy asked. She'd advanced a couple of steps closer.

'Someone had to make a decision. She appeared to be in a coma, and you were nowhere to be seen.'

'There was nothing wrong with her,' Wendy snapped. 'She was just tired.'

Ally had had enough. 'Perhaps she was tired of being fed laburnum seeds, Wendy!'

Something dangerous flashed in Wendy's eyes for a second. 'What the hell are you talking about?' she said, now glaring at Ally with renewed fury.

'I'm just curious to know why you had laburnum seeds in your bedside drawer?'

'And why the hell were you looking in my bedside drawer?' Wendy asked, her face twisted with anger, still clutching the rolling pin.

'A landlady's privilege,' Ally replied, her eye on the rolling pin. 'I was cleaning your room, and your drawer wouldn't shut properly.'

'If you must know, I'm taking the seeds home to plant in my garden,' Wendy snapped.

'Oh, good,' Ally said, 'I just wondered. Anyway, I've given a few to the paramedics, just in case it's got anything to do with Patti's strange illness. I did have another question though – were you blackmailing your own husband, Wendy?'

'You *cow*!' Wendy was now properly brandishing the rolling pin and rounding the kitchen table in Ally's direction. She gave a strange smile. 'You know what? By the time they find out what's wrong with Patti, Joel and I will be on our way home!'

'Oh, will you indeed?' Ally was now eyeing the rolling pin with some alarm. She could only hope she'd be strong enough to ward off this woman if she really planned to attack. If she could just hold her off until Amir got there... 'I don't think somehow it's going to be that easy. But, tell me, why were you trying to kill Patti?'

Wendy laughed. 'Isn't it bloody obvious? Just for a start, the silly cow was having an affair with *my husband* – who she cajoled into killing my *brother*! But my stupid husband did as he was told. He'd probably have wanted to kill me next, but I wasn't having that! He and Patti wanted to run the business together, and they didn't want Joel and me in there at all. And why the hell not? I have as much right to inherit my father's business as Archie had. More right than Patti, and Greg, who only married into it. And they didn't want Joel in there either. It's Joel's *birthright!* Let's face it, he and I could run that business with our hands tied behind our backs.' She sighed, almost as if glad to have got that off her chest. 'Stupid, bloody Greg!' she added for good measure.

Ally was aware of Flora barking to get back in, but she didn't dare move.

'So did you kill him?' Ally asked, frantically backing towards the rear door. Wendy was still advancing and brandishing the rolling pin.

Wendy laughed. 'Oh, I did, Ally, I did! At least I succeeded there. But do you know what? You're not going to be around to tell anyone any of this.' She raised the rolling pin high.

The last thing Ally remembered was a draught as the back door opened behind her as Wendy advanced, and then everything went black.

TWENTY-EIGHT

A week had passed, and Ally was back home at the malthouse. She didn't remember much about being hospitalised, only that they'd insisted she stayed there under observation. She'd had a knock-out blow to her head which could well have killed her, they said. And if Ross hadn't read her text – in between treating an elderly cat and a sickly spaniel – and alerted Amir, then she would probably not be here now.

Ally would forever be grateful to those two men.

Amir was due to arrive any minute, and Ross was filling the kettle. They'd talk about it all over a cup of tea – what else? Ally was to sit by the log burner and do absolutely nothing, Ross instructed her.

The village had again been wonderful. When the news of her confrontation had got around, she had been inundated with flowers, scones, oatcakes, shortbread and several bottles of whisky. And Linda had excelled herself, having arrived with *two* cakes. Ross had now laid all these goodies out on the table, in anticipation of Amir's visit. She owed Amir her life. If he hadn't come in through the back door at that precise moment, she most likely wouldn't be here.

'How are you feeling, Ally?' Amir asked solicitously when he arrived a few minutes later.

'I'm fine,' Ally assured him. 'Just a sore bump where the wretched woman landed the rolling pin.'

'Well, we've had a full confession,' Amir said, accepting a cup of tea and choosing a piece of shortbread. 'It was quite strange really because, at first, we thought she'd deny everything, but in the end, it all came pouring out, almost as if she was glad to get it off her chest.'

'I'm guessing it was the laburnum seeds that made Patti so sick?' Ally asked.

'Yes, it was indeed, and thank you so much for having the foresight to hand over a few of those to the medics,' Amir replied. 'Patti is recovering well in a hospital bed in Inverness, still awaiting trial for conspiracy to murder. Wendy Watson is, of course, in custody, accused of killing her own husband and trying to kill her sister-in-law and, not least, yourself. Apparently, she found out before they left Canada that Greg and Patti were having an affair and so knew that Greg probably fired the shot that, one way or the other, killed her brother.'

'What about the girls?' Ally asked anxiously.

'They refused to leave their mother and have been rescued by Patti's estranged sister, who runs a transport café in Ayrshire. She seems very kind, but also, to be honest, I think she's been looking for two waitresses. She agreed to take them in for now provided they help her out in the café, which they're apparently really excited about.'

Ally tried very hard to imagine those two serving burgers and chips to big, brawny truck drivers. Would they still be chewing gum?

'And what about Angus?'

'Well, Angus will have to appear in court charged with withholding information from the police – vital information, in fact. But the earl will doubtless get him a good solicitor. It also seems that Tom wasn't telling the whole truth to us – he *did* hear Patti asking for a gun, but he didn't hear Angus tell her where to hide it. Apparently, he was angry at Angus for favouring Gordon over him and so was trying to get his own back.'

'And Joel?'

Amir rolled his eyes. 'Joel Watson is back in Canada, where he belongs, running the cabin-making business.'

'Try as I might,' Ally said, 'I cannot see how Wendy managed to kill Greg. I worked out that it was she who was blackmailing him, but...'

Amir smiled. 'She obviously faked the injury with her boots, sped back here once she was out of your sight, then sprinted up to where she'd arranged – via the note – to meet her husband, where she killed him. She appears to be gifted when it comes to knocking people on the head.'

'She left a note to say she'd gone up to the castle early to see Greg arrive,' Ally said. 'We all thought it was because she'd have been limping.' Her thoughts turned again to Greg's body and the massive wound on his head. Wendy had plainly planned the same fate for her.

'No, she attacked the guy before she ran off, limping again, of course, as she arrived at the castle. She was extremely devious and clever,' Amir added. He accepted a slice of cake.

'Well, Amir, I owe you my life. I saw what she did to her husband...' Ally shuddered, and Ross took her hand tightly in his own.

'All part of the service,' Amir said modestly. 'You'd done such a brilliant job of solving the case, and holding Wendy off, it was the least I could do. Oh my goodness, this cake is delicious!'

'I'll get my friend Linda to make you one just like it!' Ally said, laughing.

As Ross refilled the teacups, he said, 'We're planning to

dine at the Craigmonie tonight, Amir, so why don't you join us? My treat!'

Amir looked uncertain for a moment.

'Oh, please do!' Ally said. 'And you must try their desserts – Linda makes them.'

'This is very kind,' Amir said, looking from Ally to Ross with a smile.

As she and Ross watched him drive away, Ally thought for the umpteenth time what a very lucky woman she was. Here she was, in this glorious spot, on this beautiful autumn day, surrounded by a hillside of purple heather and looking down over the golds and bronzes of the trees beneath in the funny little village she called home.

Ross took her arm. 'Come inside, Ally,' he said. 'It's getting cold.'

And, not least, Ross! Ally smiled up at this handsome man who made her life so much richer. Whatever would she do without him? She was indeed an extremely fortunate woman, and she knew it.

Holding him close, Ally let him lead her over the threshold of The Auld Malthouse, and shut the door.

A LETTER FROM DEE

Dear Reader,

Ally's at it again! She's become a very proficient sleuth since moving up to Locharran, and if this is the first 'Ally' book you've read, then do catch up with the previous ones to see how she's progressed. And if you'd also like to read any of my other books, then you can sign up at the following link. Your email will never be shared, and you can unsubscribe at any time.

www.bookouture.com/dee-macdonald

I hope you enjoyed this book, and, if so, I'd greatly appreciate it if you could write a review. Your feedback is invaluable. You can get in touch with me via social media too.

With thanks and best wishes,

Dee

facebook.com/AuthorDeeMacDonald
x.com/DMacDonaldAuth

ACKNOWLEDGEMENTS

A million thanks, as always, to my lovely, helpful – and very patient! – editor at Bookouture, Lizzie Brien. She's been brilliant at knocking this book into shape!

And thanks to my agent, Amanda Preston at LBA, for her continuing support and suggestions.

Huge thanks as well to Rosemary Brown, my writing consultant (posh expression for 'writing buddy'!) Every writer should have someone who's not afraid to say what's lacking in planning, plot and grammar. I am deeply indebted to her.

I must thank my husband too, for leaving me in peace to write, and to my son and family who sort out my technical problems.

Then there is the wonderful team behind the scenes at Bookouture. They publish and promote my books, and I am deeply indebted to them all: Alba Proko, Melissa Tran, Peta Nightingale, Mandy Kullar, Hannah Snetsinger, Hannah Wilson, Sarah Hardy, Melanie Price, Kim Nash, Noelle Holten, Jane Eastgate, Laura Kincaid and Lisa Brewster. And apologies to anyone I've omitted.

And a special mention to Samara MacLaren, the narrator of my audiobooks, whose lovely voice is so exactly right!

Last, but never least, a huge thank you to everyone who've bought my books, left reviews or sent messages.

PUBLISHING TEAM

Turning a manuscript into a book requires the efforts of many people. The publishing team at Bookouture would like to acknowledge everyone who contributed to this publication.

Audio
Alba Proko

Commercial
Lauren Morrissette
Hannah Richmond
Imogen Allport

Cover design
The Brewster Project

Data and analysis
Mark Alder
Mohamed Bussuri

Editorial
Lizzie Brien
Hannah Wilson

Copyeditor
Jane Eastgate

Proofreader
Laura Kincaid

Marketing
Alex Crow
Melanie Price
Occy Carr
Cíara Rosney
Martyna Młynarska

Operations and distribution
Marina Valles
Joe Morris

Production
Hannah Snetsinger
Mandy Kullar
Nadia Michael
Charlotte Hegley

Publicity
Kim Nash
Noelle Holten
Jess Readett
Sarah Hardy

Rights and contracts
Peta Nightingale
Richard King
Saidah Graham

RAISING READERS
Books Build Bright Futures

Dear Reader,

We'd love your attention for one more page to tell you about the crisis in children's reading, and what we can all do.

Studies have shown that reading for fun is the **single biggest predictor of a child's future life chances** – more than family circumstance, parents' educational background or income. It improves academic results, mental health, wealth, communication skills, ambition and happiness.

The number of children reading for fun is in rapid decline. Young people have a lot of competition for their time, and a worryingly high number do not have a single book at home.

Hachette works extensively with schools, libraries and literacy charities, but here are some ways we can all raise more readers:

- Reading to children for just 10 minutes a day makes a difference
- Don't give up if children aren't regular readers – there will be books for them!

- Visit bookshops and libraries to get recommendations
- Encourage them to listen to audiobooks
- Support school libraries
- Give books as gifts

There's a lot more information about how to encourage children to read on our websites: **www.RaisingReaders.co.uk** and **www.JoinRaisingReaders.com**.

Thank you for reading.

hachette UK

Printed in Dunstable, United Kingdom

81673685R00143